REX STOUT DOES NOT BELONG IN RUSSIA
Exporting the Detective Novel

Molly Jane Levine Zuckerman

Copyright © 2016 Molly Jane Levine Zuckerman

All rights reserved. No part of this book may be reproduced by any means without the written permission of the publisher, except for short passages used in critical reviews.

Cover design by M. Wayne Miller, www.MWayneMiller.com

Interior design and cover layout by Steven W. Booth,
   www.GeniusBookServices.com

Foreword

While browsing through a stack of Russian and American novels in translation on a table on Arbat Street in Moscow in 2013, I came across a Russian copy of one of my favorite books, *And Be a Villain,* by one of my favorite authors, Rex Stout. I only knew about this author because my father had lent me a copy of *And Be a Villain* when I was in middle school, and I was so entranced by the novel that I went out to Barnes & Noble to buy as many Rex Stout books as they had in stock. I quickly ran out of Stout books to read, because at the time they were out of print in America. I managed to get hold of most of them by high school, courtesy of a family friend's mother who passed on her collection of Stout novels to our family. Considering the relative difficulty I'd had in acquiring the books in America, I was surprised to find one lying on a book stand in Moscow; I bought it for less than 30 cents (which was probably around the original price of its first printing in America).

When I went back to Russia to study in 2015, I discovered that every bookstore had at least five Stout novels in translation. In America, I had been to several bookstores that had zero Stout books on their shelves. This phenomenon was curious, but I did not fully see the extent of Stout's popularity in Russia until a Russian friend, taking a literature-in-translation course at our Russian university, asked me to help him with his homework and I recognized in the exercises a passage from one of Stout's novels. I then asked around the university, and, while most of my professors had heard of him, that was nothing unusual, as most people my parents' age in America had also heard of Rex Stout. What piqued my interest beyond all else was when I discovered that Rex Stout was the second most printed author in all of Russia in 2014—Dostoevsky ranked twelfth on the list. This is when I decided to investigate my favorite author and his two favorite detectives, Nero Wolfe and Archie Goodwin, and why the heck Russians like them so much.

ABSTRACT AND METHODS

In my research, I seek to answer the following questions: Based on the inherent contradictions between a Western detective novel and Communist Russian society, why were Rex Stout's detective novels popular in the Soviet Union? What was the political appeal of the novels' plots during different periods in Russian history, from the Soviet Union to the present? What influence has Stout's Nero Wolfe series had on Soviet and Russian culture?

I will begin answering these questions by detailing a brief history of the detective genre in Russia. I will then examine the most important political themes in Stout's books, including all pertinent references to Communism and Russia. The next section will introduce the role of his books in Russia and analyze some general theories on how Western detective novels in translation affected Russian culture and the literary scene. I will intersperse quotations from people that read Stout during the Soviet period and how they felt about him and his most political novels. Many of those comments will be taken from the Russian online Nero Wolfe fan site, which I discovered during my initial research.

On the site, I found many members willing to talk with me, through their discussion forum, about Stout's influence on their lives. The makeup of the forum is such that anyone can become a member and start a new topic or add comments to a previously discussed topic. This forum consists of Russian speakers, but not all are necessarily from Russia itself. My initial query on the forum about Stout in Russia led to an explanation that members come from Ukraine, Belarus, Latvia, Kazakhstan, Armenia, Estonia, and elsewhere, and that limiting my topic to Russia was too narrow, in several users' opinions. I took this into account in my research but did not have the time or space to delve into Stout in every country mentioned; I make up for this by including information on his Russian-language publications in the wider Soviet bloc in Chapter Four.

Throughout, I will be referencing the forum discussion generated by my initial question about "Nero Wolfe, Archie Goodwin, and all that is connected with them," as well as drawing on comments made in other discussion threads.[1] I will use the comments to provide a contemporary reaction to Stout's books from the perspectives of those who either read his books in Russian during the Soviet Union or after 1990.

I will continue with an explanation of how Stout's books influenced specific Russian writers in terms of plots and characters, and then how his books manifested themselves in different

---

1 Comments will be attributed to the author with their username or actual name as they chose.

formats, including online fan clubs, a cookbook, and a television show. I will conclude by discussing the overall implications of the impression that Stout left on Russian culture through his almost forty years of popularity in the country.

VIII

Table of Contents

Acknowledgements ....**xi**

Chapter One: Rex Stout and the Hard-boiled Detective Novel....1
What is the Detective Genre?...1
Stout's Beginnings in America..6
The Detective Novel's Beginnings in Russia.....................................8
Stout's Use of the Capitalist Model in his Nero Wolfe Series 11
The Creation of Nero Wolfe and Archie Goodwin 16

Chapter Two: Stout Critiques American Politics **21**
Anti-German Attitudes and a Change of Habit in Writing 21
Stout and World Federalism 25
Stout and Racism..27

Chapter Three: Stout and His Characters Hate the "Commies" **29**
Battling Stereotypes and Promoting Democratic Liberties.............29
Stout's Anti-Communism Enters His Novels 33
The Rosenberg Trial..51
Wolfe and Archie Enter Yugoslavia 53

Chapter Four: Wolfe and Stout Enter Soviet Russia **60**
How Stout the Anti-Communist was Published in the USSR 60
Stout Critiques Yugoslavia from America 62
Soviet Critics take Offense at Stout's Plots.....................................66

Chapter Five: Why Russians Love that Stout Hates the FBI **80**
The Doorbell Rang 80

Chapter Six: How Stout's Popularity Continues after the Fall of Communism..**97**
Stout's Detective Novels in Post-Soviet Russia...............................97
The Russians Begin Writing Their Own Detective Novels 105
Russian Intellectual Backlash Against the Rise of Mass Culture and the Detective Novel 109

Chapter Seven: Stout's Novels Influence New Russian Detective Novelists 116
Aleksandra Marinina Critiques Russian Politics and Society 116
A Confluence of Circumstances: The Non-Coincidental Similarities Between Anastasia Kamenskaia and Nero Wolfe 120
Darya Donstova and the Unnamed Others 142

Chapter Eight: Stout's Influence in Contemporary Russia Goes Beyond the Literary 147
How Food and Translation Fit Together 147
Stout's Fan Base Goes Online and Eastward 155
The Russian Nero Wolfe Television Series 157

Conclusion 163

Appendix 169
Statistical Records of Printed Materials in Russia in 2014 169
Stout Collections 2000s by Russian Publishing Houses 170
Stout's Novels Mentioned in This Book 176
Darya Dontsova's Ivan Podushkin Series 178

Bibliography 180

Acknowledgments

I would first and foremost like to thank Professor Susanne Fusso for her work as my advisor on this project at Wesleyan University. Without her, my research would not have gone as smoothly and my mental state would not have remained as calm. Her willingness to meet with me as many times a week as needed (which, toward the end, meant more than once a day) and to answer all my late night emails with lengthy and thoughtful replies meant that I was not nearly as overwhelmed as I could have been. Her assistance with translations and analyses of Russian texts saved readers from having to wade through my own well-intentioned, though often incomprehensible, passages and quotations. Thank you.

I would also like to thank both the American Wolfe Pack and the Russian online Nero Wolfe fan club for their help with my research. Special thanks to Ira Matetsky for his kindness and help with the American side of my research on Stout's work. And particular thanks go to Stanislav Zavgorodnii, a Ukrainian Stout fan who reached out to me and was indispensible in the portion of my research on Stout in Russian translation. I would also like to mention Natalia Rymko, who welcomed me into her home in Moscow, stuffed me full of Russian blini and caviar, and provided valuable insight into Stout's popularity in Soviet Russia. User BleWotan, User Fox, Sergey Chervotkin, Sergey Panichev, and all members of the Russian online forum also deserve recognition for their willingness to interact with me online and answer my many questions about Stout and Nero Wolfe in Russia.

I also need to thank my invaluable translator, Gleb Vinokurov, who provided English translations for the Russian online forum members' answers, as well as provided moral support throughout the whole year with his willingness to watch Downton Abbey with me until five in the morning and send me countless Ellen DeGeneres videos when I needed inspiration.

And finally, I thank my parents, Liza Levine and Edward Zuckerman, who instilled in me a love of books from a very young age, an outcome of their race against other relatives to see whose toddler would learn to read first. I won.

My father also deserves recognition for introducing me to the world of Nero Wolfe and Archie Goodwin. He allowed me to acquire every Wolfe novel in my childhood, and, when we moved to New York, brought every single Nero Wolfe novel with him so I could have them at Wesleyan. Because of him, Nero Wolfe and Archie Goodwin will live on in my generation's mind a little bit longer.

1 | Rex Stout and the Hard-boiled Detective Novel

You are headstrong and I am magisterial. Our tolerance of each other is a constantly recurring miracle.
—Nero Wolfe to Archie Goodwin
Champagne for One

What is the Detective Genre?

Stout's Nero Wolfe books are more than just detective novels; they exhibit one man's opinion of America and all of its flaws throughout the historical period (1940s-1970s) in which they were written. His detective stories offer a glimpse into everyday life in America; foreigners who read his books are able to glean information about the US through the novels as well as absorb Stout's scathing commentary on certain aspects of life in America. The plots of the novels reveal the reasons crimes are committed, who is responsible for catching the criminals, and what happens to them once they have been caught. But Stout's books also offer Russians a distinctive look into crime in

America through the lens of Stout's own political views and his depiction of the capitalist society within which he resides.

Ammie Cannon, in a Master's thesis, makes the argument that the popularity of Stout's novels stems from both good writing and an ability to mute political messages in the stories; they are "not forced by an author seeking to infuse his novel with statements that confirm his own political agenda."[2] She argues that Stout used the interplay of his two main detectives and the conventions of the genre to advance his political messages without "threaten[ing] the sanctity of storytelling."[3] I do not necessarily agree with Cannon's point that Stout never threatens the sanctity of storytelling with his political messages. Rather, his politics and his plots are purposefully intertwined, usually subtly but occasionally repetitively, in a manner that sometimes pushes the murder investigation to the background by Stout's focus on the political aspect of motives and suspects. However, even with this caveat, I still see Stout as successfully portraying the capitalist model in his texts through the vehicle of the detective genre, without sacrificing almost any literary value.

Before the Russian Communist revolution, crime did have a place in Russian literature, most famously in Dostoevsky's murder mystery *The Brothers Karamazov*. In answer to the question of the social purpose of novels depicting crime and punishment, Dostoevsky wrote:

> It is clear and intelligible to the point of obviousness that evil in mankind is concealed deeper than the physician-socialists suppose; that in no organization of society can evil be eliminated; that the human soul will re-

---

2 Ammie Cannon, "Controversial Politics, Conservative Genre: Rex Stout's Archie-Wolfe Duo and Detective Fiction's Conventional Form" (Brigham Young University, 2006), 80.

3 Ibid., 26.

main identical; that abnormality and sin emanate from the soul itself; and finally, that the laws of the human spirit are so unknown to science, so obscure, so indeterminate and mysterious, that, as yet, there can neither be physicians nor *final* judges, but that there is only He who saith: 'Vengeance belongeth unto me; for I will recompense.'[4]

Dostoevsky's musings on the literary morality of depicting crime and criminals highlight the different role that detective fiction was forced to play in the Soviet period. He writes, "In no organization of society can evil be eliminated," which is exactly what the Soviet Communists wanted to do; their belief in a socialist utopia presupposed that the elimination of evil was possible. The discrepancy between Dostoevsky's view and the lack of acceptance in Soviet Russian society of the detective novel illustrates one significant difference in the valuation of literature during the Soviet period.

East German writer Ernst Kaemmel saw the detective novel as a "child of capitalism."[5] Although his premise that all private detective stories involve crimes solely based on economic motives can be attributed to his political background at the time of writing, he made the point that the idea of an individual private detective righting the wrongs of "a society based on exploitation" in an isolated manner "shows how strongly the defects of its [the capitalist world's] social order are felt."[6] Kaemmel believed that

---

4 Fyodor Dostoevsky, *Diary of a Writer*, vol. 2 (New York: Scribners, 1949), 788. Quoted in Anthony Olcott, *Russian Pulp: The Detektiv and the Russian Way of Crime* (Lanham: Rowman & Littlefield Publishers, 2001), 150.

5 Ernst Kaemmel, "Literature under the Table: The Detective Novel and Its Social Mission," in *The Poetics of Murder: Detective Fiction and Literary Theory*, ed. Glenn W. Most and William W. Stowe (Harcourt Brace Jovanovich, June 1983), 13.

6 Ibid., 58.

the individuality inherent in hard-boiled detective fiction did not have a place in a socialist state, and again, although he incorrectly predicted that the impending fall of capitalism would wipe out the detective novel, his analysis of how fictional private detectives do not fit the socialist model is apt.[7]

Stout's books support this analysis; while the cases his detectives solve often expose the defects of the capitalist world's social order, his detectives sometimes defend the democratic freedoms of that social order in a lone vigilante manner that violates socialist norms. With the rise of Communism came the creation of the ideal of the New Soviet man and the Soviet family; Stout's detective novels do not fit into any of these ideals in any way. Stout's detectives can even break the laws of society if required to protect overall democratic freedom, and Kaemmel sees this positive portrayal of a lone man against society as subversive to the socialist cause. From Kaemmel's point of view, the Soviet Union, as a society that built socialism into a relatively strong political entity that lasted for decades, had no place for the detective novel in its ideology.

Stout's biographer John McAleer quotes Stout as agreeing indirectly with this analysis of the democratic values inherent in Western detective fiction:

> I think the detective story is by far the best upholder of the democratic doctrine in literature… There couldn't have been detective stories until there were democracies, because the very foundation of the detective story is the thesis that if you're guilty you'll get it in the neck and if you're innocent you can't possibly be harmed.[8]

---

7 Ibid., 61.
8 John J. McAleer, *Rex Stout: A Majesty's Life*, Millenium ed. (James A Rock & Co. Publishers, 2002), 286.

Kaemmel's analysis of the detective novel as showing the defects of society is turned upside down by Stout, who sees the implicit democratic values in detective fiction as representative of a positive universal political model. While Stout doesn't mention capitalism in this quotation, only democracy, his later views on the dangers of Communism show that he conflates democracy with the necessity of residing under capitalism (as the opposite of Communism), in order to fully experience democratic freedoms.

Although Kaemmel's viewpoint is politically oriented, his overall point about the intrinsic connection between the detective novel and the values of capitalist society are correct. Detective fiction is an outlier in Communist society, which is built on the concept of communalism and a desire to move toward a society with full employment, no class boundaries, no homelessness, a controlled economy, and ultimately the disappearance of a monetary system and any form of government. Communism contains the belief that citizens can become enlightened if they follow the right path, and that crime will be eliminated as generations of enlightened people are born. The crime written about in detective novels cannot exist in this utopia. The Western detective novel contradicts this viewpoint; it presupposes the eternal existence of crime in society.

In the universal detective story, there must be a crime, an investigation, and usually a reveal of the criminal. Detective stories involving a murder and private detectives, such as those written by Stout, fit even less into a socialist utopia. There should be no crime in a perfect socialist world, because everyone will have as much as they need, according to their ability, and therefore will have no reason to commit a gruesome act like murder. Murder for gain has no place in a society where no one is supposed to be in want of anything, particularly money. Family ties are different under Communism as well, with the ideal being for the state to raise children, leaving parents fully committed to the workforce, an ideal that would also eliminate family intrigue as a motive for murder.

The essence of my argument is that ideal Communist society eliminates the motives for murder, and therefore detective novels that have these motives as the bases of their plots would be seen as subversive texts. Detective novels also have the potential to show citizens under Communism another way of life, albeit one with murder and crime, that has the potential to lead them away from the life that they are living. The choice of the detective genre by Stout to promote a capitalist, democratic society put his books in direct opposition to socialism or Communism in any form.

Stout's Beginnings in America

Rex Stout was born in Noblesville, Indiana, on December 1, 1886, and raised in a Quaker household. His whole family eventually moved to Wakarusa, Kansas, for his father's work. Stout joined the Navy in 1905 and moved to New York four years later. He began his non-military career with the 1916 invention of a school banking system that was widely used across America.[9] Having become financially secure from that invention, Stout pursued his literary interests by becoming the president of Vanguard Press from 1926 to 1928 and then vice president until 1931. The small publishing company was created with a $100,000 grant from the American Fund for Public Service (the Garland Fund) and was dedicated to publishing books that larger commercial publishing houses wouldn't take on for political reasons. Examples of the "un-publishable mate-

---
9 Ibid., 150.

rial" included seven books by Scott Nearing, a member of the American Communist Party, along with three of Stout's novels (pre-Nero Wolfe): *How Like a God* (1929), *Seed on the Wind* (1930), and *Golden Remedy* (1931).

In 1926, the same year he became the president of Vanguard Press, Stout helped start the radical magazine *The New Masses* by donating $4000 for its publication; he then served on the executive board with his sister, Ruth Stout, as office manager.[10] After Michael Gold, a Communist, took over as editor and started publishing articles supporting the Soviet Union, Stout and his sister discontinued their association with the magazine, for Stout realized "that it was Communist and intended to stay Communist."[11] This early inadvertent brush with Communist publications may have helped fuel the future FBI case against Stout after his more incendiary literary publications. Ironically, *The New Masses* was similar to the political and literary journals that would be the first to translate and publish Stout's novels in the Soviet Union.[12]

Having begun a writing career with pulp fiction stories for magazines several years before, Stout turned to writing full time after he ended his work at both the Vanguard Press and *The New Masses*. He published his first Nero Wolfe novel, *Fer-de-Lance*, in 1934, beginning a habit of turning out exactly one Wolfe novel a year. He also began to build High Meadow, a country house on the border of New York and Connecticut.

---

10 Ibid., 183; John Simkin, "New Masses," http://spartacuseducational.com/JmassesN.htm.

11 McAleer, *Rex Stout: A Majesty's Life*, 184.

12 Elena V. Baraban, "Russia in the Prism of Popular Culture: Russian and American Detective Fiction and Thrillers of the 1990s" (The University of British Columbia, 2003), 161.

The Detective Novel's Beginnings in Russia

As Stout was growing up and beginning his career in the US, political changes in Russia began affecting its native detective genre. Russia did historically have a tradition of detective fiction, but it would be incorrect to put Dostoevsky's *Crime and Punishment* in the same category as Rex Stout's *Too Many Detectives*. Russians fed their desire for less literary detective stories by borrowing from the Western canon, which contained a plethora of lowbrow detective fiction that simply did not exist on the same scale in pre-Soviet society. Before the 1917 Russian revolution, there was an influx of "quaint Russian knockoffs" of American detective fiction to Russia, referred to by the critic and translator Boris Dralyuk as "Pinkertonovshchina." He describes the popularity, especially among youth, of Nat Pinkerton novels, whose hero was an American detective who was the "scourge of the American criminal world…and sent more than one villain to the electric chair of New York's Sing Sing prison."[13] Jeffrey Brooks cites statistics of 6.2 million copies of Pinkerton novels published in Russia from 1907 to 1915, all at 15 kopecks a book (as well as 3.1 million copies of American detective Nick Carter and 3.9 million of Sherlock Holmes in novel form).[14]

After the revolution of 1917, the continuing popularity of Pinkerton novels (as opposed to the teachings of Karl Marx) among Russian youth was seen as a symptom of the failure of the Communist Party to inspire youth toward socialism, and so the desire to write Communist "Red Pinkertons" was born. In the 1920s, Nikolai Bukharin, a Bolshevik revolutionary, full member of the Politburo, and author, wanted to create a type of

---

13 Boris Dralyuk, *Western Crime Fiction Goes East: The Russian Pinkerton Craze, 1907-1934* (Brill Academic Pub, 2012) 1, 8, 10.

14 Jeffrey Brooks, *When Russians Learned to Read, Literacy and Popular Literature, 1861-1917* (Northwestern University Press, 2003), 147.

socialist realist literature that would both entertain young people and motivate them to support the Communist cause.[15] He drew on Karl Marx himself to both explain away problematic interest in Western detective novels and to create the foundation for a new type of more revolution-friendly literature. In 1922, Bukharin was quoted as saying, "Marx, as is generally known, read crime novels with great enthusiasm. What's the point here?... If we give one specific description of one of our revolutionary fighter's lives— that will be a thousand times more interesting than anything."[16]

The demand for detective stories, even socialist realist ones, can be attributed to what Dralyuk describes as a "psychological motivation [to] devour popular genres in times of flux" and what Brooks sees as conjoining an interest in foreign detectives with an interest in foreign places.[17] Michael Holquist posits the idea that people are drawn to detective novels at times when "enormous destruction is in the hands of faceless committees," for such novels demonstrate to readers that "a single man...exploiting the gifts of courage and resourcefulness ...can offset the ineffectiveness of government."[18] Catharine Nepomnyashchy, who wrote about the rise of the new Russian *detektiv* in the 1990s, connects the rise in popularity of the Western detective genre with the many cultural and political transitions in the Russian

---

15 Ernst Kaemmel, "Literature under the Table: The Detective Novel and Its Social Mission," 61. Kaemmel would call for a return to this type of literature almost fifty years later, for if detective novels portrayed crimes as against society and social order, then the genre would finally have "attained the function of transmitting knowledge" in his idea of a successful manner.

16 Dralyuk, *Western Crime Fiction Goes East: The Russian Pinkerton Craze, 1907-1934,* 5, 23, 26.

17 Ibid. 7; Brooks, *When Russians Learned to Read, Literacy and Popular Literature, 1861-1917,* 142.

18 Michael Holquist, "Whodunit and Other Questions: Metaphysical Detective Stories in Postwar Fiction," in *The Poetics of Murder, Detective Fiction and Literary Theory,* ed. Glenn W. Most and William W. Stow (Harcourt Brace Jovanovich, June 1983), 153.

state, claiming that social instability allowed a chance for Russians to freely read fiction.[19] She uses the New Economic Policy transitional period as a microcosm to be studied in the Russian history of detective novels, calling it "an unstable and inevitably temporary meeting of literary theory, highbrow parody, a more or less competitive market, and a politically motivated desire to simultaneously encourage literacy and to indoctrinate."[20] This connection between the political environment and the desire to read and write detective stories is the same confluence of circumstances that led to the inspiration for many of Stout's plots as well as the spike in his popularity in Russia in the 1970s, 1990s and the mid-2000s.

With the rise of Stalin's power in the 1920s came the fall of the mystery novel, for Russian political leaders began to forcibly direct the population's focus away from escapist novels in order to protect them from what was considered the harmful values of fiction. Western detective literature featured passion-based and private-property based crimes; they were inherently based on capitalist values that the Soviet system blamed for crime in the first place. Since the motives in Western detective stories did not fit the Soviet model that crime was a socially-fueled, curable happenstance, they held no place in Soviet society. Stalin neither allowed for the publication of detective novels nor allowed the genre to be left in libraries.[21] There were no more calls for "Red Pinkertons"; everything to do with the detective genre was simply banned.

---

19 Catharine Theimer Nepomnyashchy, "Markets, Mirrors, and Mayhem: Aleksandra Marinina and the Rise of the New Russian Detektiv," in *Consuming Russia: Popular Culture, Sex, and Society since Gorbachev*, ed. Adele Marie Barker (Duke University Press, 1999), 162. I will be referring to the detective stories written in the Soviet period and later as the distinctive *detektiv*, based on the use of the term for this time period by authors Nepomnyashchy and Olcott.

20 Ibid., 163.

21 Olcott, *Russian Pulp: The Detektiv and the Russian Way of Crime*, 4.

Some popular Soviet detective writers who were able to write detective stories to the censors' liking were Arkadii Adamov, Yulian Semyonov, Lev Ovalov, the brothers Arkadii and Grigorii Vainer, and Nikolai Leonov; however, in order to be published, they were forced to portray their heroes as "squeaky clean."[22] Stephen Wilkinson, a scholar of the detective genre in Socialist Cuba, compares the constrained style of Soviet detective writers to Cuban detective novels. As Wilkinson sees it, the use of the detective genre as a "tool of education" lessens the artistic value of the work and undermines the psychological credibility of the detectives. He quotes Adamov scholar Barbara Göbler and her analysis of Adamov's use of "pathetic" and "socially directed" lectures directed at the criminals his detectives apprehend; these detectives are so socially conscious that the novels "invariably end with the criminal being captured alive and offered a chance to reintegrate into society."[23]

With novels like these the only ones available, it seemed as if the whole Russian population was holding its breath until it could dive back into a detective genre separate from the pedagogical and didactic books it was forced to read under Stalin.

Stout's Use of the Capitalist Model in his Nero Wolfe Series

Stout, with his politically critical plots, his unabashedly eccentric and individual character, and his "failure" to push the value of reintegrating murderers back into the socialist fold, would be an attractive option for a Soviet Russian looking for an entertaining story. Stout's most famous characters, Nero Wolfe

---

22 Nepomnyashchy, "Markets, Mirrors, and Mayhem: Aleksandra Marinina and the Rise of the New Russian Detektiv," 166.

23 Stephen Wilkinson, *Detective Fiction in Cuban Society and Culture* (Peter Lang, 2006), 20.

and Archie Goodwin, adored by Americans and Russians alike, were born with the publication of *Fer-de-lance*. Although Stout would go on to create other characters (Tecumseh Fox and Dol Bonner) for a few odd novels of their own, the Wolfe-and-Archie duo would be Stout's legacy. Wolfe, a three-hundred-pound Montenegrin-born detective with a love for orchids, a disdain for women, and a fear of leaving his house, employs the young and dashing Archie Goodwin to traverse New York, doing his errands for him and bringing him suspects and witnesses that help him solve every case. Wolfe charges exorbitant fees, Archie drinks only milk, and together they became one of the detective genre's most famous crime-solving duos. Although the pair has been compared to Sherlock Holmes and Dr. Watson, as well as Hercule Poirot and Captain Hastings, they remain unique in their pairing of the puzzle-solving genius, Wolfe, and the hard-boiled sidekick, Archie.[24]

Stout's use of not one but two private detectives reinforces his novels' setting in capitalist society; the trend in Soviet and Russian detective fiction was to use police or military men as the heroes. Nero Wolfe does have a working relationship with several policemen, but he often metes out justice on an individual basis, arranging for the suicide or, more rarely, the murder of guilty parties.[25] His ability to personally deliver justice and the positive role that his working outside of the system plays in the plots highlight the values of the capitalist society wherein he resides. In *Fer-de-Lance*, Wolfe stands idly by while a homicidal son kills his homicidal father in a plane crash, an instance of sidestepping the judicial system that critic Bruce Beiderwell describes as Wolfe

---

24 Sean McCann, "The Hard-Boiled Novel," in *Gumshoe America: Hard-Boiled Crime Fiction and the Rise and Fall of New Deal Liberalism*, ed. Donald E. Pease, New Americanists (Duke University Press, 2000), 47, 48.

25 Bruce Beiderwell, "State Power and Self-Destruction: Rex Stout and the Romance of Justice," *Journal of Popular Culture* (1993), 16.

suggest[ing] that contractual theories of society can minimize his own obligations. A citizen accepts burdens as well as benefits in living in a civil society; Wolfe communicated the burdens to the criminal while saving what benefits he can for himself and (by implication) those who take pleasure in reading of his exploits.[26]

This description of how Wolfe works is the opposite of anything that could occur under Communism; a private detective self-profiting in terms of both fees from solving a crime and income from selling the story of his solving of the crime didn't make sense in a Communist society.

Nero Wolfe's extravagant lifestyle is also indicative of a capitalist world. Ammie Cannon writes that Wolfe embodies the economic structure of American society owing to his wealth and social status, implicitly accepting the following:

the right to protect personal property and liberty, the responsibility to work within the socioeconomic framework, the right to make money through whatever legal means present themselves, and the justness of acquiring wealth through the current system of economic distribution, which favors already educated, employed, and generally socially integrated members of society.[27]

The success of Wolfe and his lifestyle proves how capitalistic individuals are free to take their own paths and succeed. Wolfe's actions and lifestyle could never exist in "Red Pinkertons," for

---

26 Ibid.
27 Cannon, "Controversial Politics, Conservative Genre: Rex Stout's Archie-Wolfe Duo and Detective Fiction's Conventional Form," 43.

Wolfe does not, by any stretch of the imagination, fit the description of Bukharin's hypothetical "revolutionary fighter."

Russian speakers on online Nero Wolfe fan sites have clearly been affected by Stout's portrayal of capitalism in American society.[28] New York, the main location of Stout's novels, is an important facet of the plot for Russian readers; the city as a foreign, Western space is received in a variety of ways. Sergey Panichev, a member of a Wolfe fan club on the Russian site VKontakte, writes that his familiarity with New York remains at a surface level even after reading Stout, for he thinks that Stout's descriptions of the city are excessively sparse. However, Panichev writes that reading of New York in the Wolfe novels did spark "interest of household diversity, the multiculturalism of the city, [and] its multinational nature." Sergey Chervotkin (username Avis) looks upon the portrayal of New York and America in general "ironically, yet favorably," and User BleWotan agrees, making the distinction that "States are States, New York is New York :D."[29]

---

28 The Russian forum members' views on racism, Communism, and the FBI in Stout's novels will be discussed in detail in Chapters Three, Five, and Seven.

29 Sergey Chervotkin (user Avis), November 20, 2015 (11:32am), comment on Molly Zuckerman, "Reks Staut iz Ameriki v Rossii," *O Niro Vul'fe, Archi Gudvine, i ikh avtore, Rekse Staute* (*About Nero Wolfe, Archie Goodwin, and their author, Rex Stout*) (blog), trans. Gleb Vinokurov, October 18, 2015 (8:38pm), http://nerowolfe.info/forum/viewtopic.php?f=5&t= 522&sid=5578a875b87af57f1d92 9613a0f50979; Stanislav Zavgorodnii (user Chuchundrovich), November 23, 2015 (4:40pm), comment on Molly Zuckerman, "Reks Staut iz Ameriki v Rossii," *O Niro Vul'fe, Archi Gudvine, i ikh avtore, Rekse Staute* (*About Nero Wolfe, Archie Goodwin, and their author, Rex Stout*) (blog), trans. Gleb Vinokurov, October 18, 2015 (8:38pm), http://nerowolfe.info/forum/viewtopic.php?f=5&t=522&sid=55 78a875b87af57f1d92 9613a0f50979; User BleWotan, December 14, 2015 (2:26pm), comment on Molly Zuckerman, "Reks Staut iz Ameriki v Rossii," *O Niro Vul'fe, Archi Gudvine, i ikh avtore, Rekse Staute* (*About Nero Wolfe, Archie Goodwin, and their author, Rex Stout*) (blog), trans. Gleb Vinokurov, October 18, 2015 (8:38pm), http://nerowolfe.info/forum/viewtopic.php?f=5&t=522&start=10.

Stanislav Zavgorodnii (username Chuchundrovich), the webmaster of the main Russian Nero Wolfe online fan club and an equally intense fan of Stout and America, thinks that Stout's depiction of the US is "realistic enough." However, he does point out the class inequality inherent in Stout's work: "the majority of his characters are people of middle and higher classes of the society. The poor are practically not represented in his books about Nero Wolfe. Besides, most of the stories take place in a huge city—in New York, which also affects our impression of the country." Zavgorodnii is emphatic in his admiration and interest in America (he even created a website called prousa.info), yet his focus on class inequality in the Wolfe books perhaps unconsciously derives from the fact that he grew up in Soviet Ukraine, in a culture where class difference was considered a literary trope necessitating analysis.[30]

Russian readers especially noticed even something as seemingly inconsequential as the brief descriptions of the countryside in Stout's books. Zavgorodnii writes that countryside (or rural areas) in America are described in a "quite unusual" manner. The countryside in books like *Death of a Dude* and *Some Buried Caesar* (the first Wolfe book that Zavgorodnii read) is filled with wealthy landowners and large ranches. It is not surprising that an ex-Soviet citizen, reading Stout's books in Ukraine in the 1990s, would react to this. In *Some Buried Caesar*, a bull is one of the "murder" victims, and the animal alone is worth tens of thousands of dollars. In the 1990s, a wealthy landowner who owned acres of land and a forty-five-thousand-dollar bull in the Russian or Ukrainian countryside would have been an impossibility.[31]

---

30 Stanislav Zavgorodnii (user Chuchundrovich), November 23, 2015. Stanislav Zavgorodnii (user Chuchundrovich) is the creator and head of the Russian Nero Wolfe online forum and website.

31 Rex Stout, *Some Buried Caesar* (Farrar & Rinehart, 1939).

The Creation of Nero Wolfe and Archie Goodwin

Nero Wolfe and Archie Goodwin were not only of interest to Russian readers owing to the descriptions of their capitalist lifestyle in a democratic society—they were unique to the detective genre as a whole in that their partnership was a pairing of two people of relatively equal intelligence. Unlike Watson and Hastings, who hang around Holmes and Poirot in the roles of dimwitted sidekicks who help out their brilliant detective friends with inane comments that often inadvertently point the detective to the murderer, Archie is a useful and essential partner involved intimately in the success of Wolfe's cases.

Nero Wolfe as a character has a more complicated and checkered past than other famous fictional detectives. According to several books in the corpus, Wolfe was born in Montenegro and grew up in a small house on the side of a mountain. Stout scholar Bernard DeVoto traces out a solid timeline of Wolfe's life, beginning with his entering the Austrian secret service in 1913, when Wolfe was between 19 and 21 years of age. He travelled from Egypt to Arabia at this time, and was in Albania in 1915, jailed in Bulgaria in 1916, and joined the Montenegrin army that same year. Wolfe then adopted Carla, a Montenegrin child, having taken pity on her as a starving orphan in 1921, but left her behind when he went to America and from then on did not return to Montenegro until the adventure depicted in *The Black Mountain*.[32]

Wolfe never directly tells his life story to Archie or to the readers but instead lets it slip out, bit by bit, in various stories. In *Over My Dead Body*, he is most candid, for he must deal with

---

32 Bernard DeVoto, "The Easy Chair- Alias Nero Wolfe," *Harpers Magazine*, July 1954, 9, 12.

the inquisition of a meddling FBI agent. It is during this farcical interrogation that the reader learns about Wolfe's political activities in Europe. In the same book, Wolfe tells Archie that the reason he gained so much fat is to protect himself from his feelings after they got too strong for him on one occasion as a boy in Montenegro. Archie guesses that this could have to do with a Montenegrin woman, owing to Wolfe's negative reaction upon hearing Carla speak Serbo-Croatian.[33]

McAleer speculates that Stout received inspiration for Nero Wolfe from his grandmother, who is described as sitting "much of the time, but always in her special straight backed chair … There was always a book in her hands. On a stand beside her a mammoth dictionary lay, perpetually open … With houseplants she was a sorceress."[34] As well, Stout scholar William Baring-Gould writes that Wolfe is based on Stout himself:

> The case for Stout's resemblance to Nero improves, however, when their intellectual attributes are considered: both are formidable antagonists in verbal battle: both often stoop to irregular means to prove a point. Then, too, Nero's hobbies resemble Stout's. Nero is obsessed by orchids; Stout has won blue ribbons at country fairs for his mammoth pumpkins and strawberries.[35]

In an interview, Stout refuted any speculation (often raised) about Wolfe being either the son of Sherlock Holmes or his brother Mycroft, denouncing the ideas as nonsense.[36] Stout then delves into his own specific notions about the creation of

---

33 Rex Stout, *Over My Dead Body* (Farrar & Rinehart, Inc., 1940), 119.

34 McAleer, *Rex Stout: A Majesty's Life*, 49.

35 William S. Baring-Gould, *Nero Wolfe of West Thirty-Fifth Street* (Penguin Books, 1982), ix.

36 Beiderwell, "State Power and Self-Destruction: Rex Stout and the Romance of Justice," 15. Bobby Ray Miller and Ronald G. Burns, "It's Time Again for a New Nero Wolfe Detective Novel," Rex Stout Papers, MS1986-096, John J. Burns Library, Boston College.

good characters for novels; he claims that, although he created Wolfe, he has no idea where he came from:

> Listen, you know damn well in all fiction writing, dramatic, narrative—no matter what level of literature—all characters are of two kinds. They're either created or contrived. In the created ones, the writer really has no idea where he came from or anything else. And the others, they're made up. And, boy, how you can tell 'em apart.

In another interview by Shenker several years later, Stout cites Russian fictional characters as examples of "first degree" writing, even though his characters of Wolfe and Archie do not embody classic Russian character psychologies: "It was obvious in a paragraph the way Dostoevsky felt about Raskolnikov, or the way Tolstoy felt about Natasha, and their feeling was of a degree that I wouldn't get."[37]

There is also the case to be made for Wolfe's heritage's debt to Stout's friend Louis Adamic, a Slovenian author, whose description of Montenegrins seems to have inspired some of Wolfe's more characteristics: "Adamic describes the Montenegrin male as tall, commanding, dignified, courteous, hospitable. He is reluctant to work, accustomed to isolation from women…. He is stubborn, fearless, unsubduable, [and] capable of great self-denial to uphold his ideals."[38]

Archie Goodwin does not have as complicated a personal history as Wolfe. He grew up in Ohio and moved to New York at an unknown date and started working for Wolfe soon after,

---

[37] Israel Shenker, "Rex Stout, 85, Gives Clues on Good Writing," *The New York Times*, December 1, 1971.

[38] McAleer, *Rex Stout: A Majesty's Life*, 546.

assisting him with his cases and writing them up in the form of the books that readers know Stout really wrote. Wolfe depends on Archie for everything—reading his mail, categorizing his orchid hybrids, and bringing in (sometimes forcibly) murder suspects to the brownstone that Wolfe almost never leaves. Even when Wolfe leaves his brownstone for a case in Yugoslavia, a country where he speaks the language and Archie doesn't, he can't leave Archie behind. Wolfe says, "If I hadn't let you grow into a habit I could have done this without you."[39]

While Wolfe's style of detection is akin to that of classic literary detectives like Poirot, who depend on their intelligence alone to solve complex murder mysteries, Archie's personality is linked to the Sam Spade, hard-boiled model of detective. Archie, while often acknowledging that he does not have the same level of genius as Wolfe, is remarkable in his own intellectual capacity in that he can commit to memory long conversations between multiple people and then repeat them back to Wolfe verbatim whenever Wolfe asks. Archie is consistently described as handsome and well-dressed and, in many of the stories, he takes female suspects on dates, which fall under the umbrella of his job description of "running errands" for Wolfe. While he is out on these errands, which can range from the aforementioned dates to the illegal searching of a suspect's apartment to the procurement of a certain type of gourmet food, Wolfe often reminds Archie to always "act in the light of experience as guided by intelligence."[40]

The critic and professor Sean McCann writes that the hard-boiled detective story is central to American culture, and Archie definitely embraces the all-American, gangster-like attitude

---

[39] Rex Stout, *The Black Mountain* (The Viking Press, Inc., 1954), Location 684.
[40] *In the Best Families* (The Viking Press, Inc., 1950).

of classic hard-boiled detectives like Dashiell Hammett's Sam Spade and Raymond Chandler's Philip Marlowe. Stout's success with his novels can be attributed to his combination of Wolfe as the eccentric intellectual and Archie as the hard-boiled detective who struggles with the "tension between bureaucratic organization and personal autonomy."[41] Wolfe has his own personal set of morals and sometimes chooses to sidestep the formal processes of justice in favor of an easier way out, while Archie lives his life looking for "the chance to seize his heroic mission and remake his world."[42] Wolfe as a stand-alone character, a Montenegrin refugee in America, could easily be written into commonplace plots of international conspiracies, just as Archie could easily fit into simple plots involving American gangsters: Stout's genius in pairing these two unique figures creates the opportunity for more innovative plots and imaginative murders that feel real because of his two characters' differing backgrounds and personalities.

---

41 McCann, "The Hard-Boiled Novel," 44.
42 Ibid., 45.

2 | Stout Critiques American Politics

As I understand it, the Commies think that they get too little and capitalists get too much of the good things in life. They sure played hell with that theory that Tuesday evening
—Archie Goodwin
Champagne for One

Anti-German Attitudes and a Change of Habit in Writing

The psychology of Wolfe as a character, with his predilection for luxury and his strong views on democratic freedoms, allowed Stout to use Wolfe to promote his own political views without its seeming out of character. Stout took a very strong stance against Nazism during World War II, a stance that manifested itself through both political action and the plots of his detective novels. In 1941, Stout helped establish arguably the most important foundation of his career, Freedom House.[43] The

---

43 Martin J. Manning and Herbert Romerstein, *Historical Dictionary of American Propaganda* (Greenwood, 2004), 269.

organization was created through a merger of political groups that wanted America to enter the war, and it devoted itself to the promotion of concrete actions toward international freedom.

The many organizations to which Stout belonged throughout his life (Friends of Democracy, the War Writers' Board, the Society for the Prevention of World War III, and more) demonstrate that he considered himself a man of both actions and words; although he was a prolific letter writer and novelist, he also placed importance on making real changes in American foreign and domestic wartime policies. In an October 1941 interview with *Cue* magazine, Stout said, "Everything else of importance must be set aside—work, pleasure, family life, everything, until that man [Hitler] and machine [Nazi Germany] are destroyed. Apathy in the face of the world situation is unthinkable. Shout. Write your Congressman. Write the President. Nag. Coerce. Ridicule. Make yourself felt."[44]

In his later novels, Stout would combine political messages with the murder mysteries solved by Wolfe and Archie, but it seemed that during the peak of war everything "must be set aside." Through the war years of 1939 to 1945, Stout wrote only five Wolfe books, two fewer than he normally would have with his one-book-a-year system: *Some Buried Caesar* (1939), *Over My Dead Body* (1940), *Where There's a Will* (1940), *Black Orchids* (1942), and the two-novella collection *Not Quite Dead Enough* (1944). Two of those novels plus both novellas touch on political themes.[45] In the first of the two novellas, Wolfe himself follows Stout's directives in *Cue* magazine and gives up his gourmand lifestyle; he even begins exercising to prepare to shoot more Germans, because he didn't shoot enough last time (as he

---

44 McAleer, *Rex Stout: A Majesty's Life*, 282.

45 The only other Wolfe story that places Archie and Wolfe in roles helping during wartime is the novella *Help Wanted, Male*, published after the war in 1949.

puts it).⁴⁶ The second novella, *Booby Trap*, involves Archie working for the US Army. (*Over My Dead Body* concerns both Nazis and Yugoslav refugees and will be discussed in Chapter Five.)

In a 1943 book review in *The New York Times*, Stout discusses the way that literature can help to change the public's mind about the German people: "A large majority of us still believe that the Germans are on the whole people of good-will, temporarily misled by the Nazi gangsters. It does no good for me to say that that opinion of the Germans is utterly false. Who believes me? But a book could do it."⁴⁷ Stout's multiple negative portrayals of Germans (and later Communists and the FBI) in his novels and articles put this idea into action; he uses books to make sure that no one could think any German a person of good will.

Stout's pro-war, anti-German attitude continued with a series of radio shows that he hosted on CBS through 1943, a task that he prioritized over writing, for he did not write his annual Wolfe novel in 1943. The first program was called *Speaking of Liberty* (in 1941), then *Voice of Freedom* (1942), with the best known being *Our Secret Weapon* from (1942-43). All of the programs analyzed Axis radio transmissions and offered succinct commentary from a counterpropaganda stance. Stout's neat responses picking apart the Axis messages would later be reflected in his novels, where he gives a voice to both the American Communist left and the anti-Communist Nero Wolfe; one can connect their dialogue with words used by Stout during his broadcasts and the scripts of the actual Axis broadcasts.⁴⁸

---

46 Rex Stout, *Not Quite Dead Enough*, in *Not Quite Dead Enough* (Farrar & Rinehart, 1944), 14.

47 "Books and the Tiger," *The New York Times Book Review Spring Book Supplement* March 21, 1943.

48 *The Truth*, Podcast audio, Our Secret Weapon, 14:36 August 30, 1942, https://archive.org/details/1942RadioNews. See the deleted excerpt from the manuscript of *Home to Roost*, referenced in Chapter Three, as an example of this reflection.

Although Stout had begged the American public to give up all work and pleasure for the war effort, his manner of speaking during the program revealed that his mind never quite stopped thinking of Wolfe and Archie. McAleer describes Stout's role on *Our Secret Weapon* as a lie detective:

> Rex used the logic of Nero Wolfe and the idiom of Archie—with due allowances for "Pfui" [Wolfe's favorite], which turn up in the broadcasts every now and again. Indeed, the World Wide interviewer, watching Rex examine "with patient curiosity" the scripts of the monitored broadcasts, found him quite Neronian…. On 20 September, he spoke in pure Goodwinese: "The Germans have no good bets left. They've raked in all the easy pots and from here they're drawing to inside straights."[49]

Stout's antipathy against the German people was well recorded throughout the war in his nonfiction articles as well. His anti-Germany essay, "We Shall Hate or We Shall Fail," published in 1943 in *The New York Times*, reaffirms Stout's harsh position against Germany and Germans as a whole. Stout writes in a mockery of Hitler's words, "You can be a German, or you can accept a code of morality. You cannot do both," referencing a quotation of Hitler's: "You can be a German, or you can be Christian. You cannot be both."[50] In 1945, Stout even briefly went to Germany as a war correspondent, and while on a tour he "took a shot at a distant German soldier but 'apparently missed.'"[51] Stout's unequivocal hatred of Germans, and his conflation of all Germans with the Nazi Party, might seem

---

49 McAleer, *Rex Stout: A Majesty's Life*, 294-95.

50 Rex Stout, "We Shall Hate, or We Shall Fail," *The New York Times*, January 17 1943, 6.

51 O.E. McBride, *Stout Fellow: A Guide through Nero Wolfe's World*, (iUniverse, 2003).

narrow-minded when one looks at his later protests against McCarthyism and his strong stance against censorship. A man who was able to preach for hatred and strong government action against foreign enemies did not seem compatible with a man who would later be a loud protester against McCarthy's and the FBI's action against supposed internal US enemies. But Stout was a man of strong opinions, and, although they might have seemed inconsistent to an outside observer, he followed his personal code of morality and was never bothered by any apparent contradictions.

Stout and World Federalism

Alongside his crusade against the Germans, Stout spent a significant amount of time from before the war until much later in life promoting the idea of world federalism. Stout chaired the Writers' War Board, established in January 1942, an organization supporting World Federalism that he remained a member of until 1970.[52] World War Two led him to the belief that the best way to avoid another war was to create one global government. After the war, Stout continued his support for world federalism by joining the United World Federalists, a 50,000-member organization founded in 1947 that claimed such celebrity writers as Kurt Vonnegut and E. B. White as members. Stout, with two other members, musical comedy giant Oscar Hammerstein II and radio and television personality Clifton Fadiman, wrote and acted in a play called "The Myth that Threatens the World" that toured America in the early 1950s, sponsored and promoted by the United World Federalists.[53] When interviewed about con-

---

52 Benjamin F. Shearer, *Home Front Heroes: A Biographical Dictionary of Americans During Wartime* vol. 3 (Greenwood, 2006), 788.

53 "The Myth That Threatened the World," in *Rex Stout: Activist* (The Wolfe Pack: The Nero Wolfe Literary Society).

troversy generated by the play, which centered on the United Nations becoming the basis for a global government, Stout said,

> We were a small island of liberty in a despotic world 173 years ago when our Declaration of Independence was issued…. But this July 4th, after nearly ninety score years of great change, including two world wars in our own lifetime, we have become the leaders in a fight for a free and peaceful world. Necessarily, this means our own freedom at home has become dependent on the progress of liberty everywhere.[54]

Stout went so far as to personally invite J. Edgar Hoover, then head of the FBI, to the play, writing that Hoover would be "glad [he] came," but Hoover responded that he was "unable to accept [his] gracious invitation as previous commitments preclude [his] attendance at the event."[55] Stout also personally wrote to Eleanor Roosevelt in 1951, quoting part of an article she had written and imploring her to publicly support the movement for world government. Stout ended the letter with an appeal: "Your support of that great cause would be one of the most encouraging pieces of news that could possibly be proclaimed. May it not be that you are now ready to proclaim it?"[56]

Stout's activities with world federalism would not have been welcome ideas in the Soviet Union in the 1940s and 50s. In 1934, Stalin had declared that Communism was a success at the 17th Congress of the Communist Party, better known as the Congress of Victors. Stalin did desire a world government, but

---

54 "17 Writers Frame a World Law Plan," *The New York Times* July 4, 1949.

55 Unknown to J. Edgar Hoover, undated correspondence, FBI Redacted File, Wolfe Pack online archives, 3.

56 Rex Stout to Mrs. Franklin D. Roosevelt, "Writers Board for World Government," January 15, 1951, Wolfe Pack online archives.

in his terms that would involve an international proletarian revolt that would lead to Communism in every country. Stalin had resolved himself to building "socialism in one country," and wanted as little Western interference in the Soviet population as was possible. On the other hand, Stout was constantly dreaming of a universal capitalist order that would inevitably include Russia in its jurisdiction.

Stout and Racism

World federalism and the hope for every society to be governed by the same rules necessitated an idea of what those rules should be, and therefore Stout's concepts of morality and human rights took on a great significance in his life. This included taking a stance on societal problems he saw within America, especially the plight of African Americans. Stout had always had what McAleer referred to as a "lifelong respect and admiration for blacks," and this respect led to the inclusion of the theme of race relations in providing motives for murder in two Wolfe stories, *Too Many Cooks* (1938) and *A Right to Die* (1964). Both highlighted the senselessness of racism and its consequences in America.[57]

The first Wolfe novel to touch on racism is *Too Many Cooks*, a novel that is described as Stout's way of "clearly strik[ing] a blow for human freedom so subtly the reader never realizes he is being enlisted for a point of view in the process of enjoying a detective story."[58] The plot is an unusual one, for it takes Wolfe out of his brownstone and places him in Kanawha Spa, West Virginia, where he attends a sauce tasting and one of the chefs involved is murdered in front of him. The spa employs a black service

---

57 McAleer, *Rex Stout: A Majesty's Life*, 53.
58 Ibid., 263.

staff, and the murderer therefore wears blackface to commit the crime undetected, which brings race into the mix. While Archie casually uses racial slurs throughout the book, Wolfe does not, and during a long speech to the black service staff he convinces one of them, Paul Whipple, to divulge a secret and therefore catch the murderer.[59]

Skipping ahead almost thirty years, a race theme returns in *A Right to Die* in 1964. It is also unusual in that a character from a previous novel (who is not Wolfe's nemesis Arnold Zeck or one of the recurring policemen or freelance detectives) reappears in the form of Paul Whipple, the black man who helped Wolfe catch the murderer at Kanawha Spa. Whipple's son, Dunbar, is going to marry a white woman, Susan, who works with him at the Rights of Citizens Committee (ROCC), and Whipple wants the interracial marriage stopped. Wolfe only agrees to take the case because he owes Whipple a favor, but when Susan gets murdered and Dunbar ends up behind bars, Wolfe sets about finding the real murderer. After a second murder takes place, Wolfe manages to pin the crimes on a white woman whose son had killed himself years before after Susan had refused his romantic advances. The mother had traced Susan down and taken a job at the ROCC to be near her. She decided to kill her after she became engaged to a black man, which was an "insult" that she couldn't stand; her reason for murder was solely racially-motivated.[60] The racially-charged plot of *A Right to Die* called attention to Stout as a positive race relations advocate: after the novel's publication, Stout was elected to the National Committee Against Discrimination in Housing.[61]

---

[59] Rex Stout, *Too Many Cooks* (Farrar & Rinehart, Inc., 1938). 60 *A Right to Die* (The Viking Press, Inc., 1964).
[60] *A Right to Die* (The Viking Press, Inc., 1964).
[61] McAleer, *Rex Stout: A Majesty's Life*, 440.

3 | Stout and His Characters Hate the "Commies"

But the Communist angle comes first until and unless it's ruled out. So you can see why we're in on it. The public interest is involved, not only of this city and state but the whole country. You see that?
—Nero Wolfe and the Communist Killer

Battling Stereotypes and Promoting Democratic Liberties

Stout's main crusades, fighting what he saw as the immorality of both McCarthyism and Communism, put him in the public spotlight in America in a way that his past political projects – anti-Nazism, world federalism, and anti-racism – had not. He was first and foremost a strong anti-Communist, being against both American Communism and Communism abroad. Stout believed in the importance of democracy and used the Nero Wolfe series in order to express that belief, by among other things placing Wolfe and Archie in the middle of the war effort. In the postwar years, the ferocity of Stout's anti-Communist plots made it surprising that any of his books were allowed to be printed in the USSR.

Stout's personal battle against McCarthyism was complicated by his past and present association with several organizations that allegedly had Communist connections, such as *The New Masses*; some people mistook his far-left leanings for more "sinister" Communist ones. His FBI file in 1942 contained a memo that branded Stout as "a Communist fellow traveler and one of the prize exhibits of the [Martin] Dies House Committee on Un-American Activities."[62] When Stout met Dies, the *Amarillo Globe* reported, Stout told him "I hate Communists as much as you do, Martin, but there's one difference between us. I know what a Communist is and you don't."[63] Herbert Mitgang references a column in the *Washington Times-Herald* that also attacked Stout's alleged Communism:

> Rex Stout [is a] goat-bearded writer of mystery stories.... His long gray chin whiskers bristled against a scarlet shirt, and there was a fanatical gleam in his small brown eyes. He was like a grotesque caricature of a man.[64]

In 1944, when Stout attended a Republican political rally for New York representative Hamilton Fish and publically heckled him with accusations of spreading Nazi propaganda, Fish's response was to attack Stout's political views: "You are a Communist and are more dangerous to America than Earl

---

62 Michael Newton, *The FBI Encyclopedia* (McFarland, 2003), 325. Martin Dies was the creator of the House Committee Investigating Un-American Activities, which later became HUAC.

63 "Some Quips That Flew in from the Air Front," *The Amarillo Globe* April 26, 1945.

64 Chesly Manly quoted in Herbet Mitgang, *Dangerous Dossiers: Exposing the Secret War against America's Greatest Authors* (Open Road Distribution, 2015), Location 3037.

Browder!"⁶⁵ Stout is quoted as saying that he built his house, High Meadow, "all in Connecticut because I didn't want Hamilton Fish—so what did I get? Clare Boothe Luce!"⁶⁶ Stout's treatment at the Fish rally (and subsequently by Hoover and the FBI after the publication of his novel *The Doorbell Rang*) was a stimulus for Stout's strong questioning of unsubstantiated accusations of Communism.

Stout saw the fight against Communism and the fight against the rising influence of Senator Joseph McCarthy in the 1950s as linked causes. Although McCarthy was allegedly fighting Communism in his own particular way, with public denunciations, Stout believed that McCarthy's style actually worked against those truly fighting Communism. McCarthy's loud denunciations and calls for silencing the views of suspected Communists led to a decline in democratic freedoms in America, Stout believed. He considered democratic freedoms to be more valuable than anything gained by quelling alleged Communist sentiment. McAleer writes that "Rex saw that the methods of McCarthyism discredited democracy itself. Freedom House [where Stout worked during the height of McCarthyism] did not wish to bundle with strange bedfellows."⁶⁷ In 1952, Freedom House released a statement, drafted with help from Stout, concerning the danger of McCarthyism: "Wild exaggerations and

---

65 Earl Browder was the leader of the Communist Party USA from 1930 to 1945.

66 "Stout Nearly Causes a Riot at Fish Rally," *The New York Times*, November 3 1944; John T. Winterich and Frankel Haskel, "Private Eye on the FBI," *Saturday Review of Literature*, (October 9 1965): 54-55. Luce won the House of Representatives seat representing Fairfield Country, Connecticut, in 1942. Stout's animosity toward her is presumed to stem from her popularity with isolationists, while Stout was a staunch advocate for entering the war. Luce was also the wife of Henry Luce, the right-wing editor of *Time* magazine. Wikipedia contributors, "Clare Boothe Luce," Wikipedia, The Free Encyclopedia., https://en.wikipedia.org/w/index.php?title=Clare_Boothe_Luce&oldid=707265564.

67 McAleer, *Rex Stout: A Majesty's Life*, 370.

inexcusable inaccuracies serve to divide and confuse the country when we should be united in the task of resisting Communist aggression abroad and Communist subversion at home."[68]

Stout's dismissal of the legitimacy of McCarthyism also meant that he aligned himself against what he saw as the excessive censorship of writers spurred on by McCarthy's overzealous attitude. Stout was part of the Committee of 1,000 that signed a document, written by Harvard astronomer Dr. Harlow Sharpley and published in 1948 in *The New York Sun*, that referred to the HUAC hearings as a "trial by headlines [that] encouraged publicity seekers and sympathizers."[69] In 1952, Stout became president of the Authors' League of America (also known as the Authors' Guild), which was part of the movement against the blacklisting of writers for purported Communist connections (the specialty of magazines like *Red Channels*.)[70]

Stout was against all intrusion from above into the mind of the writer, even if the writer might be a Communist. McAleer describes a situation where an FBI man came to High Meadow to ask Stout about a friend, and once the FBI agent asked if this friend had read *The New Republic*, Stout remembered, "I wouldn't talk to him anymore. I will not cooperate with a sub-

---

68 Ibid., 376.

69 Mitgang, *Dangerous Dossiers: Exposing the Secret War against America's Greatest Authors*, Location 2056. Later seen as the American version of "show trials," the House Un-American Activities Committee (HUAC) led highly publicized hearings on the purported subversive behavior of Americans linked to the Communist Party. Wikipedia contributors, "House Un-American Activities Committee," Wikipedia, The Free Encyclopedia., https://en.wikipedia.org/w/index.php?title=House_Un-American_Activities_Committee&oldid=708565501. Novelist Philip Quarles notes in an address that Stout actually ignored a subpoena from HUAC in the 1950s. Philip Quarles, "Rex Stout Writes Detective Stories, Makes Enemies of the FBI," text of podcast audio, WNYC.org, 1:00p, 2013, 2.

70 Mitgang, *Dangerous Dossiers: Exposing the Secret War against America's Greatest Authors*, Location 3004. Although the FBI claimed in their file on Stout that there were "numerous Communists" in the Authors' Guild membership, that claim was never supported with any names or other evidence.

versive organization, and to censor or restrict what a man reads is subversive. I got so damned mad, I put him out."[71] Interestingly, Stout referred to the FBI as the subversive organization, even while the FBI was hinting at his friend's connection with Communism, an ideology that Stout also saw as subversive. Stout's advocacy of the rights of writers against censorship accentuate how his commitment to democratic values outweighed his personal feelings about Communism.

Stout's Anti-Communism Enters His Novels

Stout's aversion to groundless Communist accusations became the baseline for the characters, murder, and motive in *The Second Confession* (1949).[72] The plot revolves around James U. Sperling and his family. Sperling wishes to hire Wolfe to rid his daughter of her boyfriend, Louis Rony, because he suspects that Rony is a Communist. There is no hard evidence of his Communist sympathies, so Sperling wants Wolfe to find the proof and present it to his daughter. According to Sperling, proof of Rony's Communist leanings would be valid reason to end the relationship, which is referred to as "a fate worse than death."[73] Archie and Wolfe don't question this logic; severing ties with a person simply due to a discovery of their Communist leanings makes sense to them as well.

This plot implies a contradiction between Wolfe and Archie's views on Communism and those of Stout. Stout is against McCarthyism, for he feels that it unfairly affects innocent men, and yet he writes a novella in which Wolfe does not question

---

71 McAleer, *Rex Stout: A Majesty's Life*, 447.

72 Ibid., 364. In response to the publication of *The Second Confession*, a *Daily Worker* review lauded Stout's plotline for its discovery of "the possibilities in fusing the current anticommunist drive with the mystery formula."

73 Rex Stout, *The Second Confession* (The Viking Press, Inc., 1949), 8.

the breakup of a relationship owing to a man being a Communist. The distinction should be made here that Wolfe does not fabricate any evidence, and that suspicion alone does not make Wolfe condemn Rony, as McCarthy most likely would have done. Instead, Wolfe agrees to the case only so far as sending Archie to the Sperling home to have a look at both Rony and Sperling's smitten daughter. Even so, his acceptance of the case in the first place implies that it is not morally wrong to try to figure out if a man is a Communist, albeit if it is done in the subtler way of private detection, rather than McCarthy's public denunciations and the showiness of the HUAC trials.

Stout gives anti-Communist sentiments to all of his characters in this story, including Wolfe and Archie. Sperling says that his daughter tried out Communism in college, but then decided that it was "intellectually contemptible and morally unsound." Archie responds to this with a familiarly toned quip, "I like the way she put it. The best I can do is 'a Commie is a louse' or something like that."[74] The plot becomes complicated when Archie goes to stay at the Sperling house for the weekend, tries to drug Rony's drink, finds it already drugged and then arranges for Rony to get hit on the head so Archie can steal his wallet. The wallet turns out to contain the damning evidence of a card certifying that one William Reynolds is a member of the American Communist Party. Shortly after this discovery, Rony's body is found run over by a car in the bushes outside the Sperling home. Wolfe and Archie must then figure out if Rony and Reynolds are the same person or if the card belongs to another member of the household.

It eventually comes out that Rony worked for Arnold Zeck, the longtime nemesis of Wolfe and the only traditional evil villain in the Stout novels. This discovery is made when Zeck or-

---

74 Ibid., 6.

ders a machine-gun attack on Wolfe's beloved orchid plants. In order to expose the murderer of Rony without further incurring Zeck's wrath (although Wolfe is prepared to take him on if necessary), Wolfe arranges a complicated trick wherein he writes several anonymous exposés of Communist Party meetings to gain leverage to make the top members of the American Communist party tell him William Reynolds' real identity.

Archie's repartee as he discusses Communism with secondary characters does not improve from his initial "louse" comment. He and one of the Sperling daughters verbally spar, with her calling him a "comrade" as an insult (a device that Stout used in *Home to Roost*). Archie later says that he "wouldn't put anything beneath a Commie." He cracks jokes about Wolfe's Communist informant behind the exposés being a member of the "Union Square Politburo," refers again to this man as "telling the Commies' family secrets," and references "commissars" reading the documents of the American Communist party. When Wolfe has Archie call the Communist Party headquarters, Archie is connected with a female secretary:

> In a moment a pleasant feminine voice was in my ear. Its being pleasant was a shock, and also I was a little self-conscious, conversing for the first time with a female Commie, so I said, "My name's Goodwin, comrade."[75]

His surprise and shock is the most striking indication of his attitude toward Communism in the book. Archie jokes in every situation, never taking things seriously, so to have him be self-conscious emphasizes that something about speaking with a real Communist has jarred him in a way that only the discovery of a dead body has done before.

---

75 Ibid., 37, 220, 41, 08, 13, 12.

The plot of *The Second Confession* contains a reference to another of Stout's personal political inclinations: world federalism. One of the guests at the Sperling house when Rony is murdered is Paul Emerson, a radio personality who represents Sperling's Continental Mines Corporation. Wolfe dislikes Emerson because of his attitude concerning the World Federalists:

> Minutes later Emerson was taking a crack at another of his pet targets: … they call themselves World Federalists, this bunch of amateur statesmen, and they want us to give up the one thing we've got left— the right to make our own decisions about our own affairs. They think it would be fine if we had to ask permission of all the world's runts and funny-looking dimwits every time we wanted to move our furniture around a little, or even to leave it where it is…[76]

As mentioned earlier, Stout was an active member of the United World Federalists, and a small aside getting revenge on one of their opponents is written into the book's finale. Once Wolfe catches the murderer, Sperling calls to say that "the Continental Mines Corporation was grateful to him for removing a Communist tumor from its internal organs and would be glad to pay a bill if he sent one," but Wolfe turns down the money and asks instead for the removal of Emerson from the radio as payment. When Sperling objects, citing that Emerson had popularity, Wolfe retorts harshly: "'So had Goebbels…and Mussolini.'"[77] Wolfe compares a dislike of world federalism to Nazism and Fascism, overstating his comparison to make a point while mirroring Stout's own views on the matter.[78]

76 Ibid., 159, 60.
77 Ibid., 238, 39.
78 *The Second Confession* was published in 1949, and it was the early 1950s when Stout would tour the country as a stage actor extolling the virtues of a

Stout is, however, mostly concerned with Communism in *The Second Confession*. As part of his scheme to induce Communist Party higher-ups to help him identify the murderer, Wolfe writes several articles for *The Gazette*, the fictional New York newspaper in the Wolfe series, exposing secrets of the party organization. It is never clearly explained who Wolfe's informant is (Wolfe keeps that secret, even from Archie), but Wolfe's information is apparently accurate. The preface to Wolfe's first article reads:

> HOW THE AMERICAN COMMUNISTS PLAY IT/ THE RED ARMY IN THE COLD WAR/THEIR GHQ IN THE USA… *The Gazette presents herewith the first of a series of articles showing how American Communists help Russia fight the cold war and get ready for the hot one if and when it comes. This is the real thing. For obvious reasons the name of the author of the articles cannot be given, but the Gazette has a satisfactory guaranty of their authenticity. We hope to continue the series up to the most recent activities of the Reds, including their secret meetings before, during, and after the famous trial in New York. The second article will appear tomorrow. Don't miss it!*[79]

The articles succeed in their purpose of scaring the American Communist Party into a willingness to do anything to stop them. Wolfe assembles two of the Party leaders in his office so that they can identify one of their members from several photographs of all suspects from the Sperling house party, for Wolfe doesn't know which one goes by "William Reynolds" as an alias

---

single world government.
79 Stout, *The Second Confession*, 207, 08. "The famous trial" referenced is the Rosenberg spy trial.

for his Party membership. The Party leaders indirectly indentify the murderer by pointing him out.

Archie's description of the Party members is on par with his usual vocabulary concerning Communists; his continual surprise at the normal appearance of Communists is always insulting: "Having seen one or two high-ranking Commies in the flesh, and many published pictures of more than a dozen of them, I didn't expect our callers to look like wart hogs or puff adders, but even so they surprised me a little."[80] Dialogue between Stevens, one of the Communist Party leaders, and Wolfe underlines the idea that merely linking a man with Communism does not make him a murderer. Stevens says, "'It hasn't quite got to where you can prove a man committed murder just by proving he's a Communist.'…. 'No,' Wolfe conceded. 'Rather the contrary. Communists are well advised to disapprove of private murders for private motives.'"[81]

The last twenty or so pages of the novel have more slurs against Communism than the rest of the book combined. Archie pokes fun at the supposed gluttony of the Communist Party leaders:

> As I understand it, the Commies think that they get too little and capitalists get too much of the good things in life. They sure played hell with that theory that Tuesday evening. A table in the office was loaded with liquids, cheese, nuts, homemade pâté, and crackers, and not a drop or a crumb was taken by any of the thirteen people there [non-Communists], including Wolfe and me. On a table in the front room there was a similar assort-

---

80 Ibid., 214.

81 Ibid., 216. Wolfe's sentiment reflects the differences between Western crime fiction and Soviet crime fiction, for the latter tended to avoid motives for murder involving private or individual gain, wants, or intrigue.

ment in smaller quantities, and Harvey and Stevens [the Communists], just two of them, practically cleaned it up. If I had noticed it before the Commies left I would have called it to their attention.[82]

When Wolfe goes through his final deduction, he does not mention the actual Communist by name, and Sperling gets the wrong idea that Rony was the one who belonged to the Party. Wolfe corrects this misperception and adds, "You were as wrong…as a man can get. You may be a good businessman, Mr. Sperling, but you had better leave the exposure of disguised Communists to competent persons."[83] Wolfe is casting another stone at McCarthy with his reprimand of Sperling; McCarthy is not a competent person to weed out Communists, but Wolfe considers that he himself is.

Once the name of the actual Communist, an associate of Sperling, is revealed, Sperling's attitude is one of horror "after the terrific jolt of learning that he had nurtured a Commie in his bosom for years." Wolfe, who does not mince words in his accusation, takes the harshest tone as he addresses the culprit: "You're done as Kane [the murderer's real name], with the Communist brand showing at last. You're done as Reynolds, with your comrades spitting you out as only they can spit. You're done even as a two-legged animal, with a murder to answer for."[84] Wolfe has the evidence that Kane ran over Rony with a car, but his guilt on murder charges is separate from his Communism (even though the motive for Rony's murder was to protect Kane's undisclosed identity as a Communist).

---

82 Ibid., 225.
83 Ibid., 230.
84 Ibid., 237, 35, 36.

Chervotkin, on the Russian forum, did not like the plot of *The Second Confession*, disapproving of what he considered Stout's ignorance of the reality of Communism and the validity of Stout's source material: "There is too much exaggeration, too much bile, without any proper knowledge of the subject. What Stout is describing was characteristic of the end of the 19th century. I believe he collected the information from Marx's works and Bolshevik newspapers of the beginning of the 20th century."[85] Vk user Panichev's concise summation of Stout's views on Communism in *The Second Confession* is humorous in its accurate simplicity: "Apparently he was not impressed."[86]

Stout's anti-Communist sentiment in his plots continued with two novellas published in the trilogy *Triple Jeopardy* in 1952. The first is *Home to Roost* (originally entitled *Nero Wolfe and the Communist Killer*), which is largely concerned with Wolfe's beliefs about both the threat of Communism in America as well as the threat of the threat to Communism, McCarthyism. A murdered man is purportedly a Communist, and the same kind of harsh language surrounding the Communist Party that appears in *The Second Confession* appears with greater prevalence in this story. It begins with Mr. and Mrs. Benjamin Rackell coming to Wolfe with a problem: their nephew has been murdered, and before his death he had said he was an FBI spy posing as a Communist.[87] At first glance, it seems to be a locked-room mystery: Arthur Rackell attends a dinner with five guests, swallows a vitamin capsule, and is dead within ten minutes.

After Archie gathers the dinner guests in Wolfe's office, it becomes clear that the murder plot is hopelessly tangled in political intrigue, with FBI agents pretending to be Communists

---

85 Sergey Chervotkin (user Avis), November 20, 2015.
86 Sergey Panichev, Vkontakte message to author, March 15, 2016.
87 Rex Stout, *Home to Roost*, in *Triple Jeopardy* (The Viking Press, Inc., 1952), 1.

and Communists getting spooked by FBI agents. Wolfe sends Archie out on a willing fool's errand to provoke the murderer into revealing herself. He tries to convince one of the guests to falsely confess for money, leading to her telling the story to another murder suspect, undercover FBI agent Carol Berk. The story resolves itself with the revelation that Arthur Rackell had been a true Communist and had lied to his aunt about working for the FBI to continue following his divisive political ideology. Unfortunately for him, his aunt was secretly a member of the American Communist Party herself, and, overcome with fear at the threat of exposure through living with an FBI agent, put poison in her nephew's vitamins to save her reputation.

Although both Wolfe and Archie express strong anti-Communist views through their harsh language to the suspects, the novella's main political purpose is to take subtle jabs at the logic behind McCarthyism. McCarthyism was in its heyday in 1951 when the story was first published, for in 1950 McCarthy had given his famous speech on Lincoln Day (at a Republican Party fundraising event) during which he brandished a list of the names of supposed Communists working in the State Department (a claim he had trouble proving in the following years). Wolfe's speech to the five suspects in his office is where he pokes McCarthyism most directly: "I deplore the current tendency to accuse people of pro-communism irresponsibly and unjustly." [88] Wolfe's statement is in line with Stout's thoughts. As McAleer writes, Stout believed "that McCarthy helped Communism by making anti-Communism seem reactionary." [89] The complexity of the plot, with the supposed murder motive turning out to be false and unfounded, promotes Stout's point that McCarthyism was the wrong approach to eliminating Communism in

---

88 Ibid., 49, 50.

89 McAleer, *Rex Stout: A Majesty's Life*, 378. See Héda Kovaly's thoughts on McCarthyism in Chapter Six.

the United States. A man is murdered because of the heightened fear of exposure during the Red Scare—a family member kills her orphaned nephew just to avoid being labeled a Communist. This worst-case consequence of the Red Scare could be seen as a warning of the dangers of McCarthy's methods of fighting Communism.

Stout walks a fine line between his disgust for Communism and his disgust for McCarthyism, for, while *Home to Roost* loudly denounces McCarthyism, Stout has no qualms about denouncing Communism in even stronger terms. After the term "Communist" has been introduced to the plot by the Rackells in their first meeting with Wolfe, it is then most often shortened to the pejorative "Commie," its pejorative nature accentuated by the prevalence of its proximity to the word "murder" and other negative phrases. Mrs. Rackell is described as being "convinced not that one of them was a Commie and a murderer, but that they all were." Wolfe brings it home by comparing Communist leanings to a terminal illness: "Anyone might be a Communist, just as anyone might have a hidden carcinoma." The plot contains several more insulting references to and jokes about Communism: there is an "odium attached" to the ideology, and Archie is described as eyeing the attractive Carol Berk "with an expression of comradely interest." The jests also include Wolfe accusing the five suspects of walking out of his office in order "to call a meeting of your Politburo," and again with Carol Berk telling Archie that she will be wearing "a hammer and sickle in [her] buttonhole" on their first date.[90]

In an earlier draft of *Home to Roost*, Stout wrote an ending in which Mrs. Rackell and Wolfe had a harsh ideological showdown in Wolfe's office, as opposed to the published ending, in which Archie simply calls the police to turn over the murderer.

---

90 Stout, *Home to Roost,* 14, 18, 22, 51, 52, 28, 52, 54.

The deleted section includes Mrs. Rackell shouting at her Communist companion, who had exposed her (Mrs. Rackell's) guilt in the murder of her nephew:

> "You worm," she said with cold contempt. "He was a danger to us—I thought he was—and he had to die. And I served the cause! There is nothing but the cause—nothing, nothing. If you tell the police—are you mad, you fool?" He stared at her, at her white lipless face only inches from his, as she held him. He spoke. Staring at her, he said calmly, "I must do my duty as a citizen, Mrs. Rackell."

Wolfe responds fiercely to both Mrs. Rackell and her companion, enraged at the idea that a Communist would cite his American citizenship as any sort of reason to act morally:

> "A citizen?" he roared. "In heaven's name, a citizen of what? You owe allegiance to this country, but you give it to another. You are intellectual robots and moral imbeciles. You scorn and betray the duties and responsibilities of citizenship, but you claim the protection of its rights and privileges." His leveled finger waggled. "Very well, madam, you'll get that protection. In the service of your preposterous cause you have killed a man, and in this country whose interests you have infamously betrayed you will be tried fairly and truly. Ingrates!"

While we don't know why Stout left this argument out of the final published version, he obviously wrestled with its inclusion, for the passages quoted above were attached to the manuscript with the note to "delete lines 7 to 13 and replace with this," meaning that he added it in and then took it out again.[91] The name change of the novella as well, from *Nero Wolfe and the Communist Killer* to the more innocuous *Home to Roost*, demonstrates Stout's indecisiveness over how overtly he wanted his political beliefs to be represented in his fiction.[92] Wolfe's speech also reflects the way Stout reconciled his hatred of McCarthyism with his hatred of Communism; no matter what, democratic values came first, and Wolfe expresses that idea by saying that Mrs. Rackell would still receive the "rights and privileges" of an American citizen. This underlines the core of Stout's problems with Senator McCarthy's treatment of alleged Communists; even with their subversive ideology, Stout did not approve of McCarthy taking away their democratic rights.

Although two members of the Russian forum, Zavgorodnii and user BleWotan, do not like the plot, it is significant that they both referenced *Home to Roost* as the novella that clearly shows Stout's anti-Communist attitudes in Wolfe. Zavgorodnii writes: "No wonder that Wolfe does not like communists either."[93] User BleWotan, describing this novella as "mediocre," calls the Communism depicted in the plot as "somewhat unserious, unlike Stout's hatred for it."[94]

In the second novella from the trilogy *Triple Jeopardy*, *The Cop Killer*, two citizens from a country run by Communists come to Wolfe for a case, making a change from the American Communists Wolfe had previously dealt with. The story begins with Carl and Tina, a couple who work at the barbershop that Archie and Wolfe frequent, coming to Wolfe's office to ask him

---

91 Undated manuscript by Rex Stout, *Home to Roost*, Box 15, Folder 5, Rex Stout Papers, MS1986-096, John J. Burns Library, Boston College.

92 Wolfe's deleted speech condemning Mrs. Rackell and her Communist friend is important to keep in mind when reading Stout's 1966 article on the outcome of the Rosenberg spy trial of 1951.

93 Stanislav Zavgorodnii (user Chuchundrovich), November 23, 2015.

94 User BleWotan, December 14, 2015.

to get them out of a fix. At first, they won't tell Archie the real reason they have come (Wolfe is out of the picture here, for he leaves the front room immediately after seeing them trembling in his yellow chairs—he can't deal with emotional clients). Carl explains that he met his wife

> three years ago in a concentration camp in Russia. If you want me to I will tell you why it was that they would never have let us get out of there alive, not in one hundred years, but I would rather not talk so much about it. It makes me start to tremble, and I am trying to learn to act and talk of a manner so I can quit trembling.

Carl and Tina's descriptions of life in Communist Russia are always characterized in this manner: vague terms of horror and accompanied by Carl's trembling. Their life abroad before working at the barbershop has no positive memories associated with it, for Archie comments on them as having "run out of despair long ago" and Carl utters the heavy phrase, "we have learned so long ago to stay away from windows."[95]

After paying a visit to the barbershop, Archie finds out that a policeman on a solo investigation of a hit-and-run had been murdered there that morning, and that Carl and Tina are the main suspects due to their fleeing the crime scene. Although they proclaim their innocence, Wolfe takes umbrage at their absconding from the site of a murder, so Carl explains that

> a policeman asking questions…has a different effect on different people. If you have a country like this one and you are innocent of crime, all the people of your coun-

---

[95] Rex Stout, *The Cop-Killer*, in *Triple Jeopardy*: (The Viking Press, Inc., 1952), 58, 84, 93.

> try are saying it with you when you answer the questions. That is true even when you are away from home – especially when you are away from home. But Tina and I have no country at all. The country we had once, it is no longer a country, it is just a place to wait to die, only if we are sent back there we will not have to wait. Two people alone cannot answer a policeman's questions anywhere in the world. It takes a whole country to speak to a policeman, and Tina and I – we do not have one.[96]

Before the identity of the murderer is discovered, Archie spends time interrogating the couple in his front room, learning that they don't know how to drive a car, and therefore cannot have been responsible for the original hit-and-run and had no motive to kill the policeman. They still greatly fear any sort of confrontation with police, however; at one point Carl even attacks Archie physically. When New York police officers finally find the couple, they do not harm or hassle them in the way that they had feared, a legacy of their time in a Russian concentration camp.

While Archie has the couple hidden in the front room, Inspector Cramer (a recurring Wolfe friend and foe) comes by to demand knowledge of Carl and Tina's whereabouts. Archie uses candor as a disguise, "joking" that he has them hidden in the front room right under the Inspector's nose, and Cramer leaves in a huff. In reference to his trick, Archie says, "It's the Hitler-Stalin technique in reverse. They tell barefaced lies to have them taken for the truth, and we told the barefaced truth to have it taken for a lie," paralleling the backwardness of life under those regimes.[97] Archie eventually discovers that the mur-

---
96 Ibid., 62.
97 Ibid., 93

derer is another barber at the shop who drunkenly killed two women with a stolen car the night before and had then killed the cop who discovered his identity. The book ends with a hint that Wolfe will call in favors from Washington to get the proper legal papers for Carl and Tina to stay in the United States, an unusually kind move for Wolfe. He will go uncharacteristically out of his way to help people avoid Communism.[98]

The Cop Killer's representation of Soviet refugees is widely seen as inaccurate on the Russian online forum. Scholar Elena Baraban argues that the disconnect between an American's [Stout's] portrayal of a Russian person and the reality of a Russian person has historical significance:

> Representations of Russia in detective fiction may be far from reality. Yet, they constitute a separate reality themselves. On the one hand, they reflect history and express certain individual and collective values in response to a concrete ideological and political situation. On the other hand, they, in turn, may have an impact on public opinion and politics. [99]

Chervotkin supports Baraban's analysis with a humorous disbelief that characters like Carl and Tina could have been Soviet refugees: "It is caricature and distorted. Such downtrodden people would never make it out of the USSR." User BleWotan, who read *The Cop Killer* in English, agrees with Chervotkin: "Refugees as an archetype are described realistically enough. Yet there is a nuance: in our reality with such a set of mind they would

---

[98] Stout does not mention Communism by name, but he clearly states that Carl and Tina were in a Russian concentration camp in the English publication, and Russia was a Communist regime in the 1950s when the story was written. Stout does not clarify Carl and Tina's nationality.

[99] Baraban, "Russia in the Prism of Popular Culture: Russian and American Detective Fiction and Thrillers of the 1990s," 11.

never escape from the USSR of that time. They are too spineless." Stout's perhaps exaggerated characterization of Soviet refugees may have come about in response to the prevalence of anti-Soviet stereotypes in America in the 1950s. Only Zavgorodnii doesn't take offense to the description, perhaps through a misremembering of the plot: "As far as I recall (I read it quite a long time ago), the characters in this book were refugees not from the USSR but from some (perhaps, even unnamed) Eastern-European country. I have not had the chance to meet any emigrants from the countries of Soviet bloc who went to the West back then; I believe, however, that Stout described them accurately enough."[100]

Zavgorodnii's supposed misremembering of the nationality of Carl and Tina may be explained by reading the 1994 Russian version of *The Cop Killer*, published by KUBKa and translated by T. Danikova. The original English version says that Carl met Tina in a "concentration camp in Russia"; in the Russian version, he met her in a "concentration camp in Poland." There is a footnote attached to this sentence which reads, "In the original it was: In a Soviet concentration camp. Actually, the main heroes were Soviet political prisoners, apparently—Baltic."[101] Zavgorodnii writes in the forum that this translation change was only to be expected:

> It is not surprising that the translator has replaced "Soviet" concentration camp with "Polish." In the late eighties, when Stout began to be translated into Russian, it would be somewhat imprudent to write about Soviet

---

100 Sergey Chervotkin (user Avis), November 20, 2015; User BleWotan, December 14, 2015; Stanislav Zavgorodnii (user Chuchundrovich), November 23, 2015.

101 Sergey Panichev, Vkontakte message to author, March 15, 2016; Reks Staut (Rex Stout), *Ubiistvo Politseiskogo (the Cop Killer)* (KUBKa, 1994).

concentration camps. *The Gulag Archipelago* was published in the USSR only in the 1990s.[102]

VK user Panichev says that he "personally thought that they [Carl and Tina] are from Germany," and this can be attributed to the location change in the translation. German nationals were held in concentration camps in Poland during WWII, which had ended less than a decade before the original publication, so Panichev's answer makes sense in this historical context. Even four years after the end of Communist rule in Russia, it was still not acceptable to have accurate translations of Western detective novels that besmirched the Soviet period. It wasn't until a 2014 translation that the publisher allows Carl to have met his wife Tina in "a concentration camp in Russia."[103]

Remarkably, none of the Russian forum members' reactions to Stout's anti-Communist plots mention any of his political organizations or affiliations; they think his portrayal of Soviet refugees is a caricature, but they don't relate it to his political activities. It is the books alone, not Stout's name on Freedom House documents, which apparently were unknown in Russia, that displayed his anti-Communist sentiments. Zavgorodnii writes: "Before I read Stout's books, I had not known anything about him. Having read several of his books, I realized he was a confirmed anticommunist. Later, after I learnt more about Rex

---

102 Stanislav Zavgorodnii (user Chuchundrovich), November 23, 2015.

103 Reks Staut (Rex Stout), "Ubiistvo Politseiskogo (the Cop Killer)," in *Igra V Piatnashki (Prisoner's Base)* (Amfora, 2014). This is the earliest translation that I could find online that places the concentration camp in Russia, but I don't want to say definitely that it was the earliest published, for I was limited in my search by what copies were online. Forum member Natalia Rymko (username Rymarnica) supports this statement, for her 2008 Eksmo edition of the novel says "Poland." Natalia Rymko (user Rymarnica), April 1, 2016 (9:56am), comment on Molly Zuckerman, "Reks Staut iz Ameriki v Rossii," *O Niro Vul'fe, Archi Gudvine, i ikh avtore, Rekse Staute (About Nero Wolfe, Archie Goodwin, and their author, Rex Stout)* (blog), trans. Gleb Vinokurov, October 18, 2015 (8:38pm), http://nerowolfe.info/forum/viewtopic.php?f=5&t=522&sid=5578a875b87af57f1d92 9613a0f50979.

Stout's biography, I was convinced that my first impression was true."[104]

Most members of the Russian online forum do not see Stout's anti-Communist sympathies as an impediment to enjoying his writing, either in the 1990s or today; if they have any reaction to it at all, it is that his plots with politics sometimes bore them. Chervotkin did not learn of Stout's dislike of Communism until after reading a Wolfe novel but feels "in no particular way" about it, and user BleWotan does not care at all that Stout was an anti-Communist: "I did not know; I did not care. I figured that out upon having read some of the books." Although Chervotkin thinks that Stout's anti-Communism "does not affect the quality of his writing," he does write that "sometimes, however, there is too much bile, and those parts get boring. But this does not affect the general impression all that much."[105]

In America, some reviewers also saw his political messages as too overt, although they didn't take offense at the inaccuracy of the "spineless" portrayal of Soviet refugees like Russians did. Cannon writes in reference to *Home to Roost* and *The Cop Killer*, "Occasionally, Stout's adoring public, eager for more Nero Wolfe stories, complained about the political agendas of some of the stories.... One reader wrote a letter to Stout objecting to 'those two little stinker anti-Communist stories.'"[106] Even Stout's "long-time" friend Anthony Boucher "admitted he wished Wolfe would focus on an opponent other than Communism."[107]

---

104 User BleWotan, December 14, 2015; Sergey Chervotkin (user Avis), November 20, 2015; Stanislav Zavgorodnii (user Chuchundrovich), November 23, 2015.

105 Sergey Chervotkin (user Avis), November 20, 2015.

106 McAleer, *Rex Stout: A Majesty's Life*, 378.

107 Ibid. 378. Anthony Boucher was an American mystery and science fiction writer.

The Rosenberg Trial

Stout's attitudes toward Communism and McCarthyism could not be clearer in the novels discussed above; negative imagery and mockery runs throughout them. When McCarthyism and the fear of Communism came to a peak in America during the 1951 trial, conviction, and execution of Julius and Ethel Rosenberg, Stout's convictions led him to take a strong position on the side of the Rosenbergs' innocence, and this position manifested itself in a literary manner, as was Stout's way.[108]

Stout vents his opinion about the Rosenberg conviction most clearly in his fiction when Wolfe says in *Home to Roost* (published the year after the trial), "It is true that all five of those people [the murder suspects] may be Communists and therefore enemies of this country, but that does not justify framing one of them for murder."[109] According to Wolfe, being a Communist makes one an enemy of America, but framing American Communists for murder denies them basic American freedoms and therefore is wrong, even though they are "Commies."

Stout stepped outside constraints of a Wolfe novel to further defend the Rosenbergs more than ten years after their trial. In 1966, Stout wrote a 3000-word review of *Invitation to an Inquest* by Walter and Miriam Schneir for *Ramparts* magazine entitled, "The Case of the Spies Who Weren't."[110] This was not an ordinary review as the editor of the magazine had requested, but a critique couched in the language of a Nero Wolfe mystery, complete with an illustrated cover and a first-person narration by Archie Goodwin. The article begins with a short, italicized

---

108 Although Stout had been fine before conflating all Germans with Nazis, he was not fine conflating all Communists with lawbreakers.

109 Stout, *Home to Roost*, 25.

110 The book was a supposedly impartial study of the trial, but it took the stance that the Rosenbergs had received only a modicum of justice.

dialogue between Wolfe, Archie and, surprisingly, Stout. Archie is purportedly writing down a discussion between Stout and Wolfe concerning the Rosenberg case and the publication of *Invitation to an Inquest*, with Stout as Wolfe's literary agent. The most telling part is Archie's final sentence: "So this cramping [editing] job on their [Stout's and Wolfe's] verdict on the book is mine."[111] This is the only case where Stout's and Wolfe's political opinions are stated as being directly in line with each other by none other than Archie Goodwin. Although Stout is obviously using Wolfe and Archie in this article as a literary device to get across his opinion of the innocence of the Rosenbergs, the key phrase, "their verdict," conjoining Stout and Wolfe into one mind, must not be forgotten when reading Stout's less subtle political plotlines.[112] McAleer writes that "for readers of the saga, here was important evidence placing it in the mainstream of Rex Stout's commitment to universal order realized through the expression of democratic ideals."[113]

The review continues by giving a step-by-step summary of the reasons why each witness in the case against the Rosenbergs had either lied or misrepresented evidence, ending with a strong indictment of the FBI's role in the trial and subsequent sentencing. Stout writes that "in this extraordinary pageant of mendacity and perversion, the palm must be awarded to the FBI. So many instances of their ingenuity and versatility are documented in the book that exposition here would take too much space." The article ends with a notice that Stout's most recently published book is *The Doorbell Rang*, which deals directly with the FBI and will be discussed in Chapter Five.[114]

---

111 Rex Stout, "The Case of the Spies Who Weren't," *Ramparts*, January 1966.
112 Ibid., 31.
113 Ibid.
114 McAleer, *Rex Stout: A Majesty's Life*, 453.

Wolfe and Archie Enter Yugoslavia

Stout's 1954 novel *The Black Mountain* could be considered the fictional postscript to what went wrong when American citizens and Communists interacted in the McCarthy era (as in the 1951 Rosenberg trial) as well as a fictional precursor to the ideas that Stout would support in Freedom House's activities in the 1960s. Wolfe's attitude toward murderers, even Communist murderers, reflects Freedom House's support for the democratic judicial process; Wolfe believes that every accused person should be fairly tried in a court of law (except in the infrequent cases where his laziness overpowers his morality and he allows, or encourages, suicides to occur). Wolfe's belief in democratic freedoms is tested to the limit in *The Black Mountain*, where Wolfe's quest for vengeance against the man who killed his best friend Marko Vukcic ends with his forcibly bringing the murderer from Montenegro to New York by boat rather than leaving him in Titograd [the name given by General Secretary Tito to Podgorica] to be killed by rebel forces.

The book begins with the murder of Marko, owner of Rusterman's restaurant and one of the few men that Wolfe is on a first-name basis with. Marko is shot down by an unknown assailant in the street outside his restaurant, and Archie is the one who gets the call to identify the body at the morgue. After Archie's positive identification, Wolfe breaks one of his cardinal rules and leaves his house to go to the scene of the crime, shocking Inspector Cramer (a recurring character) with his presence. Wolfe's desire to bring Marko's murderer to justice takes him to Montenegro, his birthplace, after Wolfe's adopted daughter Carla tells him that Marko was probably killed due to his involvement with the Spirit of the Black Mountain, an anti-Communist rebel force in Yugoslavia.

The book deals with Wolfe's personal political inclinations regarding his Montenegrin origin; instead of dealing with American Communists or Soviet refugees, he is in the thick of things with Communists in Eastern Europe. When Wolfe makes faces at the mention of the Spirit of the Black Mountain, Carla erupts at him: "What do you care if the people of the land you came from are groaning under the heel of the oppressor, with the light of their liberty smothered and the fruits of their labor snatched from them and their children at the point of the sword? Stop making faces!"[115] Wolfe responds with a diatribe:

> "Apparently," he said dryly, "I must give you a lecture. I grimaced neither at your impudence nor at your sentiment, but at your diction and style. I condemn clichés, especially those that have been corrupted by fascists and communists. Such phrases as 'great and noble cause' and 'fruits of their labor' have been given an ineradicable stink by Hitler and Stalin and all their vermin brood. Besides, in this century of the overwhelming triumph of science, the appeal of the cause of human freedom is no longer that it is great and noble; it is more or less than that; it is essential. It is no greater or nobler than the cause of edible food or the cause of effective shelter. Man must have freedom or he will cease to exist as man. The despot, whether fascist or communist, is no longer restricted to such puny tools as the heel or the sword or even the machine gun; science has provided weapons that can give him the planet; and only men who are willing to die for freedom have any chance of living for it."[116]

---

115 Stout, "The Case of the Spies Who Weren't," 33-34.
116 *The Black Mountain*, Location 324-30.

Shortly after meeting with Wolfe, Carla disappears, and word soon gets back to Wolfe that her dead body has been found at the bottom of a mountain in Montenegro. It is then that Wolfe resigns himself to the necessity of travelling to Montenegro to find the murderer of both his best friend and his adopted daughter. Wolfe and Archie proceed to trek around Yugoslavia, climbing illegally across borders through the mountainous terrain, under the aliases of Toné and Alex Stara, father and son on a phony mission to donate money to either the Communists or the rebels, supposedly depending on their impressions of the parties.

Once abroad, Archie still uses the same joking banter with which he treats all Communists in America. When getting off a plane, Archie writes that he "stood guard over the bags and watched the communist boys. I assumed they were communists because they were throwing things at a cat on Palm Sunday."[117] Wolfe and Archie then sneak across the Albanian border into Montenegro, where they take refuge in a haystack for the night. Upon awakening, they find the farmhouse and ask the farmer to exchange food for money, and he refuses at first and tries to lock them outside his house. Wolfe sees this man's attitude toward them in political terms:

> Six feet tall, a jaw like a rock, an eagle's beak for a nose, a brow to take any storm. In ten centuries the Turks could never make him whine. Even under the despotism of Black George he kept his head up as a man.[118] But Communist despotism has done for him. Twenty years

117 Ibid., Location 331-38.

118 Ibid., Location 803-05. Black George was the founder of modern Serbia in the early 1800s, and nicknamed thus due to his often violent nature. Wikipedia contributors, "Karadorde," Wikipedia, The Free Encyclopedia., https://en.wikipedia.org/w/index.
php?title=Kara%C4%91or%C4%91e&oldid=70706 0032.

ago two strangers who had damaged his haystack would have been called to account; today, having espied us in trespass on his property, he tells his wife to stay indoors and shuts himself in the barn with his goats and chickens.[119]

Wolfe attributes the destruction of the psyche of the common man and farmer to Communism, which reduces strong men to weaklings who succumb to the fearful environment created by their despotic Communist leaders.

Wolfe and Archie are then brought to government headquarters in Titograd (which Wolfe only refers to as Podgorica) against their will to present their proper documentation (which they don't have) to Gospo Stritar, the boss of Titograd's political headquarters. The car they travel in is a 1953 Ford sedan, much to Archie's surprise, until he recalls the 58 million dollars lent to Yugoslavia by the World Bank. He decides not to bother questioning the car's owner as to the specifics of its acquisition; to Archie, the car is the manifestation of corruption in the form of his income tax dollars.[120]

Once at headquarters, Wolfe and Archie manage to talk their way out of imprisonment and find Marko's cousin, whom they ask for help finding Marko's and Carla's killer. The cousin is hesitant to help them but is convinced by Wolfe's almost unbelievably persuasive language, and Wolfe and Archie then enter the secret mountain lair of the Spirit of the Black Mountain. Members of the Spirit direct Wolfe and Archie to an outpost of Albanians (the enemy) where Carla was last seen alive, and so Wolfe and Archie set off on foot with the idea "just to walk in and introduce ourselves, announcing, I suppose, that we had

---

119 Stout, *The Black Mountain*, Location 1201-05.
120 Ibid., Location 1329.

about decided to hook up with the Kremlin and wanted to discuss matters," says Archie in a mocking tone.[121]

Inside the Albanian enclave they find a man, Peter Zov, hanging by his arms from a ceiling. They pause long enough to hear a conversation that proves that Zov was the man who murdered Marko and that his Albanian torturers are the ones who murdered Carla. Archie and Wolfe burst in, and Archie kills all of the Albanians in self-defense while Zov collapses on the floor. While Zov is still unconscious, Archie and Wolfe discuss what to do with him. Archie is in favor of ending the ordeal with a quick shot right then, but Wolfe strenuously objects:

> "If personal vengeance were the only factor I could, as you suggested, go and stick a knife in him and finish it, but that would be accepting the intolerable doctrine that man's sole responsibility is to his ego. That was the doctrine of Hitler, as it is now of Malenkov and Tito and Franco and Senator McCarthy; masquerading as a basis of freedom, it is the oldest and toughest of the enemies of freedom. I reject it and condemn it."[122]

Wolfe is taking the moral upper hand by not killing a defenseless man, even though he has evidence that this man is a murderer—this is Stout giving an example of how to treat even a Communist murderer with the proper democratic freedom of a trial. He also manages to compare McCarthy to several bloodthirsty dictators, including Hitler.

---

121 Ibid., Location 2042.

122 Ibid., Location 2182, 87. *Too Many Cooks* (1938) contains another instance when Wolfe mentions McCarthy directly: "A garbageman collects table refuse, while a senator collects evidence of the corruption of highly placed men—might one not prefer the garbage as less unsavory?" *Too Many Cooks*, 11.

Wolfe, Archie, and Zov then set off on foot back to Titograd to report to headquarters, for Wolfe has convinced Zov that he is on the side of Tito and wants to donate money to the cause. Once at headquarters, a plan is formed for Wolfe and Archie to head back to America, with Zov coming along as a liaison in their ruse to stimulate support for Tito in New York. Discussing this plan, Wolfe asks, "'Would you advise us to join the Communist Party of the United States and try to influence them in your favor?' 'Good God, no,' Stritar was contemptuous. 'They belong to Moscow, body and soul, and they're a nest of slimy vermin.'"[123] Stout's pitting of two competing versions of Communism against each other shows his negative opinion of Communism and its inability to join its own adherents together, even though communalism is one of its main tenets.

Russian speakers reading about Wolfe's foray into the mountains of Montenegro do not like the plot. Chervotkin objects to *The Black Mountain* due to its "unrealistic representation of Soviet special agencies," but thinks that the choice of a Montenegrin as a detective is a positive one, for it is "not a typical move for an American author. :D But Yugoslavia is a very interesting country with very peculiar people." [124] BleWotan also does not like the novel: "The caricature of Albanians as devils incarnate – no, thanks," although he does enjoy the image of "the angry Nero as a fighter with a knife." He also cares not at all about Wolfe's heritage: "A Montenegrin; so what." Zavgorodnii calls the plot "far-fetched" and not among his favorites, but he acknowledges: "I think that Montenegro was (and still is now) a sort of 'exotic' place for most of Stout's American readers back then, which inevitably added to Wolfe's mysteriousness."[125]

---

123 *The Black Mountain*, Location 2427-29.

124 Sergey Chervotkin (user Avis), November 20, 2015. Interestingly, Chervotkin read this after 2012, so the offense taken at the portrayal of Soviet special agencies takes on a different kind of significance.

125 User BleWotan, December 14, 2015; Stanislav Zavgorodnii (user

Importantly, both Zavgorodnii and user BleWotan see a historical connection between the anti-Communism in the plot and the political scene in America when it was written, saying respectively that "it fits well into the general tendencies of American anticommunism of the 50s" and that "it correlates with the general spirit of the American 50s pretty well."[126] The common theme of the contemporary Russian reaction to this novel is that Stout was successful in inserting his anti-Communist position into it but unsuccessful in his "caricature"-like depictions of Eastern Europeans.

Some Western reviewers liked the book better. One reviewer was "unsurprised[d] by Stout's political views on Yugoslavia" and considered the novel "enormously readable." Another saw the onus of the murder exactly where Stout intended, as a murder created by a place "where Reds rule and a police system tries to hinder the cause of American justice."[127] However, these positive reviews were matched with negative ones. On the negative side, another American reviewer wrote that Archie's "usual bright outlook takes on a jaundiced hue,"[128] and a Canadian review wrote that Stout "sends his massive detective halfway around the world to match wits with some evil iron-curtain specimens [and] the story suffers by it."[129]

Chuchundrovich), November 23, 2015.

126 User BleWotan, December 14, 2015; Stanislav Zavgorodnii (user Chuchundrovich), November 23, 2015.

127 Stout, *The Black Mountain*, Location 2427-29; "Nero Wolfe," *Dublin Evening Herald*, August 22 1955.

128 "Wild Places," *Daily Dispatch*, September 5, Manchester, International PressCutting Bureau, Box 39, Folder 8, Rex Stout Papers, MS1986-096, John J. Burns Library, Boston College.

129 "The Black Mountain by Rex Stout," *Battle Creek Enquirer*, December 26, 1954, Michigan, Box 39, Folder 8, Rex Stout Papers, MS1986-096, John J. Burns Library, Boston College.

4 | Wolfe and Stout Enter Soviet Russia

I decided that if and when I became a dictator I would damn well clean a town up and widen some of its streets and have a little painting done before I changed its name to Goodwingrad.
—Archie Goodwin
The Black Mountain

How Stout the Anti-Communist was Published in the USSR

While Stout was dealing with Communist and anti-Communist in America and Yugoslavia, Russians were beginning to have access to more and more detective novels from the West. Various Stout novels were translated and published in both journals and trilogies during the Soviet era, and, although it is difficult to identify precisely either the first book translated or the precise date of publication, Stout's books definitively appeared in the Soviet Union. McAleer cites a *London Sunday Times* article that says that in March of 1971, "in the Soviet Union more of Rex Stout's works were in print than those of any other American writer."[130]

The online catalog of the National Library of Russia in St. Petersburg lists seven of Stout's books in translation before 1990 as well as Stout's biography by John McAleer, which was available in 1977 (although only in English; there is still no Russian translation available). *The Doorbell Rang* was published in trilogies in the years 1967, 1969, 1973, 1981, 1986, and 1989, and *Might as Well Be Dead*, or in the Russian translation *Vse nachalos v Omakhe* (*It All Started in Omaha*), was published in 1989.[131] There are references to more of Stout's books published in serial form in journals (which would not appear in the National Library of Russia's online catalog) in a 1971 article in the Russian *Literaturnaia gazeta*.[132] Specifically, the article mentions the novel *Vse nachalos v Omakhe*, published in the journal *Nash sovremennik* in 1970. A dissertation on the Russian *detektiv* genre by Baraban says more generally that translations of Western hard-boiled detective fiction, including Stout's novels, were used in the following journals in the 1960s and 1970s to attract subscribers: *Neman, Iunost', Ural, Inostrannaia literatura, Don, Literaturnyi Azerbaidzhan, Nash sovremennik, Prostor, Podiem*, and *Zvezda vostoka*.[133] The fact that many of the journals that published Stout in the Soviet period were located in the Far East (*Zvezda vostoka*) or Soviet Socialist Republics like Azerbaijan

---

130 McAleer, *Rex Stout: A Majesty's Life*, 491. Stout wrote the previously discussed *The Second Confession, Home to Roost, The Cop Killer*, and *The Black Mountain* all before 1971, but they were not his first books to be translated in the Soviet Union.

131 See "Stout Collections in the 2000s by Russian Publishing House" on page 192.

132 Georgi Andzhaparidze, "Bogachi-filantropy i belye 'Mersedesy': chto i kak my perevodim (Wealthy Philanthropists and White Mercedes: What and How We Translate)," *Literaturnaia gazeta*, (January 20, 1971).

133 Baraban, "Russia in the Prism of Popular Culture: Russian and American Detective Fiction and Thrillers of the 1990s," 161.

(*Literaturnaia Azerbaidzhan*) speaks to the fact that his books were too potentially subversive to get away with being published in Moscow or St. Petersburg journals.

Outside of Russia, but still within Soviet-dominated Eastern Europe, several of Stout's books were published in Russian before 1990. McAleer writes generally that "Russians, Poles, Estonians, Latvians, Lithuanians, Rumanians, Bulgarians, Hungarians, and Yugoslavs" all had access to Stout's books behind the Iron Curtain. According to the Russian State Library in Moscow's database, *The Doorbell Rang* was published by Molod in Kiev in 1983 in a collection with Agatha Christie's *The Moving Finger*. Another Stout novel, *The Broken Vase*, was published by Esti Ramat in Tallinn in 1989; however, the hero of this novel was not Nero Wolfe but Tecumseh Fox, making this the first instance found of a non-Wolfe Stout novel in Russian. In a handwritten list, Stout notes that two of his books were published in Czechoslovakia before 1990: *A Right to Die* was published in 1967 in both Prague and Bratislava in Czech and Slovak, by Mladá fronta and Tatran respectively.[134] He also notes two books published in Yugoslavia: *The Golden Spiders* was published by Privreda in 1963 in Croatian translation in Zagreb, and *Prisoner's Base* was published by Državna založba in Ljubljana in Slovenian translation in 1964.

Stout Critiques Yugoslavia from America

While Stout's books were beginning to be disseminated in Russia, Czechoslovakia, and Yugoslavia, he also was actively judging the state of Communism abroad and its effect on those peoples' freedoms. Stout's connection to Freedom House

---

134 *The Doorbell Rang* and *A Right to Die* were novels the Russians chose to publish first owing to their plot lines critical of the American political scene.

in the 1960s aligned him with the organization's stance on the Soviet Union, Bolshevism, and the satellite countries; in 1965, Stout and Freedom House became involved with the creation of an oppositionist magazine in Tito's Yugoslavia (where at least two of his novels had been published in translation), a project sponsored by the previously jailed Yugoslav dissident Mihajlo Mihajlov.[135] Stout personally wrote to Mihajlov that "the news of [his] proposal to publish in Yugoslavia a magazine devoted to freedom of thought and expression has aroused great interest among American writers, editors, educators, and publicists—indeed, in the whole American community."[136] Stout's connection to Mihajlov and his fight for freedom of expression in Tito's Yugoslavia ten years after the publication of *The Black Mountain* demonstrate how Stout's writing and politics were continuously intermingled. Stout inserted himself into the political turmoil of a country that his fictional detective had done something similar in years before, while Stout's books were simultaneously being read by citizens of that same country.

While involved with Mihajlov, Stout took a step outside his fiction and wrote a letter directly to President Tito of Yugoslavia, a man that he had so negatively portrayed in *The Black Mountain* when Stout's fictional detective had refused to accept the name change of Podgorica to Titograd owing to his strong distaste for the man who had renamed it. The letter, addressed to "His Excellency Josip Broz Tito," and signed by Stout on behalf of twenty-two others, proclaims the great value of an independent editorial publication and is attached to Mihajlov's letter

---

135 Agence France-Presse, "Mihajlo Mihajlov, a Yugoslavian Dissident, Dies at 76," *The New York Times* March 7, 2010. Mihajlov was arrested in 1975 for "disseminating hostile propaganda" against Tito and sentenced to seven years, although he only served three before being pardoned and allowed to leave Yugoslavia.

136 Rex Stout to Mihajlo Mihajlov, undated correspondence, Box 21, Rex Stout Papers, MS1986-096, John J. Burns Library, Boston College.

to "Comrade Tito," in which Mihajlov stresses the importance of a magazine that would defend the principles of democratic socialism. Mihajlov's letter speaks of the "horrible practices of Stalinism" and his desire to create space for a different kind of socialism to emerge, for "opposition to the monopoly of the Communist Party over the social and political life of a nation, does in no way mean opposition to socialism as such."[137] Stout's and Mihajlov's actions led to a fiery *Philadelphia National Inquirer* article supporting Mihajlov's magazine enterprise. The article posed several rhetorical questions in a way that revealed the author's political stance quite nakedly: "President Tito and his associates face these horrendous questions: Can they accept the consequences of a free press and expect to survive? Do they dare [illegible] a degree of freedom which would almost inevitably lead to free elections and end the political monopoly of the Communist Party?"[138] Interestingly, Stout's aligning himself and Freedom House on Mihajlov's side also indirectly aligns him with socialism, albeit in a very different form from socialism in Soviet Russia.

While working with Mihajlov, Stout continued his other duties at Freedom House in his roles as either secretary or treasurer. In 1967, Leonard Sussman, executive director of Freedom House, wrote a memorandum to the creative committee, with special "Attention to: Stout," concerning the fiftieth anniversary of the Bolshevik revolution. A subsequent statement, which Stout played a role in creating, was called "The Fiftieth Anniversary of a Universal Tragedy" and detailed how things had gone

---

137 Mihajlo Mihajlov to President Tito of Yugoslavia, undated correspondence, Box 21, Rex Stout Papers, MS1986-096, John J. Burns Library, Boston College; Rex Stout to His Excellency Josip Broz Tito, from the Ad Hoc Committee for Mihajlo Mihajlov, August 1, 1966, Box 21, Rex Stout Papers, MS1986-096, John J. Burns Library, Boston College.

138 Roscoe Drummond, "Freedom Seeks Foothold Behind Iron Curtain," *The Philadelphia Inquirer*, June 17, 1966, Box 21, Rex Stout Papers, MS1986-096, John J. Burns Library, Boston College.

downhill in Russia since the revolution, citing the terror of a police state and the negative international ramifications of socialism.[139] In 1971, a report entitled "The New Shape of U.S. Soviet Relations" expressed the necessity of "contacts and exchanges" with the East and also the growing importance of presenting a Western "example which refutes Communist expectations, and options for either imitation or active East-West cooperation."[140] This anti-Communist statement was released the same year that Stout became the American writer most in print in the Soviet Union.

One undated Freedom House report (the content places it after 1972) said that President Richard Nixon's visits to Peking and Moscow, although "causes for hope," were prompted by an overall rise in fear of a global nuclear holocaust. The situation in Eastern Europe and the Soviet Union was described as "not encouraging" owing to "the Brezhnev regime's 'crackdown on dissident intellectual[s]'"; Czechoslovakia "remained repressive in the extreme" as well.[141] Again, Stout's name was attached to these statements while his novels were being disseminated both in Moscow, where Brezhnev ruled, and in Czechoslovakia.

Other Freedom House documents concerned the lack of freedom in the Soviet Union and the Soviet Union's relations with America, especially regarding nuclear weapons. In an undated letter signed by Stout, he wrote that the Helsinki accords "heighten the urgency" of coming to an agreement with the So-

---

139 Leonard Sussman to Executive Committee of Freedom House, October 18, 1967, Box 21, Rex Stout Papers, MS1986-096, John J. Burns Library, Boston College.

140 "The New Shape of U.S.-Soviet Relations," In *The Report of a Conference of Foreign Affairs Scholars*: Public Affairs Institute of Freedom House, undated, Rex Stout Papers, MS1986-096, John J. Burns Library, Boston College, 8.

141 "U.S. Bids to China and Soviet, Though Hopeful, Inspire Concern for Freedom in Europe and Asia; American Gains Continued, Though Slower Paced," Freedom House, undated, Rex Stout Papers, MS1986-096, John J. Burns Library, Boston College.

viet Union on reducing its nuclear program; he also insists "that both communists and non-communists implement the pledges to expand freedoms through scores of new programs."[142] Stout was also affiliated with the 1975 document "'Not Good' Is Not Enough," which discusses the need for Americans to have compassion for Soviet Jews and again brings up the danger of the Soviet nuclear arsenal. Another unsigned and undated Freedom House document associated with Stout says that "in the truest sense, all Soviet residents are prisoners of conscience."[143]

Stout's harsh judgments on Communist governments in his later Freedom House years were direct reflections of his novels that contained a strong anti-Communist message. Books such as *The Second Confession*, *Home to Roost*, *The Cop Killer*, and *The Black Mountain* could be seen as public indictments equal to the Freedom House documents, albeit in literary form. Wolfe sums up his and Stout's overall anti-Communist feeling when, in *Home to Roost*, Wolfe admonishes an American Communist Party member sitting in his office: "In the countries they [Communists] rule the jails are full— let alone the graves— of former comrades who were indiscreet. In America…you don't rule and I hope you never will."[144] It is ironic that the Communist countries that were so heavily lambasted by Nero Wolfe in fiction and Rex Stout in real life were the same ones that were reading and actively disseminating Stout's novels.

Soviet Critics take Offense at Stout's Plots

Stout's literature in translation in the Soviet Union, in conjunction with the increasing number of other Western detective

[142] Rex Stout to unknown, undated correspondence, Freedom House, Rex Stout Papers, MS1986-096, John J. Burns Library, Boston College.

[143] Freedom House notes on Solzhenitsyn's exile, undated, Rex Stout Papers, MS1986-096, John J. Burns Library, Boston College.

[144] Rex Stout, *Home to Roost*, in *Triple Jeopardy* (The Viking Press, Inc., 1952), 52.

novels in translation being published, began to worry Soviet literary critics. Western detective novels were rarely published as stand-alone books, but rather either in series meant for libraries or in "provincial or specialist journals such as *Vokrug sveta, Nauka i religiia, Chelovek i zakon* and *Khimiia i zhizn*."[145] In the Eastern European Soviet bloc, translations of popular fiction like detective stories were also closely monitored by the state. Andrew Wachtel writes that "Western popular literature, which…propagated values that neither communists nor dissidents would have approved of, simply had no space in the mental universe of Eastern European elites.… Official state publishers could not accept popular literature for…ideological reasons."[146]

The inclusion of such works in journals and libraries was allegedly to promote critiques of capitalism and the Western countries they represented, but Baraban writes that this inclusion sparked debate among editors over whether the stories did truly expose "the corrupt bourgeois society" the way they were intended to.[147] Party resolutions were passed that condemned the publication of foreign detective stories in the Soviet Union, an example being the 1958 resolution, "On serious defects in the content of the magazine *Ogonek*," that "criticized the weekly *Ogonek* for devoting too much space to travel writing and detective stories."[148]

---

145 Stephen Lovell, *The Russian Reading Revolution: Print Culture in the Soviet and Post-Soviet Eras* (Macmillan, 2000), 52.

146 Andrew Wachtel, *Remaining Relevant after Communism: The Role of the Writer in Eastern Europe* (Chicago: University of Chicago Press, 2006), 191.

147 Baraban, "Russia in the Prism of Popular Culture: Russian and American Detective Fiction and Thrillers of the 1990s," 161.

148 Lovell, *The Russian Reading Revolution: Print Culture in the Soviet and PostSoviet Eras* 46. *Ogonek* has published since 1899, but its reestablishment as a Soviet journal in 1923 is its best known form. Before the Soviet period, *Ogonek* was known for a Sherlock Holmes hoax in 1908, when the journal published a Russian version of Holmes' stories that portrayed Holmes as a real person writing the tales. Many Russians ended up believing that Sherlock Holmes was a living detective. Brooks, *When Russians Learned to*

One of the most outspoken critics of the trend of translating Western detective novels was Georgi Andzhaparidze, Soviet literary critic and former editor-in-chief and editor of foreign fiction at Raduga publishing house.[149] Andzhaparidze mentions Stout several times in his 1971 article (the same year Stout helped write "The New Shape of U.S. Soviet Relations"), criticizing the rising number of Western detective novels being translated and distributed in the Soviet Union. He describes them as the "detective epidemic" and questions whether it is worth it to publish "this type of book." He cites the 1970 *Nash sovremennik* publication of Stout's *Vse nachalos v Omakhe* (*It All Started in Omaha*) as an example of the type of Western detective novel that was harmful to Soviet readers. His specific reference to Wolfe's "all consuming passion for orchids" is evidence that he had a real familiarity with the Wolfe texts. Soviet critic A. Kuznetsov agreed with Andzhaparidze's negative analysis, calling the translation "epidemic" a "cunning process" whereby journals fall "prey to the chase for success."[150]

Andzhaparidze's main argument is that the mass publication of these translated detective stories does not actually "unmask the essence of the bourgeois way of life, the vices of capitalist society" in a successful manner, as the journals intended. Instead, he writes that "one must note that the tendency expressed in the majority of Western detective novels is conservative, in particular defending the fundamental basis of capitalist society—the 'sacred' right of private property." Andzhaparidze thinks that the

---

Read, Literacy and Popular Literature, 1861–1917, 116, 17.

149 Raduga was a state-owned publishing house in the Soviet Union, created in 1982 when Progress was divided into two parts, with the main Progress house publishing science and political literature and Raduga publishing fiction. Raduga published much of Stout's fiction after the 1990s. Wikipedia contributors, "Progress (Publishing)," Wikipedia, the free encyclopedia, http://ru.wikipedia.org/?oldid=75511036.

150 Baraban, "Russia in the Prism of Popular Culture: Russian and American Detective Fiction and Thrillers of the 1990s," 161.

positive descriptions of what he sees as the bourgeois lifestyles of the private detectives is more harmful than any benefit received by the Soviet public reading authors like Stout, who do include criticisms of American society in their books.

To call attention to those bourgeois vices of capitalism, Andzhaparidze discusses the use of millionaires as characters in James Hadley Chase's detective novels, and, although he doesn't mention Wolfe directly, Wolfe's wealth and upper-class tastes would be classic examples of vices that Andzhaparidze did not want described to the Soviets. Kuznetsov agreed with Andzhaparidze that this type of Western novel "was ideologically unsuitable in Soviet society."[151] The very idea of crime being "insurmountable and unconquerable" and occurring because of the "human personality" turning out to be a "plaything of its own passions and instincts" is antithetical to Soviet ideology, wherein crime is supposed to be eradicated once the Soviet citizen has become fully conscious (to borrow a socialist realism term). Andzhaparidze applies this framework of analysis to Stout's oeuvre.[152]

Cannon writes that "the constant emphasis on rationality by logical patterns within detective fiction speaks as loudly as any explicit message,"[153] an idea which indirectly supports these Soviet critics' fears; Stout's plots that neatly sum up mysteries and catch murderers with logic and rationality would serve to draw attention to contrasting inefficiencies and corruption in the Communist judicial system. Andzhaparidze's objections to the Western detective "epidemic" include the fear of exposing Soviet citizens to fictional characters that are motivated by the

---

151 Ibid.

152 Andzhaparidze, "Bogachi-filantropy i belye 'Mersedesy': chto i kak my perevodim (Wealthy Philanthropists and White Mercedes: What and How We Translate)."

153 Cannon, "Controversial Politics, Conservative Genre: Rex Stout's Archie-Wolfe Duo and Detective Fiction's Conventional Form," 72.

desire to preserve wealth and position in society and also to the haste with which the translations were done and their subsequently poor production. He ends the article by shaming the journals' publishers for their fluctuating moral choices in picking authors to translate, as well as suggesting that journals in the far Eastern parts of Russia should focus more on local literature. Andzhaparidze is not so focused on Party ideology that he wants all fiction writing to stop (although he does refer to pop culture as "the protruding ass's ears"), but that he just wants the right kind of fiction to be published.[154]

A report from Moscow in a 1981 edition of *Encounter* magazine specifically references the role of Stout's writing in Andzhaparidze's 1971 article.[155] The write-up on Stout and crime fiction is signed "D.W." and extensively quotes Andzhaparidze (though not by name). D.W. offers his own commentary on Andzhaparidze's article, a rather heavy-handed interpretation of Andzhaparidze's views on Stout. The piece begins with a description of murder as a "class phenomenon of bourgeois society" with crime being "part and parcel of capitalism." However, D.W. continues, "Nero Wolfe, continue[s] to fascinate, even under Bolshevism."

The whole piece is written in this same judgmental vein, although its switching between italics and bold fonts makes it hard to tell if D.W. is still quoting Andzhaparidze or expressing his own opinions (if he is quoting Andzhaparidze, the text is either not from the 1971 article or else is paraphrased with D.W.'s

---

154 Andzhaparidze, "Bogachi-filantropy i belye 'Mersedesy': chto i kak my perevodim (Wealthy Philanthropists and White Mercedes: What and How We Translate)."

155 *Encounter* was a London-based Anglo-American literary magazine that was associated with the anti-Stalinist left, much as Stout was. Its mission was to try to influence culture within the USSR. The magazine is best known for its controversial secret funding by the CIA, which, when tmade public, caused a rift in the editorial board. In the 1980s, when the report about Stout was published, the magazine had been supported without CIA money for more than a decade.

overly negative interpretation of Andzhaparidze's views). D.W. writes: "Everything about Nero Wolfe is darkly suspicious: from his corpulence, his passion for cultivating orchids, to his fat fees for uncovering dastardly acts" (the reference to orchids suggests that this is a paraphrased section of Andzhaparidze's article.)[156] D.W. next brings up the role of Archie, a character that Andzhaparidze does not mention. D.W. sees the role of Archie as Wolfe's assistant as one where Goodwin is "miserably exploited, and serves only to reinforce the illusion that one can be happy in America even when one is subject to exploitation."[157] The write-up ends with a warning to editors of journals in the Soviet Union that parallels, as well as deviates from, Andzhaparidze's warning with its advice for readers and editors: "Soviet readers and especially editors will just have to be more vigilant. Errors of every ideological stripe keep cropping up."[158]

D.W. then breaks from an analysis of Andzhaparidze article and Stout by citing the case of another Western writer, Graham Greene. Although Greene was once officially approved by the Kremlin as a "progressive" writer, D.W. writes that he has now become ideologically subversive due to his role in protesting human rights abuses against Soviet dissidents. The Greene example mirrors both Andzhaparidze and D.W.'s views on Stout; he was published at first because his books exposed flaws in Western society, but the tide had turned and now his characters' immersion in capitalist society was seen as too subversive for publication. D.W. concludes: "Mao Tse-tung once achieved a short-lived fame with a theory of 'reconciling contradictions', and we all

---

156 This is an example of D.W. possibly misinterpreting the original Russian article, for although Andzhaparidze mentions Wolfe liking orchids, he doesn't cite it as a criticism of bourgeois tendencies as D.W. claims.

157 Stout, *The Black Mountain*, Location 327. This thought mimics a line from *The Black Mountain* (1954), when Carla (a Montenegrin and active participant in Yugoslav politics) cries out, "And this Archie Goodwin for a slave to do all the work and take all the danger!"

158 D.W., "Crime Fiction," *Encounter*, August 1981, 26.

remember where that ended...." D.W. is saying that it is impossible to reconcile Stout's good plotlines with his bad ones; his negative Western influence outweighs any potential positive one for the Soviets.[159]

Andzhaparidze wrote another article critiquing the continuing rise in popularity of Western detective novels in translation published four years later (the same year Stout helped write "'Not Good' Is Not Enough"), also for *Literaturnaia gazeta*. He again bemoaned the device of including Western detective stories in journals as a way of attracting subscribers. Andzhaparidze cites a Soviet critic's lament that it is a shame that journals cannot find the "fullness of material, contemporary life with current social issues" in Russian authors but instead look for this in the Western literary detective canon. While Andzhaparidze still considers the detective genre a product of capitalist ideology, he has softened his views somewhat at this point. He seems to have accepted the detective genre's existence in Russia and writes in reference to Progress's Modern American Detective series and Molodaia gvardiia's one-volume tome of detective fiction that it is "commendable that the national publishing companies publish such well-known and interesting foreign detective novels," a far cry from his harsh reproof of the "detective epidemic" four years before.

However, even if Andzhaparidze does think that the selections published have improved, he cannot let go of the idea that Western detective novels will lead to the moral corruption of the Soviet people. He equates actual problems in Western society with the violence and crime shown on television and described in detective literature, connecting "greed and avarice" with the "bourgeois morality" of the detective genre. He quotes another critic's assessment of recently translated novels: "Detective work

---

[159] Ibid.

of this kind does not criticize capitalism" for it instead tries to "smooth over the social contradictions."[160]

Andzhaparidze's arguments against Western detective translations focus on the motivation for crime in these novels, which attributes to the criminal the desire to snatch at anything to make him richer. Andzhaparidze does not believe that Western authors are capable of accurately critiquing this societal problem, for they write about it in a manner that makes it seem natural; in Andzhaparidze's view, it is not natural to write about a society where people desire wealth and high social standing, implying that only Soviet authors have the ability to write detective stories that show criminals committing crimes for Communist-acceptable reasons.

The article ends with a fleshed-out critique of the problem of poorly translated detective novels. He cites several examples where the syntax of a sentence becomes nonsensical in Russian translations, including a line from Stout's *The Silent Speaker (Umolknuvshii orator):* "Obviously, he had a philosophy of keeping himself in a constant degree of intoxication."[161] The sentence in English is: "It was obvious that he had been applying the theory of acquired immunity to his hangover."[162]

Andzhaparidze's articles illustrate the contradiction that prevailed during this time of popularity for Western translations of detective fiction. On one hand, he believes from an ideological standpoint that detective novels from the West will corrupt the Soviet people by exposing them to an endorsement of capitalist assumptions in the descriptions of criminals and crimes.

---

[160] Andzhaparidze, "Bogachi-filantropy i belye 'Mersedesy': chto i kak my perevodim (Wealthy Philanthropists and White Mercedes: What and How We Translate)."

[161] Georgi Andzhaparidze, "Zigzagi belykh limuzinov (The Zigzags of White Limousines)," *Literaturnaia gazeta*, (March 26, 1975).

[162] Rex Stout, *The Silent Speaker* (Viking Penguin, 1946), 34.

On the other hand, he does write that "the best novels of Rex Stout are full of social content," this slightly positive remark presumably owing to Stout's putting his political gripes about America into his work, as detailed in Chapters Two and Three.[163] Andzhaparidze's focus on the technical problems of translation implies that he does not want the Western detective novels to stop coming in—he just wants them to have the right political message and be translated well.

Literary critic Natalia Ilyina was known for her strong opinions on literary theory and its role in society, and she often mentioned Stout in her work in the 1970s. Ilyina spent time in Harbin and Shanghai as well as in the Soviet Union, and is known for her book *The Return*, which is about the role of nostalgia in the life of Russian émigrés in China, as well as for her satirical sketches and literary criticism.[164] She was a friend of poet Anna Akhmatova, having met her in 1954 at the Writers' Retreat in Golitsyno when Akhmatova's companion, Nina Olshevskaya, had stopped her because she

> had heard that I had some English detective stories. Could I give one of them to Akhmatova to read? Akhmatova herself remained silent. Only a gentle nod of her head led me to understand that she endorsed this request. I immediately ran to my room and brought back two or three books. "My thanks," she answered slowly.[165]

In her article on Akhmatova entitled "The Last Days of Her Life," Ilyina writes that as early as 1954, she herself had already

---

163 Andzhaparidze, "Zigzagi belykh limuzinov (The Zigzags of White Limousines)."

164 Natalia Ilyina, "The Last Days of Her Life," *Soviet Literature* 6 (January 1, 1989), 119.

165 Ibid., 120.

read hundreds of English detective stories.[166] When meeting with Akhmatova in her room, Iliyna describes their first conversation as beginning with a discussion of such stories, for Ilyina had recently graduated from the Literary Institute, a school she had been accepted to with the help of "writer Simonov" (most likely Soviet author and poet Konstantin Simonov).[167]

Ilyina wrote in *Ogonek* that art should always take priority over any social message, supporting her argument with a quotation from Dostoevsky in which he "declared that, however noble an author's intentions might be, if he does not succeed in expressing them in an artistic manner, then his work will never achieve its objective."[168] She was also an outspoken critic of corruption in the literary world, often writing articles for *Ogonek* and *Literaturnaia gazeta* calling out greed among Writers' Union secretaries, as well as "blame[ing] Socialist Realism (by implication) and the conservatives (explicitly)" for what she saw as the low standard of literary criticism in the Soviet period.[169]

A discussion between Ilyina and Russian *detektiv* writer Arkadii Adamov in 1975 addressed some of Andzhaparidze's concerns about the sociological and political nature of the detective novel. Ilyina considered the detective story a "game plus literature," analysis refuted by both Andzhaparidze and Adamov. Adamov thinks that her analysis ignored the importance of the social world of the detective story, "the moral authenticity of the behavior and tempers of the personages, as well as the demand that the conflict itself should be of some social significance."[170]

---

166 Ibid., 121.
167 Ibid.
168 John Gordon Garrard and Carol Garrard, *Inside the Soviet Writers' Union* (New York: Free Press, 1990), 212.
169 Ibid. This framework of analysis is almost contradictory when compared to her praise for Stout's book deriding the FBI in Chapter Five.
170 Natalia Ilyina, "Detective Novels: A Game and Life," *Soviet Literature* 3

He did not like the Western novels in translations in Russia, referring to them as "empty, hollow, contrived plots 'sucked from one's thumbs.'"[171] Ilyina, on the other hand, enjoyed reading Western detective novels, mentioning Stout's by name, owing to their ability to allow her to forget time: "Sometimes it's so important…to forget time! And I don't think you should demand anything more of a detective novel."[172] She dismissed the idea of detective novels needing to have a strong, reality-based morality, calling it an impossible goal, for "to demand of the detective novel writer that he reveal the social roots of crime is to demand that he wrote *Crime and Punishment*."[173]

Adamov's analysis of the difference between Western and Soviet detective stories accentuates the dichotomy between the types of crimes being investigated. He writes that in Western novels it is not necessary to have crimes that illuminate the injustices of society, and therefore he only likes the few Western translations that do "give a genuine picture of the life of society and have a keenly social, denunciatory character." Soviet novels are different: "In ours we seek something more, we are beginning to handle social problems which excite the reader."[174]

Adamov's concerns about the lack of social accountability in detective novels echo those of Andzhaparidze. At the heart of Andzhaparidze's argument against the spread of Western translations is his knowledge of their popularity with the Russian public; he originally responds to this demand with a blanket command to halt their publication. Adamov, on the other hand, harkens back to Bukharin's calls for "Red Pinkertons" by stress-

---

(1975), 144.
171 Ibid. This idiom in English would be "invented out of whole cloth."
172 Ibid., 147.
173 Ibid., 149.
174 Ibid., 145, 47.

ing the importance of social issues in detective stories, thus inherently acknowledging that Russian readers will always have a desire to read detective stories. Adamov sees the detective story as universally enjoyed, a universality that can be taken advantage of:

> But the detective novel has one special feature. Everything an author can put into a detective novel, it can take to the widest, to an inconceivably wide reading public. That is why the form attracts me. For that reason our detective novels should raise the most important questions of the life of society.[175]

A decade after these critiques were published, an interview with Andzhaparidze showed that he had adapted his views. Although he didn't specifically mention detective novels, he talked about the importance of publishing houses translating all types of literature from the West to Russia and vice versa as part of what he refers to as the "friendship movement" and the "aim of helping peoples to understand each other better." This change in attitude was shared by other formerly strong critics of Western detective novels, who seemed to be steadily retreating before the avalanche of detective novels.[176] Further in the interview, Andzhaparidze discusses a US-USSR agreement to create a 45-volume library of Soviet works in English and the same number of American works in Russian. He says that the U.S. isn't proceeding with its Russian translations, but the Russians will do theirs anyway, because of what he sees as the value of showing a Western audience the Soviet perspective: "'Despite all

---

175 Ibid., 150.

176 Klaus Menhert, *The Russians and Their Favorite Books* (Hoover Institution Press, 1983), 252.

the tension in the world today, we believe our efforts are valuable' he said, 'because literature reveals the state of the mind—the spiritual state—of peoples.'"[177] Andzhaparidze's views on the translation of foreign literature into Russian follow the same line of thought, with the goal being to "show the Soviet public an objective map of world literature" by choosing books that are representative of epochs or authors.[178]

That the controversy over publishing Western writers included Stout was curious in its contradictions. His books do lay bare what he saw as flaws in capitalist society, and this explains why he was published in Russia in the first place. McAleer describes Soviet readers as pondering

> the motivations of the affluent Nero Wolfe, who relinquishes his comfort, suffers the rebukes and harassments of others, and endangers his life to uphold ethical standards, remedy social abuses, and see that the ends of justice are served, even when men of power and means must be humbled to bring about that result.[179]

However, at a certain point, the inclusion of Stout's books in translated detective serials began to worry Soviet literary critics like Andzhaparidze. It is interesting that Andzhaparidze neither mentions the politics of the author nor his strong anti-Com-

---

[177] Marilyn Bechtel, "The Soviet Peace Movement: From the Grass Roots " (The National Council of American-Soviet Friendship 1984), 38-39.

[178] Ibid., 39; Elizabeth Roberts to Russia: Lessons and Legacy- The Alexander Men Conference 2012, January 30, 2012, http://www.alexandermenconference.com/blog.html. There were widely believed rumors that Andzhaparidze was an undercover officer in the KGB, rumors that only increased after his strange death falling from "the stage at the Moscow premiere of *The Russia House*, the Hollywood movie starring Michelle Pfeiffer based on the novel by John le Carré, in which George [Georgi] appeared playing himself."

[179] McAleer, *Rex Stout: A Majesty's Life*, 491.

munist messages as problems in Stout's novels; he only discusses the issue of Nero Wolfe as a capitalist figure. As described in Chapter Three, Stout was a staunch opponent of Communism and participated in what could be viewed as incendiary political activity, with anti-Communist fictional murder plots, his open letter to Tito, and his name attached to harshly worded condemnations of Bolshevism published by Freedom House that would have been disseminated in the 1970s when Andzhaparidze wrote the articles. His political background was surely even more suspect than most Soviet writers whose work was banned (with Mikhail Bulgakov or Yevgeny Zamyatin as examples).

One ameliorating factor, perhaps, is that in his novels, Stout's characters tends to only mention the American Communist Party in their diatribes against Communism, as opposed to anything about Moscow and the Russian version of Communism.[180] It is also likely that Andzhaparidze (and other critics) did not have access to sources that would have given him knowledge of Stout's anti-Bolshevik Freedom House activities. What he did have access to were the translations of Stout in Russian, and he appears to have fixated on Wolfe's rotund, well-fed figure and expensive taste in orchids, rather than the politics of the author.

---

180 Stout only actually mentions Russian Communists directly in *The Black Mountain*, which ended up being one of the books most published in Russia in the 1990s.

5 | Why Russians Love that Stout Hates the FBI

> *I am neither a thaumaturge nor a dunce.*
> *-Nero Wolfe*
> *The Doorbell Rang*

The Doorbell Rang

Stout depicts not only Communism in a negative light; influential American institutions also fell under his critical eye. Thus, Stout's popularity in Russia was owed to more than the light pleasures of detective stories; Stout's work showed Russians the freedom that Americans had to criticize their own government. As McAleer writes in reference to Stout's *The Doorbell Rang* (1965), "No Soviet writer could attack with impunity the head of the KGB. In America, Rex Stout could lay the director of the FBI under severe reprimand, and go unpunished."[181] While *The Doorbell Rang* is Stout's most famously outspoken manifestation of his criticism of the FBI, his negative feelings toward the FBI began long before its 1965 publication and can

---

[181] McAleer, *Rex Stout: A Majesty's Life*, 491.

be traced through several of his novels and novellas in the same way that one can trace his criticism of Communism. The inclusion of *The Doorbell Rang* in the previously mentioned journals that were purportedly trying to show the downside of capitalist society by publishing Western detective fiction was one selection that definitely did help achieve that goal.

Stout's opposition to the FBI as an organization also involved a personal detestation of its director, J. Edgar Hoover, whom Stout called a man with a "self-made halo."[182] Hoover in turn developed what some would consider personal problems with Stout, and Stout's FBI file grew to hundreds of pages, with over a hundred pages alone focusing solely on *The Doorbell Rang*. Mitgang wrote that

> J. Edgar Hoover considered Stout anything but genial: as an enemy of the FBI, as a Communist or tool of Communist-dominated groups, someone whose novels and mail had to be watched, and whose involvement with professional writers' organizations was not above suspicion. In the vague, bizarre phrase of one of the documents in his dossier, Stout was described as "an alleged radical."[183]

The FBI's official documentation of Stout began as early as 1940, the year of the publication of *Over My Dead Body* and a Wolfe novella entitled *Sisters in Trouble*. Mitgang goes into the details of Stout's FBI file, calling attention to the absurdities of some of the claims made by FBI agents and informants. *Sisters in Trouble* was analyzed as if it were a code involving political

---

182 . "Nero Wolfe Vs. The F.B.I.," *Life*, December 10, 1965.
183 Mitgang, *Dangerous Dossiers: Exposing the Secret War against America's Greatest Authors*.

intrigue abroad, where the German nationality of characters is suspect – "Nero" refers to Rome, "Fritz" to the German consul in San Francisco, and the three sisters' names as a code pointing toward a July invasion of the Balkans or the Mediterranean.[184] The FBI recorded that Stout had been associated with various organizations and activities that had purported Communist influences, referencing Stout's contributions to *New Masses* as well as his position as guest speaker at an annual dinner for the League for Mutual Aid.[185] This was a group that, among other things, operated an employment agency and bail fund for members of the Communist Party and allied organizations.[186]

The paragraph describing these alleged subversive activities was attached to Hoover's letter informing Stout of his nonattendance at Stout's United World Federalists play, which Stout had personally invited him to, letting Stout know that the FBI had been keeping tabs on him. Possibly in response to this, Stout was quoted as saying, "If I were President, I'd appoint a commission to go through all the FBI files carefully, and destroy every single bit of information that doesn't pertain to U.S. international interests *right now*."[187] Stout was put on "General Watch List No. 49" at Hoover's own instruction, and his NBC Today Show appearance in 1959 was monitored by Special Agent Jones of the FBI, six years before the publication of *The Doorbell Rang*.[188] In Stout's FBI file, there is a letter to J. Edgar Hoover,

---

184 Ibid., Location 3017-22.

185 J. Edgar Hoover to Rex Stout, November 15, 1949, FBI Redacted File, Wolfe Pack online archives. This letter contained a note with this excerpt: "In 1936, the *Western Worker* carried an article which stated that Stout, among others, would be a contributor of articles or stories appearing in the 25th Anniversary issue of *New Masses*."

186 J. Edgar Hoover, November 15, 1949. 3. Ironically, Stout lambasted this type of foundation in his description of the activities of the American Communist Henry Jameson Heath in *Home to Roost*.

187 McAleer, *Rex Stout: A Majesty's Life*, 449.

188 Mitgang, *Dangerous Dossiers: Exposing the Secret War against America's*

the writer's name censored, stating that while watching Stout's appearance on the Today Show the author was "saddened and sickened at the effort put forth by Hugh Downs [interviewer] and Rex Stout to discredit the FBI during this time.... P.S. I am also writing the Hon. Strom Thurmond and telling of this incident."[189]

In 1940, Stout wrote *Over My Dead Body*, which contained subtler criticism of the FBI than *The Doorbell Rang*, while at the same time setting the stage for the later book. The story begins with a young foreign woman, Carla Lovchen, coming to ask Wolfe for help; her friend Neya Tormic has been wrongly accused of stealing diamonds from a member of the fencing club where they both work, and she appeals to Wolfe for help as a fellow Montenegrin. The plot becomes complicated when a man at the fencing club is found with an epée through his heart and the two Montenegrin girls are the main suspects. Murders multiply, and it is revealed that the murdered men have ties to foreign powers, for one corpse turns out to be a Nazi spy and the other a British spy. Wolfe's knowledge of Yugoslav politics and the current struggle for control of that country lead him to wire abroad for a photo of the Yugoslav royal family, and it is revealed that Neya Tormic is really the Princess Vladanka Donevitch. The princess had come to the United States, bringing her family's poor ward, Carla, with her, in order to make a deal giving the Nazis political control of Yugoslavia in exchange for financial gain for herself. In a further twist, Carla turns out to be the daughter that Wolfe had adopted years before in Yugoslavia when she was very young.

Greatest Authors, Location 3118.

189 Censored to J. Edgar Hoover, October 12, 1965, FBI Redacted File, Wolfe Pack online archives. Strom Thurmond was a segregationist, Democratic Senator of South Carolina (who later became a Republican). Wikipedia contributors, "Strom Thurmond," Wikipedia, The Free Encyclopedia., https://en.wikipedia.org/w/index.php?title=Strom_Thurmond&oldid=708355684.

The opening scene involves Carla reading one of the books in Wolfe's library, *United Yugoslavia* by Henderson.[190] Shortly after she leaves, an FBI man named Stahl (who will be a recurring FBI agent throughout the Wolfe series) pays a call on Wolfe.[191] Archie immediately describes Stahl in a derogatory manner, saying that the "G-man...certainly had fine manners, something on the order of a high-class insurance salesman."[192] The purpose of Stahl's visit is to inquire whether Wolfe is an "agent of a foreign principal," in Stahl's words, in which case Wolfe would have to officially register with the Department of State. Since Wolfe had just turned down Carla's plea to save her friend from the diamond debacle (he did not accept the case until after the first murder), Wolfe denies representing any foreign person and sends the man away.

After the first murder, Stahl returns to Wolfe's office a second time to ask if Wolfe is now an "agent of a foreign principal," which he defines as "the government of a foreign country, a person domiciled abroad, or any foreign business, partnership, association, corporation, or political organization." Wolfe replies that he is the agent of a Montenegrin woman, but she isn't domiciled abroad, she is sitting in front of both of them in the room, and then asks what that means in terms of registration. Stahl doesn't know how to take this and says, "It's a situation I haven't met. I'll have to get an opinion from the attorney general. I'll let you know." Inspector Cramer is there for the whole conversation and throws his hands up and "paw[s] the air" in frustration with the FBI.[193]

---

190 Stout, *Over My Dead Body*, 2. Nothing I have found shows that *United Yugoslavia* is more than a title made up by Stout to complement the plot.

191 Ibid., 9.

192 Ibid., 10.

193 Ibid., 114.

The book ends dramatically, with the Princess Donevitch rushing into Wolfe's study with a dagger in her hand, only for him to crack her skull and kill her with a beer bottle without leaving his seat. As the people in the room look at the recently deceased foreign woman lying on Wolfe's carpet, Stahl returns with the news that he "may expect a ruling from the attorney general on that point in about a week," in apparent reference to the now lifeless "foreign principal." Archie looks up at him and "sat back on [his] heels and howled with laughter."[194] This ending could be seen as a precursor to the less violent ending of *The Doorbell Rang*, which ends with less blood but a similar embarrassment of a member of the FBI, albeit a much more dramatic one.

The next Wolfe story to contain slights against the FBI is the previously discussed novella, *Home to Roost* (1952), in which the FBI is presented in a negative manner on the very first page. During a description of the client's confrontation with her nephew: "He told her he was secretly working for the FBI, spying on the Commies, but he wasn't. He thought the FBI was practically the Gestapo."[195] The FBI's practices are compared to those of the Gestapo, and the organization is described as being "capable of sacrificing the rights of a private citizen to what they consider the public interest," two statements that parallel Stout's own complaints against the organization.[196] The only reason Wolfe takes on the client is his intense dislike for the FBI, which overcomes his initial reluctance: "'If you mean you want me to investigate the police and the FBI, that's too big a bite.'"[197] Wolfe hates to work, but he will work if it involves embarrassing

---

194 Ibid., 252.
195 Stout, *Home to Roost*, 18.
196 Ibid., 21.
197 Ibid., 2.

the FBI, a situation that will also occur in *The Doorbell Rang* (although in that case, it also took $100,000 as a retainer to finish the convincing).

The Doorbell Rang, Stout's most "subversive" book according to the FBI, was published in Russian in 1973, eight years after its American publication, in a trilogy containing a novel by Ross MacDonald and one by John Ball. It was the most often published of all Stout's books before the fall of the Soviet Union. The book is a combination of murder mystery and scathing critique of the FBI and was of great interest to Russian readers who could not imagine the existence of the freedom from censorship that Stout enjoyed. There is no popular Russian detective novel that has so negatively examined the KGB or the FSB. Looking beyond the idea of the novel as a demonstration of freedom of speech, the plot paints a highly critical portrait of the FBI and J. Edgar Hoover, and would be considered the most unflattering of Stout's novels in its portrayal of the Western political system. That this book is the one that the Russian state publishing companies published first is no surprise.

The plot of *The Doorbell Rang* is unlike those of most of Stout's other works, in that the client does not want or need a murder solved, because no murder has yet taken place. Instead, Mrs. Barry Rackham comes to Wolfe's office with an unusual request; she wants him to get the FBI to leave her alone after she sent out 10,000 copies of the book, *The FBI Nobody Knows,* to "the members of the cabinet, the Supreme Court justices, governors of all the states, all senators and representatives, members of state legislatures, publishers of newspapers and magazines, and editors, heads of corporations and banks, network executives and broadcasters, columnists, district attorneys, educators, and others— oh yes, chiefs of police."[198] Wolfe begins the job by

---

198 McAleer, *Rex Stout: A Majesty's Life,* 447; Rex Stout, *The Doorbell Rang*

looking into recent small criminal cases involving the FBI, presuming that in at least one of them, owing to the untrustworthy nature of the organization, there must have been some type of misconduct that Wolfe could expose and use as blackmail to stop the surveillance of Mrs. Rackham. Inspector Cramer, deviating from his normal role as the cantankerous police officer who gives Wolfe a hard time, divulges information to Archie about a death by shooting where the bullet went missing before the body was found, and tells him that not only are there witnesses who saw FBI men leaving the apartment but that he has been stopped on orders from above from investigating the case.

While Wolfe and Archie don't assume that FBI men committed the crime, they begin an investigation into the murder on the premise that the FBI was somehow involved, and they turn out to be correct. The murder itself was committed by the murdered man's girlfriend, and, in an unlucky coincidence, FBI men entered his apartment shortly after the crime to confiscate material he had uncovered while writing an exposé about the FBI. Spooked by the unexpected sight of a dead body and worried about the exposure of the illegality of their activities, the men had taken the bullet and left without reporting the murder.

In the course of their investigation, Archie and Wolfe become worried that their house is bugged and go to extreme lengths to avoid being overheard, only speaking when they are in the basement with both the television and radio on at top volume. Cramer brought on this suspicion by informing them that the FBI was looking for a way to take away their detective licenses. Wolfe then tricks the FBI into thinking that he and Archie are out of town, catches FBI men breaking into his apart-

(The Viking Press, Inc., 1965), 3; Fred J. Cook, *The FBI Nobody Knows* (New York: MacMillan Company, 1964). McAleer writes that Stout was inspired to write the novel after reading Fred Cook's *The FBI Nobody Knows,* but that the author of the book did not know of the plot of *The Doorbell Rang* until his daughter sent him a copy.

ment red-handed, and convinces an FBI higher-up, Wagg, to give the bullet to the police and stop harassing Mrs. Rackham in exchange for his silence about both instances of breaking and entering that Wolfe now has evidence of.

The plot of the book is weaker than those of Stout's other novels from the viewpoint of the detective genre, since the search for a murderer is only secondary to the embarrassment of the FBI; the focus seems to be on having every character badmouth the FBI as many times as they can. Wolfe refers to J. Edgar Hoover as "a bully" without ever mentioning him by name, and to the FBI as a whole as "that goddamn outfit and that bunch of grabbers." In a drawn-out joke, Archie explains to the cook Fritz that "We're going to push his [Hoover's] nose in. Just a routine chore, but he's touchy and will try to stop us. So futile."

> "But he—he's a great man. Yes?"
> "Sure. But I suppose you've seen pictures of him."
> "Yes."
> "What do you think of his nose?"
> "Not good. Not exactly épaté, but broad. Not bien fait."
> "Then it should be pushed."[199]

At other points, Archie jokes about shooting Hoover and makes fun of a "G-man's" appearance, describing him as having a "manly mug with a firm jaw."[200] Wolfe also makes many sweeping statements about the FBI in the grandiose vein reminiscent of Stout's sweeping statements concerning the German people:

---

199 *The Doorbell Rang*, 17, 57, 20.
200 Ibid., 43, 69. Also a possible reference to the comic strip *Dick Tracy*.

> The Federal Bureau of Investigation is a formidable foe, entrenched in power and privilege. It is not rodomontade but merely a statement of fact to say that no individual or group in America would undertake the job I have assigned myself. If an agent of the FBI killed your son there is not the slightest chance that he will be brought to account unless I [Wolfe] do it.[201]

The book ends with one of Stout's most iconic scenes, in which J. Edgar Hoover, still unnamed, comes from Washington himself to talk to Wolfe. Archie writes:

> The doorbell rang. I got up and went to the hall and saw a character on the stoop I had never seen before, but I had seen plenty of pictures of him. I stepped back in and said, "Well, well. The big fish." He frowned at me, then got it, and did something he never does. He left his chair and came. We stood side by side, looking. The caller put a finger to the button, and the doorbell rang. "No appointment," I said. "Shall I take him to the front room to wait a while?" "No. I have nothing for him. Let him get a sore finger." He turned and went back in to his desk. I stepped in. "He probably came all the way from Washington just to see you. Quite an honor." "Pfui. Come and finish this." I returned to my chair. "As I was saying, I may have to tell her privately …" The doorbell rang.[202]

After the publication of *The Doorbell Rang*, the FBI intensified its focus on Stout. In fact, the FBI did not have to wait until its publication date to read the novel. A page of Stout's FBI file

---

201 Ibid., 80.
202 Ibid., 178.

contains a memorandum, declassified in 1980, reporting that a Photostat of the manuscript was confidentially obtained by the FBI from a source at *The New York Times* and already perused in May of 1965, seven months before its official publication date. Excerpts from the FBI review of the book and subsequent recommendations read as follows:

> This vicious book depicts the FBI in the worst possible light.... Rex Stout concludes this book with a contemptuous reference to the Director....[It is recommended that] Stout be designated as a person not to be contacted without prior Bureau approval... Any inquiries received concerning the book should be answered with a statement that the FBI has no comment other than that the book is a fictional work which presents a false and distorted picture of the FBI and that any Agents conducting themselves in the manner depicted in this book would be subject to immediate dismissal.[203]

The FBI's book review continues, "The plot of this book is weak and it will probably have only limited public acceptance despite Stout's use of the FBI in an apparent bid for sensationalism to improve sales."[204] This did not end up being the case. While Mitgang references several examples of those who strongly disagreed with Stout and sent personal letters to Hoover in support, and John Wayne sent a letter to Stout saying "Goodbye," Viking Press ran a print run of 30,000 copies of *The Doorbell Rang*, double the printings of previous Wolfe novels.[205]

203 M.A. Jones to Mr. DeLoach, May 20, 1965, *"The Doorbell Rang" New Mystery Novel by Rex Stout*, FBI Redacted File, Wolfe Pack online archives.

204 Ibid. This quotation is reminiscent of Andzhaparidze's charge that Soviet journals used Western detective novels, including Stout's *The Doorbell Rang*, to improve sales.

205 Mitgang, *Dangerous Dossiers: Exposing the Secret War against America's Greatest Authors*, Location 3103.

Even with the growth of intense scrutiny, which Stout must have anticipated, McAleer writes that "Rex was more than ready to confront the implications of his book. He thought it childish that the FBI wrapped itself in the American flag and adopted the assumption of infallibility."[206] A review of *The Doorbell Rang* quotes Stout as connecting his distaste for Hoover to his already well-documented distaste for McCarthy:

> I got my first idea from the newspapers years ago when I learned that he frequently went to the races with Senator McCarthy. I was astonished that a man—Hoover—whose function it is to preserve and uphold the law would take as a social companion a man who was so obviously a threat to the very basis of democracy.[207]

Another interview quotes Stout as saying that the FBI is an "odious, overbearing and unprincipled" organization but that he is not afraid of it because it "can't touch a writer and I'm not worrying about it. All I need is a typewriter."[208] The attention Stout received for the book was only distasteful to him in one way; Philip Quarles wrote that Stout was annoyed at "having achieved wealth and fame in a genre of writing not seriously regarded by most critics, that he is in the news not because he wrote a 'good story'; but because he took on the FBI."[209]

Although the book is an obvious slam of the FBI and its practices, Stout was always vague in his interviews about its political message. Asked about his intentions when writing the novel, Stout replied, "[In] *The Doorbell Rang*, I knew that the

---

206 McAleer, *Rex Stout: A Majesty's Life*, 451, 47.

207 Haskel and Winterich, "Private Eye on the FBI," *Saturday Review of Literature*.

208 "Nero Wolfe Vs. The F.B.I.," 128.

209 Quarles, *Rex Stout Writes Detective Stories, Makes Enemies of the FBI*.

bullet wouldn't be found in the room, but I didn't know why. Later, when it turned out that the FBI took it, I was delighted."[210] In another interview:

> I didn't think of *The Doorbell Rang* as an attack on the FBI while I was writing it. I hadn't the faintest idea of attacking. Have you ever read a Sherlock Holmes story? Did you consider it an attack on Scotland Yard? *Now* I'm beginning to think that the book may lead people to stand up and speak out against the FBI.... It is conceivable to me that the FBI might tail me or tap my phone because of this book. I think it is wonderful I've written so often about ditching tails. I'd like to try to do it.[211]

Stout's crack about being tailed has the ring of truth to it. When Herbert Mitgang requested Stout's file from the FBI, he only received 183 pages of the 301-page dossier, and most of them were censored. Mitgang writes that the hesitancy of the FBI to turn everything over to him stemmed from a reluctance to disclose the identity of a "confidential source," which implies that Stout was being actively watched. The Church Committee, a Senate committee that investigated illegal intelligence gathering by the government, found that Stout's name was included in the 332 names on the FBI's "do not contact list," which was evidence in its search to prove misconduct by the FBI.[212]

The Russian trilogy, *Contemporary American Detective*, which contains *The Doorbell Rang* as well as novels by Ross

---

210 "Nero Wolfe Vs. The F.B.I.."

211 Haskel and Winterich, "Private Eye on the FBI," *Saturday Review of Literature*.

212 David Monroe to Seeking In The Zeitgeist, Februrary 2, 2012, http://seekinginthezeitgeist.blogspot.com/2012/02/doorbell-rang-by-rex-stout-myrating-4.html.

MacDonald and John Ball, includes an introduction by literary critic Natalia Ilyina.[213] (With her strong background in English detective fiction, she was a natural choice.[214]) She begins the section on Stout by declaring him "one of the oldest and the most popular representatives of the detective genre in modern America."[215] She compares him to Agatha Christie, Sir Arthur Conan Doyle, and Dorothy Sayers, asserting that Wolfe is closer in nature to his British counterparts than to his American ones. She also addresses the ideological differences between Soviet and Western detective novels: "Nero Wolfe, in particular, did not hide the fact that he was working for money." This was a major contrast; in most, if not all, Russian detective fiction at the time, the heroes were not private detectives working for fees, but instead were either policeman or other members of the state apparatus working for low salaries.[216] Wolfe's reluctance to work for anything other than high fees and his lavish household were topics to be specially noted in the Soviet Union in the 1970s; a lifestyle this incompatible with socialism should be remarked upon.

The duplicitous role of the FBI is described in detail in the introduction, for Ilyina has the same negative view of the institution that Stout did. She writes that "the growing penetration of the Federal Bureau of Investigation in the private lives of US citizens is reflected in the novel *The Doorbell Rang*. Not high

---

213 Ilyina and her views on the detective novel are discussed in Chapter Four.

214 In the introduction to *The Doorbell Rang*, Ilyina's long description of the characterization of Tibbs, a black policeman in another novel in the volume, shows the interest that the Soviet people had in race relations in America. See Chapter Two for more information on this.

215 Reks Staut, "Sovremennyi amerikanskii detektiv," in *Zvonok v dver'* ed. Natalia Ilyina (Moscow: Progress, 1973), 2.

216 Aleksandra Marinina's police lieutenant Anastasia Kamenskaia is an example of a popular Russian crime fiction series with a non-private detective working for the state.

position in society, not wealth—nothing can protect one from the FBI." Ilyina writes that the FBI could be considered "an oppressive force, brazen because of its impunity, 'a state within a state,' which crushes everything in its path," and that only Nero Wolfe would be able to put the "mighty FBI" in a position of vulnerability.[217] Ilyina considers the FBI an institution that illegally uses its unlimited resources, which could simply reflect her agreement with Stout but might also involve an unconscious coupling of the FBI with the reality of the KGB in Russia in the 1970s.

The Soviet inclination to dislike the FBI because it infringed citizens' privacy was of course ironic and contradictory. While the Soviet state was objecting to the capitalist society's organization that entered every facet of peoples' lives, its socialist organizations were doing the same thing. An insight into this contradiction comes from Héda Kovaly, who wrote about her persecution under Russian Communism in the former Czechoslovakia. Her husband was a high-ranking Communist official at the beginning of the Czech purges in the 1950s, and she explains how both she and her husband did not immediately see the government's actions against its citizens as menacing. She writes:

> Every government had an obligation to defend itself against its enemies. Look at America and Joseph McCarthy's witch hunts! It was only when someone we knew well was arrested, someone we knew could not possibly be guilty of any crime, that we began to pull our heads out of the sand.[218]

---

217 Staut, "Sovremennyi amerikanskii detektiv," 5.

218 Héda Margolius Kovaly, *Under a Cruel Star: A Life in Prague, 1941-1968* (Holmes & Meier Publishers, Inc, 1997), 95, 166. At the height of her family's persecution in Prague, Kovaly turned to the detective genre for

Kovaly's initial attitude toward the Czech purges helps explain why a Soviet critic like Ilyina could denounce the FBI without making a connection between the FBI and the KGB; she could condemn the FBI's censorship without condemning her own political system's censorship of detective novels, and worse.[219]

In her introduction to *The Doorbell Rang*, Ilyina also writes: "Risking it all puts Nero Wolfe in the fight against the FBI in the role of David, battling Goliath. The strength is on Goliath's side, but the truth is on the side of little David. And the sympathies of all honest people are on that side…"[220] In this, Wolfe is (somewhat ironically) seen as the "little David" fighting a corrupt governmental system, rather like the proletariat fighting against exploitation by the upper classes, which might be seen as an indirect endorsement of socialism. While Ilyina does not mention Stout's politics, and it is unclear if she knew the extent of Stout's persecution by the FBI, Stout's experiences with the organization would supplement Ilyina's view of it.

After the 1973 Russian publication of *The Doorbell Rang*, the novel was published many more times in Russia. It appeared in twenty-one mystery trilogies before 1999 and six more after 2000. Russians who read *The Doorbell Rang* in the 1990s took away the same negative impression of the FBI as Ilyina did in 1971. These readers took what Stout wrote about the FBI as

comfort, describing her reaction to authors like Raymond Chandler as being "enthralled by the beauty of an exact word which blends flawlessly with a clearcut idea."

219 Viktor Marakhovskii to Kul'tpul't, June 14, 2015, http://www.kultpult.ru/Niro-Vulf-pobeditel-gomofobov-Ob-evolyucii-cennostej-233. Russian blogger Viktor Marakhovskii also addresses Stout's animosity against the FBI. He is freer to make the connection between the FBI and the Soviet government given that he is writing in 2015, long after the worst Soviet repression has ended. Marakhovskii believes that Stout read Solzhenitsyn's *The Gulag Archipelago* before writing *The Doorbell Rang,* and that Stout is therefore comparing what the FBI does with the repression of the Soviet government. It is highly plausible that Stout had read Solzhenitsyn, for in *Death of a Dude*, Wolfe is reading Solzhenitsyn's *The First Circle*.

220 Staut, "Sovremennyi amerikanskii detektiv," 6.

gospel truth, because they wouldn't yet have had any other reliable source of information about the FBI.

Members of the Russian Nero Wolfe online fan site and the Vk site have only negative things to say about the FBI. Rymko, Panichev, and Zavgorodnii all read *The Doorbell Rang* as their first Stout book. Rymko found the book accidentally, and Panichev, who refers to the 1973 trilogy as a "good translation," read the book at the suggestion of his librarian. Chervotkin wrote that he saw through Wolfe's hatred of the FBI to Stout's own hatred of the FBI: "I suppose that Stout disliked Hoover personally and the FBI in general. The FBI is presented as the absolute evil. The FBI uses means of any degree of impurity. Therefore, any measures against it are acceptable."[221] User BleWotan agrees with Chervotkin's opinion of the realism of the plot: "My vision of the FBI and their methods at that time was close enough to what Stout described in his books," and Panichev writes that the FBI was "displayed as unattractive, like an organization violating the laws."[222] Zavgorodnii more specifically addresses Hoover's role in the novel, agreeing with Stout's negative opinion of the man: "I think that for that period of American history Hoover's FBI was shown realistically."[223]

---

[221] Sergey Chervotkin (user Avis), November 20, 2015; Natalia Rymko (user Rymarnica), October 19, 2015.

[222] User BleWotan, December 14, 2015; Sergey Panichev, Vkontakte message to author, March 15, 2016.

[223] Stanislav Zavgorodnii (user Chuchundrovich), November 23, 2015.

6 | How Stout's Popularity Continues after the Fall of Communism

It was about the idea that a novelist should just create his characters and let them go ahead and develop the action and the plot. This guy was dead against it. He claimed you should plot it yourself. I was thinking that a detective working on a case can't plot it himself. It has already been plotted.
—Archie Goodwin
Plot it Yourself

Stout's Detective Novels in Post-Soviet Russia

Critics had lost some of their moral ground when the blanket ban on the detective genre during the Stalin period ended in the 1950s. The "Red Pinkertons" did not return but were instead replaced when middlebrow non-literary journals like *Iskatel'* and *Podvig* began publishing detective fiction (but still only certain authors). More than fifteen of Agatha Christie's novels were translated into Russian between 1966 and 1970, and 630,000 collections of "It's elementary, my dear Watson," were "insufficient to meet demands" in Russia.[224] Lovell writes that Agatha Christie (and Sir Arthur Conan Doyle) were safe choices for Soviet publishers at this time.[225] In 1983, the foreign literary journal *Zarubezhnyi detektiv* (*Foreign Detective Stories*) had a print run of 200,000 copies, and between 1986 and 1993 more than 30 million pirated copies of Christie's novels were translated and published in Russia.[226] These numbers confirm that Nepomnyashchy, the *detektiv* scholar, was correct when she wrote that "well before glasnost Russians were reading a great deal of detective fiction, and were clamoring for more."[227]

Progress Publishers, publisher of the 1973 trilogy that included *The Doorbell Rang*, was a Moscow-based publishing house founded in 1931. It was most best known for its English-language publication of books about Marxist-Leninism, which is interesting to note because of its decision to publish Stout. An article written in February of 1991, several months before the Soviet Union was dissolved, details the importance of American books at that time to Progress Publishers. The article describes how the formerly politically-inclined, propaganda-producing

---

[224] Nancy Gryspeerdt and Sam Kinchin-Smith, "Curious Incidents: The Adventures of Sherlock Holmes in Russia," *The Calvert Journal*, 2014; "Sherlock Holmes Is Favorite in Russia," *The Washington Post*, April 15 1967. Humorously, there was also a Russian band in the 1980s called Agata Kristi (Agatha Christie) whose sound is described as a reflection of the name, a "mysterious, eccentric, and at times sadistically spooky mix of glam, goth rock, and techno-like electronics." Wikipedia contributors, "Agatha Christie (Band)," Wikipedia, The Free Encyclopedia., https://en.wikipedia.org/w/index.php?title=Agatha_Christie_(band)&oldid=703557998.

[225] Lovell, *The Russian Reading Revolution: Print Culture in the Soviet and PostSoviet Eras* 51-52.

[226] Menhert, *The Russians and Their Favorite Books*, 252. Lyndall Morgan, "Darya Dontsova's 'Sleuthettes': A Case of the Regendering of the Post-Soviet Russian Detektiv?," *Australian Slavonic and East European Studies* 19 (2005), 95.

[227] Nepomnyashchy, "Markets, Mirrors, and Mayhem: Aleksandra Marinina and the Rise of the New Russian Detektiv," 165.

company had switched to publishing Russian-language editions of popular American best-sellers such as "How to Win Friends and Influence People" and George Bush's autobiography, in order to be seen as a "modern publishing house." The US government gave $230,000 in grants to buy rights to American books (although if a book was printed before 1973, it could be legally published in the USSR without buying the rights).[228] The Text Cooperative, a private publishing house, published Stout in a collection (with no date given) with Ed McBain and Raymond Chandler in a print run of 200,000 to 400,000 copies; each book cost from four to eight rubles ($2.50 to $5). The article's author writes that "even anti-communist U.S. academics Richard Pipes and Robert Conquest will have works published in the Soviet Union this year." He doesn't include Stout in this list, even though he would be considered an anti-communist writer, if not an academic one.[229] Even with the plethora of new translations that had grown exponentially since the publication of *The Doorbell Rang*, there were still very few copies of translated Western detective novels in bookstores, for demand was always greater than supply. And so a book exchange system became universal. A reader would bring in a book and request another book in exchange, but the book he traded had to be one of the ones "in demand" in order to receive a foreign *detektiv* from publishers like Progress and Molodaia gvardiia or the 'Podvig' series from 'Zhizn' zamechatel'nykh liudei (Lives of Remarkable

---

228 McAleer writes that Stout did not receive any royalties for any edition "behind the Iron Curtain," for they were all unauthorized. However, Stout did not care; the fact that his ideas were influencing people under the suppression of Communism was enough for him. McAleer, *Rex Stout: A Majesty's Life*, 491.

229 Greg Gransden, "Yanks Write New Chapter in Soviet Publishing: Books: Onetime Propaganda Mills Still Carry the Works of Lenin. But American Favorites, Such as 'the Godfather,' Are the Top Sellers.," *Los Angeles Times* February 19, 1991.

People)."[230] In 1989-1990, the official ban on detective novels (which by then had only slight effect) was lifted, and Russian publishers began issuing Western novels in earnest. The growing demand for publishing houses increased their number from 230 in Soviet times to over 7,200 by 1995.[231] However, the book exchange system was still in use in the 1990s as the economy sorted itself out, and Western detective novels were still considered valuable currency in the book trade (even though the oversaturation of Western novels in general caused publishers to limit their issuance).[232]

Baraban explains that in the 1990s "crime fiction soon accounted for the greatest percentage of translated Western popular literature flooding the Russian book market .... Rex Stout…and other authors covered *lotki*, stalls at makeshift outdoor book markets."[233] Scholar Lyndall Morgan lists Stout as one of the most popular writers translated during this period of *lotki* (1990s), alongside Raymond Chandler and James Hadley Chase (who had been lambasted by Andzhaparidze for his millionaire cast).[234] The popularity of these books can be explained by the fact that the Soviet version of the detective genre portrayed its heroes in a stereotypical socialist realist style; with the collapse of the old system, these characters now represented the corruption of the past, and Western translations were easily

---

230 Lovell, *The Russian Reading Revolution: Print Culture in the Soviet and PostSoviet Eras* 61.

231 Olcott, *Russian Pulp: The Detektiv and the Russian Way of Crime*, 3. Lovell, *The Russian Reading Revolution: Print Culture in the Soviet and Post-Soviet Eras* 133.

232 *The Russian Reading Revolution: Print Culture in the Soviet and Post-Soviet Eras* 132.

233 Baraban, "Russia in the Prism of Popular Culture: Russian and American Detective Fiction and Thrillers of the 1990s," 162.

234 Morgan, "Darya Dontsova's 'Sleuthettes': A Case of the Regendering of the Post-Soviet Russian Detektiv?," 99.

able to edge them out.[235] Wachtel writes, "These books rapidly overwhelmed the local cultural production and, to the dismay of former communists and dissidents alike, became the reading matter for the masses."[236]

Although Baraban writes that Stout's books made up a large part of the *lotki* book markets, Chervotkin, Zavgorodnii and user BleWotan only rate Stout's popularity in the 1990s at "3+", "2", and "4" respectively. BleWotan's relatively high "4" is because of a subscription that delivered BleWotan's Stout books, which meant that "the audience did exist and it was big enough for the edition to be profitable."[237] And Zavgorodnii, even with his 2 rating, has an important historical and political reason why he began reading Stout's books after the collapse of the USSR:

> The attitude towards communism (my personal and generally in the country) had changed significantly. I had never been a confirmed communist, and the access to the information that appeared during the "Perestroika" (Solzhenitsyn's books, etc.) changed my attitude for this ideology even more; therefore, I treated Stout's anticommunism calmly, as a conscious choice of a sensible man.[238]

Panichev agrees that Stout's anti-Communism took on a new significance in the post-Soviet era, writing that "hostility to

---

[235] Nepomnyashchy, "Markets, Mirrors, and Mayhem: Aleksandra Marinina and the Rise of the New Russian Detektiv," 166.

[236] Wachtel, *Remaining Relevant after Communism: The Role of the Writer in Eastern Europe*, 192.

[237] Sergey Chervotkin (user Avis), November 20, 2015; Stanislav Zavgorodnii (user Chuchundrovich), November 23, 2015; User BleWotan, December 14, 2015; Sergey Panichev, Vkontakte message to author, March 15, 2016.

[238] Stanislav Zavgorodnii (user Chuchundrovich), November 23, 2015.

the Communist practice and ideology was opened for us after the translation of all of his [Stout's] books" in the 1990s.

Wolfe novels were not the only new publications in that period. A collection of detective stories called *Detektivy Veka (Detective Novels of the Century)* was published in Moscow by Polifakt publishing in a series called Itogi Veka, Vzglyad iz Rossii. *Detective Novels of the Century* covered one hundred years of detective novels from all over the world, in translation. Its introduction describes the selections as books that opened a new page in literature and goes on to discuss the rules and secrets learned from this century of detective novels.[239] Intriguingly, Georgi Andzhaparidze, the same Soviet critic who in the 1970s so harshly criticized the increasing influence of Western detective translations in the Soviet Union, edited the series.

Twenty years after his first condemnation of Western detective stories, and fifteen years after his interview with a milder view of the detective genre, Andzhaparidze wrote an afterword to this new collection. In it he discusses in detail several detective characters, namely Poirot, Miss Marple, and Maigret, in terms that show both his breadth of knowledge of the detective genre as well as an admiration for the writing that created these detectives. Andzhaparidze mentions Soviet-era detective novels, like those of Leonov, the Vainer brothers, and Semenov, which he does not think are worse than their Western counterparts, just different in principle:

> The problem with all of these obviously talented people was that they were working not only within the framework of a genre but were also in the grip of a brutal ideological oppression, and therefore they were forced not to

---

239 *Detektivy veka* (*Detective Novels of the Century*), Itogi veka, Vzgliad iz rossii (Total Century, Glance from Russian), (Polifakt. Itogi veka, 1999), 5.

enthrall and entertain but to educate readers in the spirit of socialist class morality, which has consistently been contrasted to "bourgeois" abstract humanism. [240]

Thus Andzhaparidze's 1971 criticism Western authors for their bourgeois character is turned upside down when he writes disparagingly in 1999 about the "Soviet detective genre's propagandist function of teaching class morals."

Menhert's previously quoted statement that the literary critics of the Soviet era had to "steadily retreat" from their previous Party-line positions on the detective genre before "the avalanche of detective novels" is an apt description of what Andzhaparidze has done.[241] Andzhaparidze had once referred to the impossibility of novels about crime to flourish in a society without private property, seemingly ignoring the fact that the detective novel did in fact flourish (albeit in an underground manner) in Soviet society. Now he describes the current trend in *detektiv* to "reflect the current level of criminalization in our society" rather than the traditional detective genre's dependence on the ten commandments for morality (in his opinion).[242] This comment about the new type of morality that a writer like Marinina observes in Soviet society retains the style of some of Andzhaparidze's older, more critical quips about the failure of society to deal with literature and morality in ways that he saw fit.

Stout's writing is included in the *Detective Novels of the Century* collection, but it is not a Nero Wolfe novel—it is not even

---

240 Georgi Andzhaparidze, "Zhestkost' kanona i vechnaia novizna (The Rigidity of the Canon and Perpetual Novelty)," in *Detektivy veka* (*Detective Novels of the Century*), Itogi veka, Vzgliad iz rossii (Total Century, Glance from Russian), (Polifakt. Itogi veka, 1999), 902, 910.

241 Menhert, *The Russians and Their Favorite Books*, 252.

242 Andzhaparidze, "Zhestkost' kanona i vechnaia novizna (The Rigidity of the Canon and Perpetual Novelty)," in *Detektivy veka* (*Detective Novels of the Century*), 909.

a detective story. Instead, editor Andzhaparidze chose to include Stout's satirical article on Sherlock Holmes, which had caused an uproar when given as a speech by Stout to the Baker Street Irregulars in 1941. The article, entitled "Watson was a Woman," is based on the singular premise that since neither Holmes nor Watson is ever described as going to bed in the stories, Watson must be a female lover or mistress of Holmes. Stout goes into elaborate detail about the ways that Conan Doyle subtly hid the truth of Watson's gender; the speech ends with an acrostic of several titles of Holmes's stories that spells out "Irene Watson."[243]

Stout quotes several passages from Conan Doyle's stories in the article, and the Russian translator, V. Voronina, had access to several different Russian translations of the passages Stout quotes. Voronina had difficulties, however, since English doesn't have gendered nouns and adjectives while Russian does. The Russian masculine endings for "Watson" had to be replaced when it made more sense for feminine endings to describe Stout's "Irene Watson."[244] The translation of the article also leaves out (for unexplained reasons) the final three paragraphs, which describe Holmes marrying Watson.

"Watson Was a Woman" is an unusual example of the problems that arose when translating Stout's work; the problems encountered in this instance are more of a technical and linguistic nature, as opposed to problems that arise from ideological issues.[245]

---

243 Rex Stout, "Watson Was a Woman," *The Saturday Review of Literature* (March 1, 1941).

244 Staut, "Uotson byl zhenshzhinoi (Watson Was a Woman)," 703.

245 To be clear, though, the translation problems of Stout in the early 2000s was largely due to a lack of knowledge of the vocabulary surrounding Wolfe's food and meals.

The Russians Begin Writing Their Own Detective Novels

Once Russians were able to write detective stories without needing to conform to particular political ideals, the linguistic problems of literal translation turned into the trickier ideological problems of translating a genre. Wachtel writes that these new *detektiv* writers created "low- or middlebrow" novels that have a "layer of metageneric commentary: postmodern pulp, in a word."[246] These writers were entering a time where everything that they had previously believed in had crumbled; they had to both restart their lives and reinvent their ways of approaching culture. Arkadii Adamov wrote in 1975 that Western detective novels would always be inherently different from their Soviet counterparts because "due to the traditions of Russian literature—we are beginning to load the detective novel with much more moral, social and public weight than Western authors do," and this idea remained pertinent even after censorship was lifted.[247] Russian *detektiv* scholar Anthony Olcott writes that the main question of the Russian *detektiv* genre is "Who is guilty," as opposed to the Western, "Whodunit."[248]

The new concepts of individuality in a capitalist society introduced into Russian culture in the early 1990s did not immediately show themselves in the Russian *detektiv*, for it was a

---

246 Wachtel, *Remaining Relevant after Communism: The Role of the Writer in Eastern Europe*, 193.

247 Ilyina, "Detective Novels: A Game and Life," 148.

248 Olcott, *Russian Pulp: The Detektiv and the Russian Way of Crime*, 7. In fact, one of the books written in the "Red Pinkerton" era, *Miss Mend: Yankees in Petrograd*, also turned the "Whodunit" formula into a Russian version: "How will vengeance be exacted?" The book was criticized for its bourgeois decadence, but the author, Marietta Shaginian, went on to win the Lenin award in 1972 for her novels about Lenin's life. Boris Dralyuk, Western Crime Fiction Goes East: The Russian Pinkerton Craze, 1907-1934 (Brill Academic Pub, 2012). 65.

concept "to which the Bolsheviks were deeply hostile" and Russians in the 1990s could not rid themselves of the influence of their upbringing overnight.[249] Olcott explains that, in the *detektivy*, good guys lie, cheat, steal, and even kill, while bad guys do things like work two jobs, manufacture goods consumers want to buy, and

> wear nice clothes. The key to understanding such apparent contradictions, however, is to see the larger purpose for which the actions are committed. At least the *detektiv* genre, and presumably the Russian readership, will consider actions committed for an individual end or benefit to be bad, while actions committed for some larger communal purpose—even if these violate laws or have tragic consequences—are going to be seen as good.[250]

Since private property was a new concept to Russians in the early 1990s, their detective storylines reflect somewhat older, more Communist-oriented ideas concerning possession and acquisition of private property as a motive for crime; the message seems to be that "possessions themselves are bad." The very definition of crime differs between Western and Russian society. What the West sees as illegal action the Russians may see as "simply human weakness, or an inescapable part of an imperfect world."[251] Olcott notes that in some Russian *detektiv* novels, when the police must investigate the crime of theft of private property "their sympathies clearly run against the victims."[252]

---

249 Olcott, *Russian Pulp: The Detektiv and the Russian Way of Crime*, 5.

250 Ibid., 140. See Olcott's Chapter Four on punishment and rehabilitation in the Russian *detektiv* for examples of these contradictions.

251 Ibid., 185.

252 Ibid., 68, 70.

In addition to ideological differences between the Western detective genre and the new Russian *detektiv*, there were differences in literary depictions of the actual processes of criminal courts and the judicial system. The idea of confession, and making the criminal confess, is traditionally very important in the Russian system and therefore plays a large role in *detektiv* novels.[253] A fictional senior official in a 1990s Russian *detektiv* novel describes the changed role of confession in the post-Soviet period. When he created a new detective team, he had to

> adapt to "working under a legal government," as he expressed it. That is, they had to pursue and prosecute criminals without using such tried and true methods as physical coercion, extended periods of detention, threats, and so on. It was incredibly difficult to operate without the help of these tools, but on the other hand [his] team got on well with the detectives and prosecutors, who could find no fault with their work.... He always performs his work reliably and well.[254]

The types of heroes that appear in the Russian *detektiv* also differ from the stereotypical Western private eye; the *detektiv's* heroes tend to be individuals working within a larger apparatus, like a police department or the military.[255] A 2001 article in *The Moscow Times* observes that the Russian *detektiv* emphasizes the "unshakeable faith of the Russian reader in the strength and impartiality of at least one state structure," the state polic-

---

253 Ibid., 118.

254 Alexandra Marinina, *A Confluence of Circumstances, The Soviet and Post-Soviet Review* 29, no. 1, 2 (2002), 156.

255 Wilkinson, *Detective Fiction in Cuban Society and Culture*, 120. Göbler had written that in the Soviet *detektiv* genre, there was only one type of detective character allowed: "the diligent policeman who never questions the social order." The 1990s *detektiv* heroes appear to be a holdover from this time.

ing apparatus, while in the Western genre characters like Nero Wolfe, Hercule Poirot, and Miss Marple are private individuals solving crimes, not "confined to the narrow corridors of state service." Russians look for faith in their police system in their *detektiv* novels, while American detective fiction tends to favor the strong individual fighting the system (shown by the popularity of writers like James Patterson).

Olcott does describe, however, one type of Russian *detektiv* hero that does resemble Nero Wolfe. The *syshchik* detective, which he translates into English as "the searcher," plays a role similar to that of the Western private investigator – first establishing the existence of a crime and then gathering evidence needed to convict the criminals. Olcott explains that the *syshchik* role differs from a Western detective in that he (or she) must conform to the formal administrative processes. *Detektiv* writer Yulian Semyonov creates a senior *syshchik* who, like Wolfe, never seems to leave his office but is indispensable in coordinating the efforts of other investigators, making sure that they are observing Russian laws in the course of their investigation, and, most important, that they are moving toward the solution of the mystery, one that he, the *syschik*, seems almost to know in advance.[256] (Nero Wolfe's meting out of justice in the novel *Fer-de-lance* by orchestrating a murder-suicide can be seen as a reflection of the sedentary lifestyle of a *syshchik*, for the murder-suicide eliminates the need for Wolfe to take an hour-long drive to testify at a trial. This is also one of the times that Wolfe departs from letting democratic processes take their course).

The *syshchik* model for a Russian *detektiv* hero only became possible in the late Soviet period, as writers began experimenting with how independent their heroes could be.[257] However,

---

256 Olcott, *Russian Pulp: The Detektiv and the Russian Way of Crime*, 28.
257 Ibid., 29. Russian *detektiv* writer Aleksandra Marinina is well known for

even though Russian *detektiv* writers in the 1990s were no longer living under Communism, they still were not able to fully embrace the idea of the individual as a positive character. Olcott sums it up in the conclusion of his book on Russian pulp fiction: "The unit of measurement that the western genre finds supreme—the individual—is to the Russian genre, at best, a solipsism, and, at worst, a criminal, actively working to destroy the Russian basic unit, an amorphously defined but acutely felt larger community."[258]

Russian Intellectual Backlash Against the Rise of Mass Culture and the Detective Novel

Not all Russians were pleased with the new phenomenon of homegrown detective novels and their new type of relatively independent hero. Natalia Ivanova, the editor of the journal *Znamya*, which was one of the journals that first published Stout in the Soviet era, worried about an increasing lack of emphasis on serious literature:

> We can all accept the idea that the only people reading now are the ones who read for non-political reasons…. Now you see the rise of advice columns, personal ads, Harlequin romances. Well, that's OK. What is unexpected is the general degradation of culture and of the intelligentsia itself.[259]

---

having *syshchik* detectives working in conjunction with senior officials.
258 Ibid., 185.
259 David Remnick, *Lenin's Tomb: The Last Days of the Soviet Empire* (New York: Random House, 1993).

Boris Dubin, a Russian sociologist and literary translator, agrees that the rise of the *detektiv* has contributed to a decline in the role of the intellectual in Russian society.[260] He refers to the years 1992-1998 as a time when the social role of the intelligentsia was up in the air, for works of the greats no longer held the same place of reverence in society, and names such as Solzhenitsyn, Bulgakov, and Tolstoy were replaced by Christie, Conan Doyle, and Marinina. Dubin wrote in 1998 that "the loss of the social mission...of interest in contemporaneity with the exclusion of immediate tasks and concerns, and decline in the creative potential of the former leaders" were all forms of social deterioration that resulted in a flood of violence-ridden television shows and crime novels that were both "anti-intelligentsia and anti-'democratic.'"[261]

A literary critique of the Russian *detektiv* genre, published in 1988 in *Literaturnaia gazeta*, the journal that had published Andzhaparidze's critiques more than two decades before, offers insight from a different perspective into how widespread the genre's popularity had become. The article discusses the creation of the new Association for Mass Literature (of which Dubin was a leader) encouraged by critics, sociologists, and philosophers. An organization based around mass literature would have been unthinkable when Andzhaparidze first criticized translated detective stories; there simply wasn't enough mass literature. In 1988, the Association for Mass Literature found that 70 to 80% of domestic Russian writers worked in the *boevik* (adventure) and detective genres, as opposed to 20 to 30% in the first years of perestroika, with individual detective books being published

---

[260] Dubin had worked with both Progress and Raduga as a translator and is now the head of the sociopolitical research department at the Levada Center.

[261] Boris Dubin, "Russian Intelligentsia between Classics and Mass Culture" (Moscow: VCIOM (Russian Public Opinion Research Center), 1998), 10, 12.

in runs of up to one million copies.²⁶² This is a large difference from journals in the 1970s publishing ten detective stories a year, which at the time was a seemingly high number lamented by critics like Andzhaparidze.

The sociologist A. Zueva observed that in the mid-1970s literary critics were still saddened by the popularity of the *detektiv* genre.²⁶³ By 1995, according to a Russia-wide survey, that popularity had only grown. Its results are displayed in a bar graph labeled "Scale of Preference (%)," which shows what percentage of survey respondents like what. "*Detektiv*/adventure" is preferred by 26.95% of women and 31.82% of men. Zueva analyzes the type of people who buy these *detektiv* novels in terms of their financial situation. She finds that those who mainly buy *detektiv*, romance novels, and fantasy are less affluent; those who spend less than $200 a year on books purchase the most *detektiv*.²⁶⁴ This shows that it was the lower class that read the most *detektiv*, which supports Dubin's point that "social deterioration" spread to all strata of Russian society.

Pulitzer Prize-winning American journalist David Remnick described a very grim political and cultural situation in Russia during this 1990s boom of *detektiv*. He observed that the Russian public was trying to figure out how to transition out of Communism without creating another dictatorship, and that confusion led people to crave the safety of authoritarian rule and

---

262 O. Vronskaia, "Na podstupakh k 'zolotomu pistoletu'," *Literaturnaia gazeta*, no.9 (1998).

263 A. Zueva, "Kto vy, pokupateli knig?," *Knizhnoe obozrenie* 33 (1996). The survey was produced by KOMON-2 and involved 14,000 families across 45 cities in the Russian socialist research Target Group index, with presumably each participant being asked to list more than one of their preferred literary genre.

264 After *detektiv*, recipe books are next in popularity (19.26% for women and 9.94% for men), a statistic that will support the popularity in Russia of Nero Wolfe cookbooks.

simultaneously the comfort of detective stories.[265] This brings up the question of why, during times of national duress, people turn to detective stories for comfort. Dubin points to the role that retribution played in the popularity of detective novels in the 1990s in Russia, using Marinina as an example. He argues that the real emphasis of Russian *detektiv* lies in redemption from the "guilt and sin of the parents' generations, people of the 'Brezhnev era.'"[266] Their children, now living without Soviet rule and with free access to the *detektiv* genre, savor the *detektiv* novel where "the criminal who is trying to hide will be inevitably discovered and punished" and his retribution will be "painted in magic colors."[267]

Edmund Wilson wrote earlier that the popularity of the detective novel can be linked to an "all pervasive feeling of guilt and…a fear of impending disaster which it seemed hopeless to avert because it never seemed conclusively possible to pin down the responsibility." This analysis is easily applied to Russia after the fall of Communism; citizens experienced a similar fear of impending disaster and an inability to identify those responsible for the problems of their new society. Although Wilson wrote disparagingly of Stout's novels, he observes that the way Wolfe unfailingly catches criminals in every novel (most often in his own office) makes readers feel relief at the fallibility of seemingly uncatchable criminals who had previously blended into society:

> He is not, after all, a person like you or me. He is a villain—known to the trade as George Gruesome—and he has been caught by an infallible Power, the supercilious

---

265 David Remnick, "Letter from Moscow: The Hangover," *The New Yorker*, November 22 1993, 53-54.
266 Dubin, "Russian Intelligentsia between Classics and Mass Culture," 15.
267 Ibid., 1, 5.

and omniscient detective, who knows exactly how to fix the guilt.[268]

This would be a reassuring concept for Russians who in the early 1990s watched their economy transition into the free market while simultaneously observing "with fury and envy" the people who took advantage of the transition in order to grow "gaudily rich." Remnick, who was in Moscow in the 1990s, wrote that "the economy hardly merits the name of capitalism at all, since it operates largely outside the framework of the law."[269] In one Marinina *detektiv* novel, a "syshchik" character directly addresses this phenomenon:

> The type of criminality we grew up with, we became accustomed to, we adapted ourselves to: it's all passed. It had its own laws and its own rules of the game, but these are no more. The country is changing. Politics is changing, and economics, and with them crime is changing. There are completely different criminals now, and we don't know how to pursue and convict them.[270]

Corruption is not built into the American justice system in the same way that it was built in the 1990s in the Russian system, and Baraban sees this burgeoning "feeling of uncertainty about good and evil" in Russian society as partially fueling the interest in *detektiv*.[271]

---

[268] Edmund Wilson, "Why Do People Read Detective Stories?," *The New Yorker*, October 14, 1994.

[269] David Remnick, "Letter from Moscow: The Hangover," ibid., November 22 1993, 55.

[270] Marinina, *A Confluence of Circumstances*, 181.

[271] Baraban, "Russia in the Prism of Popular Culture: Russian and American Detective Fiction and Thrillers of the 1990s," 268.

The popularity of Stout's novels in this era can thus be attributed in part to the neat finales of his books, where every criminal is caught and punished. Taking it one step further, Stout's plots not only put the murderer in jail, they often put the Communist in jail. Stout's books that attack Communism and Communists the most harshly – *The Black Mountain, Over My Dead Body*, and the several novellas mentioned in Chapter Three – were some of the first to be published in the 1990s by state publishing companies. The country was transitioning out of Communism, the youth were disappointed in their parents, and Stout's books were a way for people to view their past society from an opposing viewpoint. Remnick's interview with Leonid Radzikhovsky, a political writer for the weekly magazine *Stolitsa*, specifically addresses why Stout's novel, *The Black Mountain*, in which a lot of Communists are slandered and then slaughtered, was popular during this era. Radzikhovsky says, "Many people in Russia think they admire Pinochet [the Chilean dictator], but they have no idea why....All they know is that Pinochet shot a lot of Communists, and they would like to shoot Communists. But that's all they know."[272] This desire to revenge oneself on Communists everywhere for the pain caused by Soviet Communism is one explanation for the official publication of Stout's novels and their increasing popularity.

A mystery novel blog, The Thrilling Detective, asserts that the adventures of Wolfe and Archie over five decades accurately depict the many changes America went through during those years.[273] In this time of transition in Russia, when former literary idols were being thrown over for pop culture, a glimpse into the success of the American societal model might finally

---

272 Remnick, "Letter from Moscow: The Hangover," 54.

273 Marcia Kiser to The Thrilling Detective,, February, 2003, http://www.thrillingdetective.com/non_fiction/e002.html.

be welcomed by the Russian government. But Remnick offers another explanation for the success of the Wolfe books when he quotes an unnamed writer who says "Rex Stout may now be the most popular novelist in the country." The writer explains: "People want a little pleasure. If they have to read about one more concentration camp, they'll die."[274] Stout gave them the light pleasure of a detective story along with the more complicated emotion of reading about the dangers and consequences of Communism.

---

274 Remnick, *Lenin's Tomb: The Last Days of the Soviet Empire*, 539.

7 | Stout's Novels Influence New Russian Detective Novelists

Look at Kamenskaia, the blue-blood, she doesn't help carry out raids, doesn't participate in arrests, doesn't do any undercover work. She just sits in her warm office and sips coffee and tries to make herself out to be some brilliant Nero Wolfe.
—*A Confluence of Circumstances*

Aleksandra Marinina Critiques Russian Politics and Society

Stout's popularity alongside the rise of the homegrown Russian detective novel led to his plots and characters exerting an influence on some Russian writers. Aleksandra Marinina, a pseudonym for Marina Anatolyevna Alekseyeva, is one of the most popular *detektiv* writers in contemporary Russia as well as one of the few Russian *detektiv* writers who directly mentions Nero Wolfe's name in the text.[275] Marinina was worked as a po-

---

275 Since only one of Marinina's books, *A Confluence of Circumstances*, has

lice lieutenant when she began writing and uses her experience dealing with crime in real life in her books (unlike Stout, who had no real-life experience solving murders). Her novels have insight into the "day-to-day" activities of both the burgeoning criminal underworld and the police who fight it.[276]

Marinina was able to write in a time where she had a relatively large degree of control over what her characters did and said; she did not have to censor her plots as she would have had to do only a few years before. Marinina writes freely about corruption in the upper echelons of the police force in the same manner that Stout wrote about corruption in the FBI. He also had no one to fear in any real sense (he claimed no fear of J. Edgar Hoover), but he was still persecuted in the form of FBI surveillance. Marinina, on the other hand, was and is not persecuted for her writing. Nepomnyashchy writes that Marinina can "hardly be called a political writer" in comparison to the "Russian-Rambo" writers of her time, but that her novels still do contain motives for murder "implicitly traced to lapses in the Soviet past that are tied to the post-Soviet present by the thread of financial gain, charting a disturbing continuity between the systemic abuses, earlier political and later economic, of the two periods."[277]

Wachtel writes that Marinina's popularity comes in part from her success in incorporating nostalgia for the past into her work while creating something new. Marinina's success shows

been translated into English, I will rely on other authors' descriptions of the plots of her novels and will not go into specifics on her Russian work.

276 Anatoly Vishevsky, "Answers to Eternal Questions in Soft Covers: Post-Soviet Detective Stories," *Slavic and Eastern European Journal* 45, no. 5 (2001), 734.

277 Nepomnyashchy, "Markets, Mirrors, and Mayhem: Aleksandra Marinina and the Rise of the New Russian Detektiv," 177. Another popular Russian *detektiv* writer is Boris Akunin, whose mystery novels are often set in Tsarist Russia, showing that a different use of Russian nostalgia also engenders popularity. Akunin uses the classic detective prototype in his character of the brilliant Erast Fandorin (who shares many of Hercule Poirot's eccentricities involving the importance of the "little grey cells").

something important about the Russian public; they like her books because they are not just Russian versions of Western detective stories but contain Russian-specific ideas and motivations.[278] Nepomnyashchy adds that "the key to her works' popularity may lie at least partly in their overt confrontation with the anxieties and threats posed by the instability of life in Russia today, which are thereby rendered manageable and therefore less frightening."[279] Remnick's interview with Vladimir Rushailo, the chief of the Moscow Police Department, supports this view: "Even if we manage to jail an influential member of the Mafia, his fellow-bandits immediately unleash a campaign pressuring victims, witnesses, judges, public assessors. And they do this quite freely. Clearly, the criminals are much more inventive than the lawmakers."[280] As a police lieutenant, Marinina saw this crime wave unfold firsthand; her novels often aim to reassure Russians that their police are capable. Criminals getting rich from the economic transition are lambasted in Marinina's novels; she often connects their acquisition of money with evil. The moral judgments that she passes in her books "provide hope" to the Russian public.[281]

Marinina's Russian orientation does not exclude of all Western influences from her writing. She emulates the style of European mysteries by having her detective solve crimes with her intellect rather than physically going out and looking for clues: like Wolfe, Marinina's main detective, police lieutenant Anastasia Kamenskaia, rarely leaves her office. Marinina also alludes to

---

[278] Wachtel, *Remaining Relevant after Communism: The Role of the Writer in Eastern Europe*, 195.

[279] Nepomnyashchy, "Markets, Mirrors, and Mayhem: Aleksandra Marinina and the Rise of the New Russian Detektiv," 182.

[280] Remnick, "Letter from Moscow: The Hangover," 57.

[281] Baraban, "Russia in the Prism of Popular Culture: Russian and American Detective Fiction and Thrillers of the 1990s," 230, 19.

Stout and other American authors. In *A Confluence of Circumstances* she references Robert Penn Warren's *All the King's Men* on two occasions. One of her characters quotes Warren's character, Governor Willie Stark:

> "Do you remember what Governor Stark replied to his assistant, Berden [Jack Burden in English], when Berden refused to dig up any compromising material on a crystal-clean judge?" Nastia answered without hesitation, almost without thought: "Man is conceived in sin and born into depravity. His path is from stinking diaper to shit-stained shroud. There is always something to find."[282]

Marinina's use of Warren's book takes on a deeper significance when one looks again at Andzhaparidze's 1971 critique of Western literature in translation. He describes Warren as painting a broad and truthful picture of American society, for the plot of *All the King's Men* is about the moral corruption inherent in American politics.[283] Marinina's references to Warren may point to her as well favoring Russian society over the Western.

Marinina has written, "It is not for nothing that Americans say that crime is the price that society pays for democracy," which fits aptly with the situation of Russia in the 1990s when Marinina began writing. Russia was turning into a democracy, and it was paying for that transition with a crime wave that seemed unstoppable. A 1998 *New York Times* article analyzes Marinina's books in response to the fear of crime in Russia at the time. The author writes that in Marinina's books, "The detective

---

282 Marinina, *A Confluence of Circumstances*, 87.

283 Andzhaparidze, "Bogachi-filantropy i belye 'Mersedesy': chto i kak my perevodim (Wealthy Philanthropists and White Mercedes: What and How We Translate)."

actually solves the mystery, which doesn't happen very often in Russia anymore." When it appears that Russian oligarchs are getting away with crimes scot-free, "ordinary citizens seek satisfaction in a tidy, if fictional, resolution."[284] The neat endings that Stout writes for Wolfe and Marinina writes for Kamenskaia offer their Russian readers a chance to enter a world where the bad guy is caught and disaster is always averted, which would be a calming release for those living in Russia in the 1990s; Moscow had twice as many murders as New York in 1997.[285]

Marinina addresses her use of satisfying endings – and real criminal outcomes – in an interview: "My heroine always solves the crime, and sometimes my villains do go to prison…but not always – that would be too unbelievable."[286] Even if the murderer is not apprehended, however, Marinina's detective Kamenskaia will at least find out his identity by the end of the novel, and the reveal is "a particularly consoling message at a time when radically changing values have unsettled long-held assumptions about definitions of the self."[287]

A Confluence of Circumstance: The Non-Coincidental Similarities Between Anastasia Kamenskaia and Nero Wolfe

Marinina's main hero, police lieutenant Anastasia Kamenskaia, shares many traits with Nero Wolfe: she is lazy, sedentary, and has an almost unbelievable aptitude for solving

---

[284] Alessandra Stanley, "The World: In Its Dreams; Russia Solves Its Crime Problem," *The New York Times* March 15, 1998.

[285] Ibid.

[286] Ibid.

[287] Nepomnyashchy, "Markets, Mirrors, and Mayhem: Aleksandra Marinina and the Rise of the New Russian Detektiv," 182.

the puzzles of crime detection.[288] Nepomnyashchy writes that "Kamenskaia certainly owes her image as a sedentary intellect safely ratiocinating within an interior space locked off from the outside world of crime and criminals in part…to Rex Stout's Nero Wolfe, who also passed on to her his proverbial laziness, if not his bulk or refined palate."[289] Kamenskaia's laziness paints her as the "ultimate armchair detective," for she rarely leaves her office on business and prefers to send her subordinates out when needed.[290] While part of the reason behind her sedentary lifestyle is her crippling back pain (she sometimes must lie on the floor and wait for someone to help her up), her reluctance to leave her office is more of a lifestyle choice than a physical necessity. Baraban describes Kamenskaia's physical prowess as nonexistent:

> Nastia [Russian nickname for Anastasia] neglects her body. She does not work out, does not allow her body to expect "any help from her".… She can hardly "drag herself up" in the morning…and never goes jogging, has backaches, and does not know how to shoot a pistol.[291]

Wolfe's physical abilities are limited in a similar manner. Although he had been active in his youth in Montenegro and does know how to use a gun, the Wolfe that readers see in the stories

---

[288] Morgan, "Darya Dontsova's 'Sleuthettes': A Case of the Regendering of the Post-Soviet Russian Detektiv?," 96. Marinina's creative choice of a woman detective also added to her popularity, for the new Russian *detektiv* genre in the 1990s tended to favor female detectives (also seen in Donstova's work with a non-Wolfean female detective).

[289] Nepomnyashchy, "Markets, Mirrors, and Mayhem: Aleksandra Marinina and the Rise of the New Russian Detektiv," 171.

[290] *The Greatest Russian Stories of Crime and Suspense*, Pegasus Crime (Pegasus Crime, 2012).

[291] Elena Baraban, "A Little Nostalgia: The Detective Novels of Alexandra Marinina," *The International Fiction Review* 32, no. 1, 2 (2005), https://journals.lib.unb.ca/index.php/IFR/article/view/7802/8859.

is a sedentary man. When he goes to Yugoslavia in *The Black Mountain* and spends the night hiking through mountains to surreptitiously enter Montenegro, his body physically fails him the next morning:

> "My legs ache, of course, and my back; indeed, I ache all over; but that was to be expected and can be borne. What concerns me is my feet. They carry nearly a hundredweight more than yours; they have been pampered for years; and I may have abused them beyond tolerance. They must be rubbed, but I dare not take off my shoes. They are dead. My legs end at my knees. I doubt if I can stand, and I couldn't possibly walk. Do you know anything about gangrene?"[292]

Although Kamenskaia is a thin woman and Wolfe a large man, they have similarly described abilities in terms of what their bodies can do—not much at all. In *A Confluence of Circumstances*, a colleague describes Kamenskaia's laziness in a joking manner when she tells him, "Don't be so lazy":

> "Ah, who's that talking?" drawled Zakharov with a smile, then leaned back and stretched out. "Take a good look at yourself, you Hero of Socialist Labor. Kettle, safe, typewriter, all within reaching distance so you don't have to get up. You're too lazy to even empty your ashtray." Nastia laughed. "True. My laziness is legend around here. But not when it comes to mental work."[293]

---

292 Stout, *The Black Mountain*, Location 1158, 69.
293 Marinina, *A Confluence of Circumstances*, 77.

There is, however, an ideological difference between the two detectives' laziness. In a socialist society, a good worker could never be someone who sat around and thought all day; he or she had to be constantly moving and building (often physically) the new socialist paradise. Kamenskaia's modus operandi of sitting in an office while everyone else runs around collecting evidence is humorous in the early 1990s because of its proximity to the era of socialism. Wolfe's is just humorous; his lifestyle is not incompatible with the political and economic sphere where he resides.

Kamenskaia, while working within the policing apparatus, has freedoms similar to those of a Western private investigator owing to her boss's allowing her laziness to be augmented by a staff willing to run all over town for her. Nepomnyashchy writes that while Kamenskaia sits in her office

> drinking cup after cup of coffee and chain smoking… she then solves what are devilishly complex crimes by subjecting the material the men gather to cold, machinelike logic combined with an extraordinary imagination, which allows her to (re)construct multiple narratives based on the evidence and ultimately arrive at the "correct" story.[294]

Wolfe works in a similar manner when solving a crime; he remains in his brownstone, drinking beer after beer, and then uses the material that Archie brings him to solve complex cases.

Similarly, in the larger Western detective canon, investigators like Poirot and Holmes had their assistants, Hastings and Watson respectively, do some of their work or thinking with them.

---

294 Nepomnyashchy, "Markets, Mirrors, and Mayhem: Aleksandra Marinina and the Rise of the New Russian Detektiv," 169.

Not much attention paid to the private lives of these assistants outside of the cases.[295] Marinina on the other hand pays unusual attention to the background and private lives of Kamenskaia's colleagues and assistant. Baraban notes that Marinina ignores the tradition of a lack of depth in surrounding characters

> and on the contrary, introduces many passages on how much Nastia's colleague Kolia Seuinov suffers, or about the hard unhappy family life of her other colleague, Yura Korotkov; about the life of Volodya Lartsev after his wife's death, as well as about Nastia's family.[296]

In some Stout novels Archie's love affairs with women play a significant role, separate to the cases, even moreso as Archie's main love interest, Lily Rowan, became a regular character. Marinina goes further than Stout, however, in the depth of the background stories for the characters running around bringing evidence to Kamenskaia in her office. Although Stout does devote plenty of space to Archie's personal life, he avoids anything but generalities about Archie's past and skimps on specific details of the present (when Lily Rowan gives Archie a key to her apartment, it is mentioned only in passing); Marinina goes into explicit detail about the lives and loves of almost every policeman in Kamenskaia's department.[297]

---

295 For example, when Hastings marries "Cinderella," they immediately move to Argentina, putting their personal relationship as far away from Poirot as possible. In subsequent novels, the married Hastings can now leave his wife behind when he goes to England to see Poirot, for their move takes her entirely out of the picture. There is also much controversy about how many wives Watson had, showing inattention by Conan Doyle to consistency in the specifics of Watson's private life.

296 Baraban, "Russia in the Prism of Popular Culture: Russian and American Detective Fiction and Thrillers of the 1990s," 226, 27.

297 Rex Stout, *The Father Hunt* (The Viking Press, Inc., 1968).

One way to explain the effort Marinina expends on her secondary characters is to consider the Communist Russian model of *detektiv* fiction. D.W.'s previously mentioned article on Andzhaparidze and the critique of Western translations of detective literature included a reference to Archie being "miserably exploited, and serv[ing] only to reinforce the illusion that one can be happy in America even when one is subject to exploitation."[298] Marinina's insistence on readers knowing every detail of Kamenskaia's subordinates' lives can be seen as her trying to show that they aren't exploited but are working together for a greater cause. She evokes some nostalgia for the Soviet past; she wants to reassure readers that the worker is not going to be exploited under the new capitalist system.

Although Kamenskaia depends on her colleagues to do the physical work, her machine-like mind is often compared to a computer; Marinina's writes that Kamenskaia "had a phenomenal memory and the accompanying ability to instantly extract whatever she needed from it."[299] In *A Confluence of Circumstances*, Kamenskaia figures out the identity of a hit man based on a glance several days before at a photograph, when she noticed the slight displacement of figurines on a shelf in a murdered woman's apartment; this intellectual capacity is just as far-fetched as Wolfe figuring out the murderer's identity in *A Right to Die* based on the fact that her pseudonym and real name had the same diphthong.[300]

Both Kamenskaia and Wolfe are creatures of habit in their genius. Kamenskaia's inability to go more than two hours without a cup of coffee or cigarette parallels Wolfe's inability to go without his beer, of which he drinks five quarts, or twelve bot-

---

298 D.W., "Crime Fiction," *Encounter*, August 1981, 26.
299 Marinina, *A Confluence of Circumstances*, 2.
300 Stout, *A Right to Die*.

tles a day.³⁰¹ In *A Confluence of Circumstances*, Kamenskaia is described as a person with a specific daily routine. When she has to spend some days living in another person's apartment for safety reasons, the change is almost unbearable to her: "The week dragged out to be perhaps the most difficult in Nastia Kamenskaia's life. Living in someone else's apartment with no opportunity to carry on her usual way of life, doubt and uncertainty ate away at her insides."³⁰² To Wolfe, living in another person's apartment would be almost impossible; his routine is rarely unbroken: 8 a.m. breakfast in his yellow silk pajamas, 9-11 a.m. in the plant rooms where he cannot be disturbed, 11 a.m.-1 p.m. office work, 1:15.p.m. lunch, 2-4 p.m. back in his office, 4-6 p.m. in the plant rooms, 7:15 p.m. dinner, then coffee, a book, and bed, with his customary number of bottles of beer distributed through the day.

While much of Wolfe's daily routine revolves around food, Kamenskaia's weekly routine involves groceries; the most significant way that Kamenskaia's lifestyle differs from Wolfe's is in terms of her salary and the food she buys with it. The description of Kamenskaia's shopping trip in *A Confluence of Circumstances* is a lesson in frugality:

> When she received her monthly salary she divided it up into portions, and then subdivided the grocery portion by the number of days in the month…so it worked out that the longer she delayed going shopping, the more delicious and expensive grocery items it was possible to

---

301 *Fer-De-Lance* (Farrar & Rinehart, Inc., 1934), Location 2241. Fritz pours Wolfe's beer into a glass for him, and he always watches the foam go down to the correct level before he will take a sip. On one occasion, Wolfe's eyes are closed, deep in thought, when Fritz brings his beer, and Archie watches closely as Wolfe, without opening his eyes, takes the first sip of beer at exactly the right foam level.

302 Marinina, *A Confluence of Circumstances*, 146.

buy. If she went to the shops every day, she could only really afford bread, milk, and omelettes with tomato. But if she put it off to one day in every five —or better, once per week —then she could permit herself smoked chicken, cheese, yogurt, or even some watermelon."[303]

A description of Wolfe's kitchen is absurd by comparison. Archie writes that in 1957 Wolfe's kitchen and Fritz's salary together "cost only slightly less than the plant rooms on the roof bulging with orchids,"[304] which is no surprise when one examines how Wolfe shops for groceries with his

> Olympian standards: the Georgia ham from pigs fed only on peanuts and acorns, the starlings shot by an upstate farmer and driven directly to Wolfe's kitchen within two hours, the custom sausage from Bill Darst at Hackettstown, and on, and on, and on, and on.[305]

Even with their radically different access to food, both Kamenskaia and Wolfe enjoy a gourmet meal. The description of food in the Kamenskaia novels mimics the many references to Fritz's recipes throughout the Wolfe corpus. Marinina not only includes the types of food Kamenskaia buys, but she also includes recommendations for how to eat the food correctly:

> [she] often describes cooking and gives advice on appropriate drinks for particular dishes: one is advised that pizza should be consumed with red Chianti and never,

---

303 Ibid., 33-34.

304 Rex Stout, "Poison Á La Carte," *Three at Wolfe's Door* (Viking Penguin, 1960). Location 103.

305 Ed Zuckerman, "Toast to Fritz" (paper presented at the The Black Orchid Banquet, December 5, 2015), 1.

God forbid, with beer—a sign of provincialism according to a character-aesthete....We discover the names of exotic dishes (spaghetti Bolognese and shrimp cocktail) and find a recipe for eggs Neapolitan.[306]

Food and drink pairings are also very important to Wolfe; he has similar rules for the specifics of what he will and will not cook. He won't fry eggs, potatoes, or chicken, advises a dinner guest to consume nice whiskey with Fritz's apple pie, and claims to be able to smell from his office if Fritz has added a spice he disapproves of to a pasta sauce.[307] While both Wolfe's and Kamenskaia's relationship with food is mainly contained in their individual kitchens, in several novels Wolfe does travel to his friend Marko Vukcic's restaurant, Rusterman's. Kamenskaia does not often go to a restaurant, for the idea of going out to eat a gourmet restaurant meal was unusual in the Soviet era, the post-Soviet era, and even today in modern Russia. The inclusion of a dangerous villain keeping a restaurant just for gourmandizing in Marinina's *Small Fry Die First* can thus be seen as an allusion to Wolfe's Rusterman's.[308]

In *A Confluence of Circumstances*, Kamenskaia's role as the sedentary detective is challenged when she must not only leave her office to solve a murder but must also disguise herself to become bait for an assassin.[309] The plot of the book is complex and

---

306 Vishevsky, "Answers to Eternal Questions in Soft Covers: Post-Soviet Detective Stories," 735.

307 Stout, *The Father Hunt*, 50; *And Be a Villain,* (The Viking Press, Inc., 1948). Examples of Wolfe's "exotic dishes" could be shad roe or corned beef hash with chitlins, both very American dishes that would have been unfamiliar to a Russian in the 1990s, or even today.

308 Olcott, *Russian Pulp: The Detektiv and the Russian Way of Crime*, 135.

309 In discussing Marinina I refer mainly to *A Confluence of Circumstances*, as this is not only her only book translated into English, but also the book where Kamenskaia is referred to as a Nero Wolfe-esque character. That this was the only book of Marinina's translated into English is a very lucky "confluence of circumstances."

political: a female PhD researcher named Irina Filatova has been murdered, and Kamenskaia and her team must not only figure out who murdered her and for what reason but must circumvent most normal methods of communication among police officers because of the suspicion that a high-ranking police official hired the assassin. The book is written in both first- and third-person, which is different from Stout's exclusive use of Archie's first-person narration. However, Marinina's fluctuations between first and third person do allow the reader to notice clues at the same time as the detectives, just as Stout does in his choice of Archie (instead of Wolfe) as narrator. It is in this Marinina mystery that Kamenskaia is directly compared to Nero Wolfe:

> "Look at Kamenskaia, the blue-blood, she doesn't help carry out raids, doesn't participate in arrests, doesn't do any undercover work. She just sits in her warm office and sips coffee and tries to make herself out to be some brilliant Nero Wolfe." Nastia knew that people didn't just think that about her; many also said it behind her back.[310]

Kamenskaia's fear of leaving the safety of her office mirrors that same fear in Wolfe; he rarely leaves his office on business and only ventures out for non-business related trips to either flower shows or gourmandizing events. While Marinina writes that "outwardly, Nastia's work did very much resemble loafing around the office," she is actually highly respected by her boss as well as one of the most feared investigators by the criminal population.[311] Marinina's allusion to Wolfe does demonstrate, however, how she uses the dichotomy between the old Sovi-

---

310 Marinina, *A Confluence of Circumstances*, 20.
311 Ibid.

et and the new capitalist views of an individual investigator to poke fun at her Kamenskaia. Her reference to Kamenskaia as a "blue-blood" shows that she is willing to borrow from the Western canon for character inspiration, but that doesn't mean that she presents what she borrows as the correct way to live.

The book begins with a description of Kamenskaia doing mathematics and language games in the shower to wake herself up; she is described as knowing "about five hundred words from every European language."[312] Wolfe, too, is a polyglot; he does not speak every European language, but in various books he is described as knowing at least seven. Kamenskaia's morning ritual involves icy cold orange juice— but only when she has the money to afford it, which can only happen if she takes on side jobs as a translator.[313] Wolfe, on the other hand, drinks orange juice every morning in a leisurely manner with no thought as to cost: "He [Wolfe] never says a word if he can help it until his orange juice is down, and he will not gulp orange juice."[314] This is one example of how the similarities between the two detectives become differences in their respective societies; Wolfe can afford juice in his capitalist country, Kamenskaia cannot in hers.

The murder of PhD researcher Filatova is not the only crime investigated in the story. While Kamenskaia's department is working that case, they are simultaneously investigating the rape of a twelve-year-old girl. The girl's father had served on a jury had convicted a drunk driver for crashing his car and injuring two people four years before, and every year since then, on the anniversary of the accident, a relative of one of the jury members has been attacked by an unknown assailant. This most recent assault has been the most severe, and, since the girl is

---

312 Ibid., 2.
313 Ibid., 11.
314 Rex Stout, *Murder by the Book* (The Viking Press, Inc., 1951), 91.

too traumatized to speak, the rest of the story is spent figuring out how to prove that the convicted drunk driver is behind all of these revenge incidents.[315] This plotline becomes increasingly complicated and disturbing when the father of the rape victim, Kovalev, arranges for the rapist to be put away in a rehab center, safe from arrest, because he owes the father of the rapist, Vinogradov, for some sort of unexplained business transaction.[316] Viktor Alekseevich Gordeev (nickname Kolobok), Kamenskaia's boss, comments on this:

> Let rapists go free, let them rape and kill others' children, just so long as his child is well…he doesn't care. But he'd rip out his own veins with his bare teeth to help Vinogradov, and Vinogradov doesn't owe him a thing. If Averin [another character] becomes Premier then Kovalev will be riding high in the saddle, and Vinogradov will have Averin's eternal gratitude for helping him get there. If it doesn't come off, Vinogradov has already organised Kovalev a position in some Russian joint business venture. Yes, Kovalev is going nowhere without Vinogradov. He has to play along with everything to demonstrate his loyalty. It's a nightmare.[317]

A father protecting the rapist of his twelve-year-old daughter is a dark concept in a murder mystery, and it brings a pointed message from Marinina own experience. Having lived through the crime wave of the early 1990s, she saw in her job as a police lieutenant the ways that people broke all moral boundaries in order to get ahead. This storyline presents in a drastic way the

---

315 Marinina, *A Confluence of Circumstances*, 18.
316 Ibid., 73.
317 Ibid., 85-86.

immoral lengths that people were willing to go to protect their new wealth and standing in the nascent capitalist economy.

Stout comments on the political situation in America during McCarthyism in a similar manner. In the previously discussed *Home to Roost*, a woman murders the son of her deceased sister to protect her reputation and prevent her Communist affiliation from becoming known. Stout's use of his plot to highlight problems he saw arising from the McCarthy era mirrors Marinina's use of her plot to highlight problems she saw arising from the post-Soviet era. Nepomnyashchy writes that Marinina often uses economic problems in the transitioning Russian society as fodder for her motives, which are "implicitly traced to lapses in the Soviet past that are tied to the post-Soviet present by the thread of financial gain, charting a disturbing continuity between the systemic abuses, earlier political and later economic, of the two periods."[318]

In *A Confluence of Circumstances*, Gordeev ultimately confronts Kovalev about the immorality of his protecting daughter's rapist. In response, Kovalev and his allies arrange for Gordeev's father-in-law to be denied the funding he needs for his dream job. In response to this devastating news, Gordeev says,

> "Governor Willie Stark [referring to Warren's *All the King's Men*] was right: there is always something to dig up. I don't believe that a person who can spit on justice, on the lives of his own child and others' children, can also have lived an honest life. I don't believe it for a second. And this is why I hope to find a weapon we can use to stop him."[319]

---

318 Nepomnyashchy, "Markets, Mirrors, and Mayhem: Aleksandra Marinina and the Rise of the New Russian Detektiv," 177.
319 Marinina, *A Confluence of Circumstances*, 88.

His desire to avenge this abuse of power is similar to Wolfe's desire to avenge what he sees as the overreach of power by the FBI in *The Doorbell Rang*. In Gordeev's case, he is furious because a politician has taken away his father-in-law's livelihood to protect a rapist; in Wolfe's case, he is working for a fee for Mrs. Rackell, who is furious because the FBI has taken away her right to privacy. The manner in which the detectives go about fighting the nebulous monster of bureaucracy and corruption is similar; both look for any way to poke holes in its shield.

Gordeev, the head of the Moscow Criminal Investigation department, plays an important role as mentor and friend to Kamenskaia, echoing another Stout character, Inspector Cramer. While Gordeev's personality is unlike that of the blustery Cramer, who more often than not threatens to arrest Wolfe and Archie for withholding evidence, the descriptions of his intelligence and physique are similar to those of Cramer. Gordeev is "short with a sizeable paunch, and his round head was almost completely bald," while Cramer is described as having a "round red face and burly figure," and, more specifically, "his middle, though it would never get into Wolfe's class, was beginning to make pretensions."[320] The similarity in physical descriptions of the two characters hints at a deeper similarity in their roles; Cramer may often threaten Archie and Wolfe with arrest, but he invariably ends up assisting their investigation in the end.

As the investigation into the murder of Filatova continues in *A Confluence of Circumstances*, Kamenskaia runs into the problem of deciding whom to trust: it becomes increasingly obvious that a senior official is somehow involved in the murder and she doesn't know how to conduct an investigation without tipping that person off. A talk with her stepfather, who also worked for

---

320 Ibid., 11; Stout, *The Doorbell Rang*, 43; *And Be a Villain*, Location 1503-04.

the police, breaks down the problem of corruption in Moscow policing in the 1990s:

> "The circle is so tight that it's impossible to ask anyone anything. Note that I don't even use the term 'question,' because what kind of serious questioning can be done with one of your own? You speak with someone you suspect of a crime, and he answers everything with the same reply: 'It's okay, leave us alone, we're your people, remember that.' And then he claps you on the back and invites you to have a drink with him. If this doesn't happen, you can be sure that he's putting a call through to your superior, Gordeev. They probably know one another from a holiday sanatorium, or they drank vodka together at a banquet, or are connected in some other way. 'What's going on, Viktor Alekseevich? You've got to rein in your men, it just won't do. They're offending me, do you understand?' You'll end up in tears."[321]

The motive for the murder turns out to be a straightforward matter of greed and corruption. Aleksandr Evgenevich Pavlov, a police official, had wanted to get a doctorate to be eligible for promotion, but he didn't want to do any of the work himself. Instead, as was usual at the time, he hired someone to write his dissertation for him, promising her ten thousand rubles upon completion—this person was Irina Filatova. But, greedily, Pavlov did not pay Filatova the money after she sent him the manuscript, and since all arrangements had been conducted anonymously, she had no way to find him or turn him in. Ten years later, while doing research, she came across the manuscript she had written and discovered her cheater's name. Filatova, being

---

321 Marinina, *A Confluence of Circumstances*, 47-48.

an upright citizen, did not try to blackmail Pavlov; instead, she told him that she would publish the dissertation to get her own doctorate under her own name and allow the world to notice the plagiarism on its own, thus exposing him and the people who had arranged the transaction years before. Her fury caused her to disregard any possible consequences from exposing her role in the affair.

Why Pavlov so feared being exposed is never fully explained, but it has to do with his fear of a man behind the scenes that he never names, a man so powerful that Pavlov has Filatova killed to prevent the manuscript from being published in her name, and thus saving his own life. Ironically, the dissertation that Filatova died for was on the issue of corruption in Russian society. That the dissertation itself is a commentary on the corruption inherent in a market economy, while the plot of the whole novel is a commentary on the same corruption, is a clever use of the detective story to express political messages.[322] Pavlov, who is introduced to a room of reporters as a scientific consultant on corruption, describes it thus: "Corruption is, in essence, a commercial transaction, in which there is a product, a vendor, and a buyer. Market forces, the forces of supply and demand,

---

322 In the same subtle manner, Stout uses the books Wolfe reads in the novella, *Booby Trap,* previously mentioned as one of Stout's war-time novellas, to get in jabs at Communism. The plot of *Booby Trap* involves wartime secrets and treason, with both Archie and Wolfe working for the US government in some capacity, and is unrelated to Communism or Russia (except when Wolfe is playing with field commanders on his battle map of Russia). The jab occurs when Wolfe is said to be reading the book *Under Cover* by John Roy Carlson, which contains the passage, "I agree somewhat with Rex Stout, chairman of the Writers' War Board: 'The political ethics of the American Communists still are about as low as anything ever observed in these parts, including the Ku Klux Klan.'" Wolfe reads several books either about Russia or written by a Russian elsewhere in the corpus: in *Method Three for Murder* he is reading John Gunther's *Inside Russia Today*, in *Please Pass the Guilt* he is reading Turgenev poems, and in *Death of a Dude* he reads Solzhenitsyn's *The First Circle*. The inclusion of Solzhenitsyn is mentioned in Makharovskii's blog. Rex Stout, *Booby Trap*, in *Not Quite Dead Enough* (Farrar & Rinehart, 1944), Location 722; McAleer, *Rex Stout: A Majesty's Life*, 318; Marakhovskii to Kul'tpul't, June 14, 2015.

determine the intrinsic worth of the product, its asking and selling prices."[323] His economic analysis of corruption is repeated by Nepomnyashchy, who writes in an analysis of Marinina's villains that "the political ills of the past continue to be visited on the present in the form of violent, economically motivated crime.... In other words, while the old Soviet system turned people into political chattel, the new market chaos transforms individuals …into commodities, valued according to their salability."[324]

The book ends without a specific elucidation of what or whom Pavlov fears; readers are left with the feeling that the larger bad guy may still be on the loose behind the scenes. Gordeev tries to reach that villain by his plan to capture the killer hired by Pavlov in such a way that will expose the inner workings of the killer-for-hire process. He has Kamenskaia, who is both famously plain looking and secretly known for her ability to change her appearance at will, dress up as a sexy, alluring journalist who has a copy of Filatova's manuscript and wants to blackmail Pavlov with it. Gordeev's aim is for Pavlov to become so scared that he will hire the killer again to kill this false journalist, "Larisa Lebedeva", giving Gordeev a chance to apprehend the killer and expose the inner workings of the upper strata of criminal society.

The previously mentioned archvillain Arnold Zeck in the Nero Wolfe novels is exactly the type of behind-the-scenes super villain that Gordeev wants to uncover. Stout's novel *In the Best Families* puts Wolfe in an unusual role, outside his comfort zone, just as *A Confluence of Circumstances* does to Kamenskaia. Like Kamenskaia, Wolfe must put on a disguise to get close to the criminal Zeck without his knowledge so that he (Wolfe) can figure out how Zeck's criminal organization works and thus how

---

[323] Marinina, *A Confluence of Circumstances*, 79.

[324] Nepomnyashchy, "Markets, Mirrors, and Mayhem: Aleksandra Marinina and the Rise of the New Russian Detektiv," 178.

it can be destroyed. (Kamenskaia's disguise is hair dye and make-up, while Wolfe's is the loss of over one hundred pounds and the addition of a patchy beard.[325]) Gordeev explains the importance of catching this type of master criminal in a meeting:

> "We've come across the rarest opportunity, the opportunity to capture a killer who works in the highest echelons. We've never encountered this before, because we've never been able to boast the skills and abilities to tackle such a task. The risk of making a mistake is huge, and the chance of succeeding is extremely small. I want us all to understand this."[326]

The hired killer in *A Confluence of Circumstances* is not the only Zeck-like character in the book.[327] Evsei Ivanovich Dorman, a semi-retired criminal, is mentioned as occasionally helping Gordeev out in cases from an unexplained sense of kindness (unlike Wolfe, who refuses to ask Zeck for help even when it is obvious that Zeck's men could identify a murderer for him).[328] When Gordeev goes to visit him to ask for information about hired killers in Moscow, Dorman asks:

> Do you want the truth, Gordeev? I'm afraid of you. Of all the cops I've met in my life, you're the only one who could ever handle me. Retire and I can breathe easy. Maybe I'll still manage to execute the crime of the cen-

---

325 Stout, *In the Best Families*. Wolfe uses an alias to get close to a criminal only one other time, when he becomes Toné Stara in *The Black Mountain,* while Kamenskaia uses her ability to disguise herself often through the books.

326 Marinina, *A Confluence of Circumstances*, 129.

327 Baraban, "A Little Nostalgia: The Detective Novels of Alexandra Marinina". Baraban describes how the Russian Mafia and other behind-the-scenes villains, like Zeck, are often the perpetrators of the crimes that Kamenskaia must solve.

328 Stout, *And Be a Villain*, Location 2381.

tury in my twilight years. Something big, beautiful, and elegant.[329]

His speech is similar to one by Zeck in *In the Best Families*. Wolfe has disguised himself to infiltrate Zeck's criminal organization, after tricking Zeck into thinking he had run away in fear months before. Unaware of this, Zeck says to Archie about Wolfe: "There was one man who matched me in intellect—the man you worked for, Nero Wolfe …If you communicate with him give him my regards. I have great admiration for him."[330] Wolfe is the only man who can match Zeck in intellect, just as Gordeev is the only man Dorman is afraid of.[331]

Funnily enough, Dorman also shares characteristics with Wolfe. As Gordeev enters Dorman's *dacha*, they must past through some "splendid flowerbeds":

> Dorman didn't enjoy physical labor; he detested "grubbing in the dirt." He didn't grow fruit or vegetables at his dacha because he had more than enough money to buy them at the local market. He cultivated only flowers, which he had adored even in his childhood.[332]

The adoration of flowers in a book that mentions Nero Wolfe must be seen as an allusion to the great detective's passion for orchids, and Marinina ruthlessly plays with his allusion by attributing a love for flowers to the kind of villain that Wolfe would despise.

---

329 Marinina, *A Confluence of Circumstances*, 155.

330 Stout, *In the Best Families*, 82.

331 This pairing of villain and detective is also seen in the Moriarty and Holmes dichotomy.

332 Marinina, *A Confluence of Circumstances*, 152.

Dorman, a criminal, is surprisingly open in his explanation of how criminality and corruption is built into the Russian system. An argument between him and Gordeev over how policing has changed since the fall of Communism is illuminating when compared to the real crime crisis in Russia at the time of writing. Dorman explains that, under Communism, the police system was purposely designed to keep policemen needing favors and money, in order to build a system where bribery and the owing of favors to your coworkers became essential to getting anything done. He concludes by saying that "the life that awaits you [policemen] is more terrible than ever." Gordeev questions this in a fatalistic manner by replying that "there isn't anything much more terrible that can happen," and Dorman responds with a long explanation of what "terrible, terrible things [are] to come."[333]

Dorman's explanation breaks down the realities of new free market forces and the effect they will have on corruption in the justice system. He says: "Someone has come up with the brilliant idea to assemble a lawful government and introduce an open market at the same time. What an absurd thing to do…. Your detectives are going to be crushed by market forces, by the weight of commerce and big money." He says that policemen, already working inefficiently due to the old system of favors and comradeship, will be further hindered by the new system:

> "Who's going to be left in the police? First, those who are stupid, inefficient, and lazy … in short, the ballast. And secondly, those entrepreneurs who work for us now, the ones who have learnt how to take bribes; that is, those of you who are satiated and secure. The young guard, the students from the institutes, won't be able to

---

333 Ibid., 154.

do anything. The only thing they'll learn is how to fall in with the entrepreneurs and bribe-takers…. And, in tandem with this happy prospect, you're organizing the assembly of a legal government. A government where prosecutors oversee and observe, but don't permit arrests. Lawyers defend from the moment of arrest. Judges don't commit cases to trial, they simply dismiss them. A heavenly life! Well, for us at least. But for you, a succession of nightmares. Who of you will be able to get any work done, considering that any effort you muster will be counteracted by those above you? If someone wanted a criminal catastrophe to befall our country, they could hardly think up a better one than this."[334]

Marinina's use of politics in her books connects her solidly with Stout.[335] The long speeches given by several characters in *A Confluence of Circumstances* are integral to understanding the plot, and the plot itself cannot be understood without an understanding of the corruption within Russian society at the time. The problems and motives her detectives deal with are unique to Russian society in the 1990s.

In the same way that it might be hard for Americans to fully understand the motives for the crimes in Marinina's *detektiv* novels, Russians had a hard time understanding the racist motives in Stout novels. Regarding the plot of *A Right to Die*, Chervotkin doesn't find the racial motive for the crime credible: "Personally, I think that the motive of the murder in *The Right to Die* is over-thought and insufficient for such hatred and murder."

334 Ibid., 155.

335 Marinina also inserted political commentary into the plots of *Death for the Sake of Death, Death and a Little Love,* and *Playing on Another's Field.* See the Nepomnyashchy article for more detail of these plots. Nepomnyashchy, "Markets, Mirrors, and Mayhem: Aleksandra Marinina and the Rise of the New Russian Detektiv," 177.

Russians could not comprehend the idea of killing someone over their skin color. This lack of understanding of the history of racism and its implications in America led to some Russians seeing these plots as overly didactic. Chervotkin writes that the race storyline has "too many slogans and too much moralization for a book of fiction. There is too much of the idealization of some and demonization of others."[336]

Zavgorodnii, however, with his strong interest in American history, appreciated Stout's books for helping him to contextualize the civil rights movement: "Now, as I can imagine the status of Afro-Americans in the 30s (*Too Many Cooks*) and the 60s (*A Right to Die),* knowing about their fighting for civil rights, about Martin Luther King, the town of Selma, about the 'Nine from Little Rock' —now I see these books differently, more seriously. I think that Stout undoubtedly was not racist; on the contrary, he was supporting Afro-Americans and other minorities."[337]

Chervotkin and Zavgorodnii's reactions to these books are thought-provoking when considered in light of the common Soviet practice in the 1960s, which was "to respond to any criticism from the United States with the ultimate: 'And you beat the Blacks.' Articles with such titles such as 'Shame on America' were typical of the 1960s when the antiracist movement in the United States was at its peak (*Namedni 1963*)."[338] *Two Many Cooks* and *A Right To Die* were distributed in Russia for a political purpose, to "reveal flaws in capitalist society."[339] Their Russian publication may be seen as equivalent, and more powerful, than an article entitled "Shame on America." The tendency to criticize America as a country that treated some of its citizens as

---

336 Sergey Chervotkin (user Avis), November 20, 2015.

337 Stanislav Zavgorodnii (user Chuchundrovich), November 23, 2015.

338 Baraban, "Russia in the Prism of Popular Culture: Russian and American Detective Fiction and Thrillers of the 1990s," 31.

339 Cannon, "Controversial Politics, Conservative Genre: Rex Stout's Archie-Wolfe Duo and Detective Fiction's Conventional Form," 40.

less than human had long been promoted by the Soviet government; it is interesting to note how Stout's books were used to promote that aim.

Darya Donstova and the Unnamed Others

On the Russian forum, users did not mention Marinina, nor did they cite any other specific author influenced by Stout. Chervotkin sees similarities between Stout and Russian literature only in terms of genre; he does not believe that Stout's influence exists in "anything that can be considered literature – no. There are some very weak imitations of his style in all kinds of 'pulp' literature. The style is 'criminal novel'; in fact – 'pulp fiction.'" Zavgorodnii mentions what seems to be a typo in reference to one of Stout's characters: "A contemporary Russian author, Oleg Divov, has mentioned recently that one of his characters, a police inspector named Kruger was mistakenly called "Kremer" [a typo-ed reference to Stout's Inspector Cramer?] once somewhere in the text." User BleWotan has a vague idea of another reference: "I've got a feeling that I recall the characters of some sci-fi novel refer to Archie once, but I remember neither the author nor the title."[340]

There is, however, another Russian author who was strongly influenced by Stout and Wolfe, even though the Russian online fans did not recognize it. Agrippina Arkadyevna Dontsova, known more commonly as Darya Dontsova, is a *detektiv* writer who began writing in 2000, nine years after Marinina, and has surpassed many writers in both popularity and the number of published novels over the last sixteen years.[341] Dontsova's *detektiv* stories mostly fall into the category of the female-based sec-

---

[340] Sergey Chervotkin (user Avis), November 20, 2015; Stanislav Zavgorodnii (user Chuchundrovich), November 23, 2015; User BleWotan, December 14, 2015.

[341] "Darya Dontsova," http://www.forbes.ru/profile/darya-dontsova.

tion of the genre, with the exception of her fourth series, which Morgan describes as featuring "a male detective in a reprise of Rex Stout's Nero Wolfe series." Dontsova's work includes descriptions of material goods and brands that her readers would not have had access to in the early 1990s, and through them shows another side of life under capitalism, much as Stout did with Wolfe's lifestyle or what Marinina does with her descriptions of gourmet food.

Dontsova's books also contain self-referential material; one character shares a maiden name with the author and speaks French as she does, and that character's children have the same names as Dontsova's children.[342] Her use of her own biography in her fiction mirrors both Stout, who uses his political background (rather than his name) in his texts, and Marinina, who uses her police background in hers. Marinina and Dontsova share more similarities than their use of biography. Like Marinina, Dontsova includes references to the Soviet past in her works and explores the dichotomies inherent in the nascent non-Communist Russian society in her plots. Morgan writes that Dontsova's "narrative is built on the overlapping binary contrasts of Russian/Soviet, Russian/Western, real/unreal, truth/falsehood which provide a dynamic and ever changing backdrop for the action."[343]

Dontsova's fourth series has two main characters that recall Wolfe and Archie (with one sex change): an old woman named Eleanora (Nora) and a man named Ivan Podushkin respectively.[344] These characters appear in eleven novels, including *A Bou-*

---

[342] Birgit Beumers, Pop Culture Russia!: Media, Arts, and Lifestyle, (ABC-CLIO 2005), 304.

[343] Morgan, "Darya Dontsova's 'Sleuthettes': A Case of the Regendering of the Post-Soviet Russian Detektiv?," 112.

[344] Sergey Panichev, Vkontakte message to author, March 18, 2016. VK user Panichev is the provider of most detailed information about this fourth series of Dontsova, due to the lack of any English translations. This lack has

quet of Beautiful Ladies*, *The Apple of Monte-Cristo*, *A Fish Named Darling*, and *Ali Baba and the Forty Female Thieves*.[345] Beumers writes that "as Nora has chosen for herself the role of Nero Wolfe, she casts Podushkin in the role of Archie for her 'cases.'"[346] However, Podushkin is similar to Archie only on a surface level, for Beumers also writes that "Podushkin is the most incompetent and dim of [Dontsova's] 'four investigators.'"[347] He lives at his boss Nora's home and works as her private secretary for the charity fund she runs, checking the claims of people in need, and works as well as the secretary for the detective agency they created together called "Nero." This arrangement is similar to that of Archie and Wolfe (Archie also lives and works with his boss), but the similarities end there, as Archie is neither incompetent nor dim; his intelligence and quick thinking are often vital to solving cases.

The references to Wolfe in the novels are not limited to the name of the agency. In *Tushkanchik v bigudiakh [Jerboa in Curlers]*, an interrogation of a nurse turns into a discussion of the merits of Stout's Nero Wolfe series:[348]

> "So you're from the cops!" the nurse [Iraida] spat out. "Why did you try to fool me?"
> "I'm not connected to the official structures, look here: 'Private Detective Agency "Nero."'"
> Iraida started to examine the document carefully.

---

left me unable to discuss the specifics of Donstova's work in the same manner that I did with Marinina.

345 See "Darya Dontsova's Ivan Podushkin Series" on page 198.

346 Beumers, *Pop Culture Russia!: Media, Arts, and Lifestyle*. 305.

347 Ibid.

348 A jerboa is a desert-dwelling rodent native to North Africa and Central Asia. 349. Darya Dontsova, *Tushkanchik v bigudiakh*, (Litres, 2015), unknown page number.

> "So you're something like that fat guy . . . uh . . . Wolfe! Right?"
>
> I was extremely amazed: "You've read Rex Stout?"
>
> "I've never seen such a book," the nurse shook her head, "I really like Nero. Up to the very end you can't figure out who did it, but you take some other book, and you immediately figure out who the criminal is."
>
> "Nero Wolfe is just a literary character invented by a writer named Rex Stout."
>
> "I don't care who wrote it," Iraida shrugged, "as long as it's interesting. So you're like him?"
>
> "Well, not quite," I smiled, "I'm not such a genius, but our agency is named in honor of Nero Wolfe."[349]

Another character, later in the story, says: "I went to the room, lay on the bed, took a book, but did not have time to delve into the adventures of Nero Wolfe and Archie."

The cases that Podushkin and Nora solve only occasionally resemble those of Archie and Wolfe. In one, an unknown twin sister is involved, which harkens to the unknown or hidden identities of murderers in *Over My Dead Body* and *A Right to Die*. In others, the role of marital infidelities by the main characters contrast with Wolfe's his refusal to touch such cases. Even though Nora and Podushkin refer to themselves as Wolfe and Archie, and even name their detective agency "Nero," their personality traits do not match Wolfe's as Kamenskaia's do.

Through mentions of Stout's writing in her other series, Dontsova again shows her familiarity with the Wolfe corpus. In the novel *Dobryi doctor Aibandit [The Good Doctor DooEvil]*, which is not part of the Ivan Podushkin series, one of the char-

---

349 Darya Dontsova, *Tushkanchik v bigudiakh*, (Litres, 2015), unknown page number.

acters, to get the attention of a friend, attends detective literature fan clubs with him, "pretending to be a fan of Rex Stout, who was adored by Vasil'ev. [She] had to read all of the books about Nero Wolfe." There is a footnote attached to Stout's name that describes him as "one of the great founders of the ironic detective genre."[350]

It is obvious that Dontsova does not have to pretend to be a fan of Rex Stout; her numerous allusions to the author and his detectives show his strong influence in her work.

---

[350] Darya Dontsova, *Dobri doktor Aibandit*, (Litres, 2015), unknown page number.

8 | Stout's Influence in Contemporary Russia Goes Beyond the Literary

> *"You live in the wrong country." Wolfe lifted his brows. "Yes? Wait till you taste terrapin Maryland. Or even, if I may say so, oyster pie à la Nero Wolfe, prepared by Fritz Brenner. In comparison with American oysters, those of Europe are mere blobs of coppery protoplasm."*
> —*Too Many Cooks*

How Food and Translation Fit Together

The rush to translate the Stout novels in the 1990s that so influenced Marinina and Dontsova yielded poor results in translation; years of little to no contact with the West left translators unable to accurately convey the gourmand lifestyle of Wolfe and Archie. Stout was no longer primarily a political writer in the 1990s but a writer who both influenced the Russian *detektiv* genre and introduced gourmet meals to readers like Marinina. Terms for food were often mistranslated, for Fritz's kitchen was filled with ingredients that would have been foreign to a Russian translator. Olga Voronina writes that the translators of the 1990s were unable to "visualize or comprehend the ingredients Nero Wolfe and Fritz Brenner used in their cooking …. Soviet 'cuisine' was devoid of any sophistication…. They translated recipes incorrectly because they simply did not know better."[351] Thus the desire to retranslate Stout that emerged in the early 2000s was accompanied by a complementary desire for a retranslated Russian Nero Wolfe cookbook; much like Kamenskaia's introduction of spaghetti Bolognese to readers, Russians wanted an opportunity to learn how to cook what Wolfe liked to eat.[352]

Stout's 1973 *The Nero Wolfe Cookbook* was translated into Russian in 1995. The cookbook was broken up into sections by meal type: for example, "Breakfast," "Lunch on a Hot Day," and "Lunch on a Cold Day," and each recipe cited the novel it was taken from. The cookbook was published in Russia in a collection with three Stout novels: *Red Threads* (Nero Wolfe), *The Broken Vase* (Tecumseh Fox), and *Double for Death* (Tecumseh Fox). On an online forum, user Lorika wrote that food played a big role in her love of Stout novels: "I like it a lot how the process of their consuming all the delicious foods is described; back in 1992 I didn't even know what Parmesan cheese, cress-salad, Marsala, consommé and so forth were."[353] For these reasons, many Russian collections of Stout's work contain either *The*

---

351 Olga Voronina, e-mail message to author, October 30, 2015. By recipes, Voronina does not mean actual step-by-step instructions in the Stout novels, but rather the specificity of the ingredients in individual dishes in Wolfe's kitchen. BleWotan writes that "the names of the dishes are mentioned constantly," so the lack of knowledge about what these dishes were was a glaring omission for Russian readers.

352 Stout wrote an American Nero Wolfe cookbook in 1973.

353 User Lorika, December 22, 2009 (4:33pm), comment on "Niro Vul'f i Archi Gudvin Reksa Stauta (Nero Wolfe and Archie Goodwin of Rex Stout)," *Mir liubvi i romantiki* (*World of Love and Romantics*) (blog), trans. Gleb Vinokurov, http://worldof-love.ru/forum/archive/index.php?t-16988.html.

Nero Wolfe Cookbook in Russian translation or a half-cookbook, half-translation commentary called *Za stolom s Niro Vul'fom, ili sekrety kukhnii velikogo syshchika: kulinarnyi detektiv (At the Table with Nero Wolfe or Secrets of the Kitchen of the Great Detective: A Culinary Mystery)*.

Three Russian publishing houses, Tsentrpoligraf, Eksmo, and Amfora, were responsible for the large series of retranslations of Stout's novels and cookbooks.[354] Tsentrpoligraf published a sixteen-volume series of Wolfe books in the early 2000s, and a twenty-five volume series in 2002, with the twenty-sixth volume being the first edition of *At the Table with Nero Wolfe*. Eksmo released a series in 2006 called "Ves' Staut" (All Stout) made up of forty-three Wolfe novels as well as Rex Stout's 1973 cookbook in translation, *Kulinarnaia kniga Niro Vul'fa (The Cookbook of Nero Wolfe)*.[355] Amfora published a series called "Velikie syshchiki" (Great Detectives) in 2014 that included Stout novels and the second edition of *At the Table with Nero Wolfe*.[356] In Sergey Sinelnikov's words [coauthor and co-editor of *At the Table with Nero Wolfe*], the demand for the books was high enough that "all copies were sold out very fast." Amfora also published the third edition of this cookbook in 2015, which contains more edits by the authors and which Sinelnikov describes as "drier but more accurate."[357]

At the Table with Nero Wolfe was written, translated, and arranged by Ilya Lezerson, a Moscow-based chef; Tatiana Solomonik, an encylopaedist and translator; and her husband, Sinel-

---

[354] See "Stout Translations in the 2000s by Publishing Houses" on page 192.

[355] Reks Staut (Rex Stout), *Kulinarnaia kniga Niro Vul'fa (The Cookbook of Nero Wolfe)*, trans. by E. Zaitseva, Ves' Stout, (Moscow: Eksmo, 2009).

[356] The series included eleven non-Wolfe novels besides the cookbook, books with Tecumseh Fox, Dol Bonner, and Alphabet Hicks as detectives, as well as several pre-Wolfe, pulp fiction novels

[357] Eksmo is also responsible for publishing Dontsova and Marinina.

nikov, who describes himself as "just a man who can write well in Russian and who's been fond of cooking for a long time," and whom Wikipedia describes as "an author of many books and articles of culinary matters, tourism, a journalist, a geologist-geophysicist, and bard."[358] Voronina writes that by the early 2000s, after

> almost a decade of European and cross-Atlantic travel, open contacts with the US, and unrestricted access to Western literary and culinary sources, [Russians] were proud of their newly acquired culinary finesse and breadth of cultural and linguistic experiences. They wrote commentaries on mistranslated texts, recipes included, and translated [Stout's] books much more closely to the original.[359]

At the Table with Nero Wolfe offers readers both a comprehensive list of recipes from forty-eight Wolfe novels and a commentary on the mistranslation of the ingredients in the Russian version of the novels. The cookbook begins with introductions (taken from his 1973 American cookbook) by Stout as both himself and also in the voices of Archie, Wolfe, and Fritz. The Russian authors then explain that their recipes are based on the Russian translations of Stout's books and the original English as well, noting that their task of compilation was complicated by the many "omissions" and "distortions" of Wolfe's meals in past translations (but promise not to be too hard on those translators).[360]

---

358 Wikipedia Contributors, "Sergey Markovich Sinelnikov," Wikipedia, The Free Encyclopedia . http://ru.wikipedia.org/?oldid=76834152.

359 Olga Voronina, e-mail message to author, October 30, 2015.

360 Ilya Lezerson, Tatiana Solomonik, and Sergey Sinelnikov. *Za stolom s Niro Vul'fom, ili sekrety kukhni velikogo syshchika: kulinarnyi detektiv (At the Table with Nero Wolfe or Secrets of the Kitchen of the Great Detective: A Culinary Mystery)*. Velikie syshchiki (Great Detectives). 3 ed. St. Petersburg:

The recipes in *At the Table with Nero Wolfe* are divided chronologically by novel, with each section giving the date of the original US publication as well as the date and name of the publishing house that published the Russian edition. The recipes are titled in both Russian and English, and each has a short summary of its origin book in Russian, with quotations from the 1990s translation of the book, mainly the sections where the dish is described. This is followed by a linguistic analysis of the problems in translation in the quotations, and then the details of the recipe are given. Sinelnikov writes that the cookbook has been the subject of several dissertations on translation, for its appeal spans beyond those who cook to those who translate.

For example, the section describing Wolfe's breakfast in *Over My Dead Body* begins with a short quotation from the point of view of Archie, who walks into Wolfe's room in the morning and observes him eating off a tray in bed. The Russian-translated excerpt in *At the Table with Nero Wolfe* is taken from the 2000 Tsentrpoligraf edition and reads (in translation) that Wolfe is breakfasting on "orange juice, eggs *au beurre noir*, two slices of smoked ham, finely chopped fried potatoes, hot golden *pyshki* [Russian donuts] with blueberry and a pot of steaming chocolate— not a bad start to the day, yes?"[361] In the English original, Wolfe is eating "orange juice, eggs *au beurre noir*, two slices of broiled Georgia ham, hashed brown potatoes, hot blueberry muffins, and a pot of steaming cocoa."[362] The differences in the two versions are then detailed by the authors, prefaced by a short explanation of the "juice boom" in twentieth century America. The authors do not, however, address the Russian translator's addition of "not a bad start to the day, yes?" One explanation

---

Amfora, 2015, 12.
361 Ibid.,142
362 Ibid.,159

for this addition might be that the translator was impressed with Wolfe's meal, for it contained food unusual in a Russian breakfast, and wanted to highlight his impressed reaction as well as the foreignness of the food.

A description of American hash browns precedes the recipe, with a list of other American names for the food as well as a discussion of the combination of the French "hacher" with the American "brown." After the hash browned potatoes recipe is an explanation of how Russian *pyshki* differ from an American muffin, with very specific details as to an American muffin's average size, which, according to the cookbook, is about seven centimeters in diameter and three centimeters thick.[363] Before the blueberry muffin recipe is given, the cookbook includes information on the trend in America to name foods after the company that makes them, citing the Gem Company and the tendency to call their blueberry muffins "blueberry gems."

Stout fans from the online Russian Wolfe forum and Vk site have only positive things to say about the cookbook, although Chervotkin writes, "I wouldn't have the patience for most of them" in reference to the recipes, and Panichev writes that the professional nature of Fritz's cooking also discourages him from attempting any.[364] Zavgorodnii calls *At the Table with Nero Wolfe* "excellent" and agrees that the recipes seem difficult, but he attributes that to Fritz's being "a professional cook of the highest level," mirroring Panichev's language.[365] Zavgorodnii mentions the ingredients being strange in their specificity to America, citing shad roe and clams as well as squirrel stew.

The issue of how to translate "squirrel stew" is addressed in *At the Table with Nero Wolfe*. The reference appears in *The League*

---

363 Ibid., 144

364 Sergey Chervotkin (user Avis), November 20, 2015; Sergey Panichev, Vkontakte message to author, March 15, 2016.

365 Stanislav Zavgorodnii (user Chuchundrovich), November 23, 2015.

of Frightened Men, where Archie drinks rye to accompany the black sauce in Fritz's squirrel stew, cooked in the original English manner.[366] In the 1993 Triller house Russian translation, Archie is eating "hot lamb stew with onion" and drinks rye to accompany the "lamb milk." The authors of *At the Table with Nero Wolfe* correct this translation and then go into detail about the history of eating squirrel in America.[367]

The large number of translations and series with Stout's cookbooks and novels led to his being the second most published author in Russia in 2014 (his first inclusion in the top ten), with 72 books and 1,132,8000 copies in circulation. In the same list, Dontsova was first and Marinina was fourth.[368] A possible explanation for Stout's inclusion for the first time on the 2014 list is that Amfora's "Great Detectives" collection of Stout was published that year.

Opinions about Stout's popularity (and his failing to appear on the most-published list in years other than 2014) were offered by members of the online Russian Wolfe fan club. Chervotkin writes that Stout's popularity in 2015 would be ranked only five out of ten, because "his name has not been advertised enough, and people are not used to his style." He says that Sir Arthur Conan Doyle and Agatha Christie stories were what people were used to in the Soviet period, rather than Stout's more hard-boiled kind, but that "this is neither good nor bad. It just happened to be this way."[369] Zavgorodnii gives an identical

---

366 Lezerson, Solomonik, and Sinelnikov. *Za stolom s Niro Vul'fom, ili sekrety kukhni velikogos yshchika: kulinarnyi detektiv (At the Table with Nero Wolfe or Secrets of the Kitchen of the Great Detective: A Culinary Mystery)*, 34.

367 Ibid., 33-34.

368 See the appendix for Stout's printings in Russia in 2014, the Russian Stout collections in the early 2000s, and a table of his books republished in the 2000s, on page 190. Sadly, E.L. James (author of the *Fifty Shades* series) was eleventh, one higher than Dostoevsky.

369 Sergey Chervotkin (user Avis), November 20, 2015.

score and analysis: five out of ten and the inability of Stout to compete with Christie or Conan Doyle in terms of popularity.[370] Vk user Panichev gives Stout the highest rating, 8 to10 on the ten-point scale.[371] User BleWotan is unable to give an answer to the question, citing "our digital age" to explain his lack of knowledge about Stout's popularity.[372] It is worth noting that Stout's books are easily available, in unauthorized copies, on the Russian language internet. Chervotkin writes that he downloaded his first Stout book in 2012. A quick Google search will find several websites offering downloads in any format of every one of Stout's books, both in Russian and English, including all editions of the cookbooks.

Even with the large number of Stout books in print today, none of the users on the Russian forum describe the translations as excellent; they are always called either "fair," "not very good," or "incomprehensible." Zavgorodnii explains the problem in translating Stout by linking it to a general lack of knowledge of America: "Many mistakes come from the translators' unawareness of American life (for example, baseball rules and terminology.) All the flaws have become especially apparent to me this year, as I am learning English and am trying to read Stout's books in the original." However, even the poor quality of the translations does not discourage Russian readers; Rymko writes that "even though those were not always good-quality editions and good translations, I became imbued with the characters of this author."[373]

---

370 Stanislav Zavgorodnii (user Chuchundrovich), November 23, 2015.
371 Sergey Panichev, Vkontakte message to author, March 15, 2016.
372 User BleWotan, December 14, 2015.
373 Stanislav Zavgorodnii (user Chuchundrovich), November 23, 2015; Natalia Rymko (user Rymarnica), October 19, 2015.

Stout's Fan Base Goes Online and Eastward

The advent of the digital age led to a plethora of Stout and Wolfe-related online resources for Russian speakers, whose interest in Stout was encouraged by the retranslation surge in the 2000s. There is a Russian Nero Wolfe fan club on both Facebook and VKontakte (a Russian Facebook-like website), but the main site for Russian-speaking Nero Wolfe fans is nerowolfe.info, which models itself on the site of the American fan club, the Wolfe Pack. The often-quoted (in this book) Zavgorodnii is the creator and webmaster for the whole site as well as the discussion forum attached to it. In the "About the Site" section, he writes how, after reading *The Doorbell Rang* in the early 1990s, he began to seek out Stout's books in libraries and from friends and acquaintances. When he realized there was nothing on the *RuNet* [Russian internet] that served as a "specialized resource dedicated to [his] heroes," he created nerowolfe.info in 2009.[374]

The website has pages of information about Stout and each of his characters, from his two main detectives to Lily Rowan, Lieutenant Rowcliffe, Doctor Vollmer, and every single minor character that has ever recurred in the Wolfe stories. There are pages for radio and film adaptations of Wolfe stories, a table and graph charting Wolfe's recorded weight in every novel, and a three-page series on what Wolfe and Archie drink in the novels, broken down by beverage and accompanied by photos of American ads for the brands of beverage discussed, as well as a brief linguistic study of "stout" as an adjective and as a type of beer.[375]

---

374 Stanislav Zavgorodnii, "O saite," *Niro Vul'f i Archi Gudvin*, http://nerowolfe.info/about.

375 Ibid, "Staut i staut," *Niro Vul'f i Archi Gudvin*, http://nerowolfe.info/beer.

The website includes a forum for posting topics and discussing the Wolfe novels in detail. There are 173 users registered to the forum, all of whom actively comment on forum topics such as "Nero Wolfe, Archie Goodwin, and everything that is connected with them" and "In the kitchen of Fritz Brenner." The fans celebrate Stout's birthday online, post photos of orchids in honor of Nero Wolfe, and ask each other detailed questions about the American slang Archie uses. My posts in the forum as an American who had read every Stout novel in English drew questions from Russian readers about Archie's vocabulary. User Avis questioned me about the rubber silencer that Archie uses in one novel, asking me to clarify its definition and use by linking me to another discussion thread on the site about what an American silencer looks like, complete with pictures of different types of guns combined with various definitions of "rubber silencer," which included descriptions of weaponry as well as biological terms.[376]

One of the first posts on the forum in 2009 was a biography in Russian of J. Edgar Hoover, meant to be read with the Russian translation of *The Doorbell Rang*. Early posts also included a page of memes of Archie, including a Soviet-era polling poster of a Soviet woman with the words "I will vote for Archie" superimposed over the background.[377] More recent discussion threads (from 2015) include user-posted sketches of horses, in reference to *And Be a Villain* where, in an aside, Wolfe sketches a horse

---

376 Sergey Chervotkin (user Avis), November 20, 2015.
377 User RAMZES, "Biografiia Edgara Guvera" *O Niro Vul'fe, Archi Gudvine, i ikh avtore, Rekse Staute* (*About Nero Wolfe, Archie Goodwin, and their author, Rex Stout*) (blog), April 27, 2009 (10:33am), http://nerowolfe.info/forum/viewtopic.php?f=5&t=48; Stanislav Zavgorodnii (user Chuchundrovich), "Kubok luchshego detektiva- u Archi Gudvina," *O Niro Vul'fe, Archi Gudvine, i ikh avtore, Rekse Staute* (*About Nero Wolfe, Archie Goodwin, and their author, Rex Stout*) (blog), April 28, 2009 (9:55pm), http://nerowolfe.info/forum/viewtopic.php?f=5&t=49.

because he had recently read that the way a person draws a horse shows something about his character.[378]

Users posted often on the site in the years from 2009 to 2016, but the posts have slowed down in the most recent years. That does not mean that the site is defunct or no longer useful; it maintains an important place in the life of Stout's Russian-speaking fans. In 2013, one user wrote, "This site corresponds to my perception of the spirit of the novels about Nero Wolfe, I'm going to become a frequent visitor.... Thanks again."[379] The American Wolfe Pack holds regular meetings in several cities, organizes excursions to Stout's home and the archives of his biographer in Boston, and hosts a large annual banquet celebrating Stout's birthday. None of this is available to Russian-speaking Wolfe fans, who live on the other side of the world and do not necessarily speak or read English. For Russian speakers in Russia and elsewhere, this site is the only way for them to connect with one another.

The Russian Nero Wolfe Television Series

The cookbooks, retranslations, and fan club are not the limit of Stout's influence in contemporary Russia, for he has entered the Russian television sphere as well. Two series of a Russian Nero Wolfe television show were broadcast in 2001-2002 and 2005.[380] Members of the Russian Nero Wolfe online fan club,

---

378 Natalia Rymko (user Rymarnica), "A kak vy risuete loshad'?," *O Niro Vul'fe, Archi Gudvine, i ikh avtore, Rekse Staute* (*About Nero Wolfe, Archie Goodwin, and their author, Rex Stout*) (blog), March 28, 2013 (6:39pm), http://nerowolfe.info/forum/viewtopic.php?f=14&t=459.

379 User Ol'ga T., January 27, 2013 (2:49pm), comment on user MsBulavkapetek1855, "Blagodarnost'," *O Niro Vul'fe, Archi Gudvine, i ikh avtore, Rekse Staute* (*About Nero Wolfe, Archie Goodwin, and their author, Rex Stout*) (blog), December 19, 2011 (2:48pm), http://nerowolfe.info/forum/viewtopic.php?f=8&t=301.

380 There have also been Russian television adaptations of Marinina's

however, had an overwhelmingly negative view of them. Both User BleWotan and Chervotkin wrote that they "unfortunately" had seen them (in separate responses) and Chuchundrovich "did not like it."[381] VK user Panichev wrote that the series "failed in translating Stout's books. America in the serial looked very pale and superficial."[382] The first series was five episodes long: "Poka ia ne umer" (*Before I Die*), "Letayushchii pistolet" (*Gun with Wings*), "Golos s togo sveta" (*The Silent Speaker*), "Delo v shliape" (*Disguise for Murder*), and "Voskresnut', shtoby umeret'" (*Man Alive*). The second series in 2005 was four episodes long: "Podarok dlia Lili" (*Black Orchids*), "Posledniaia volia Marko" (*The Black Mountain*), "Ochen' mnogo zhenshchin" (*Too Many Women*), and "Taina krasnoi shkatulki" *(The Red Box)*.[383] The cast featured Donatas Banionis as Nero Wolfe, Sergey Zhugunov as Archie Goodwin, Sergey Parshin as Inspector Cramer, and Sergey Migitzko as Fritz Brenner. Both the writer of the series, Vladimir Valutskiy, and the scorer, Vladimir Dashkevich, had worked on the 1980s Russian Sherlock Holmes show. Dashkevich's take on the score for the show's opening was to play the opening music of the Sherlock Holmes series backwards, an unexplained and humorous stylistic move that reflected the Russian Stout fans' opinions of the large popularity of Holmes in Russia compared to Stout.[384]

Kamenskaia and Darya Dontsova's Podushkin.

381 User BleWotan, December 14, 2015; Sergey Chervotkin (user Avis), November 20, 2015; Stanislav Zavgorodnii (user Chuchundrovich), November 23, 2015.

382 User BleWotan, December 14, 2015; Sergey Chervotkin (user Avis), November 20, 2015.

383 Stanislav Zavgorodnii, "Rossiia, 2001-2002, 'Niro Vul'f i Archi Gudvin,' 2005, 'Novye prikliucheniia Niro Vul'fa i Archi Gudvina,'" *Niro Vul'f i Archi Gudvin*, http://nerowolfe.info/movies.

384 "Poka ya ne umer (2001)." IMDb.com, Inc., http://www.imdb.com/title/tt0368157/.

The opening credits of the Wolfe series are very America-centric, with the Statue of Liberty shown twice (once with a man literally building her) alongside repeated views of the New York skyline. Although the plots of the episodes do mainly follow those of Stout's stories, the show takes a much more comical slant than the books. There are several simple factual inaccuracies in the portrayal of Wolfe, Archie, and New York City, which could have come from a mistaken ideological standpoint or a lack of reliable information about America. In some episodes, Archie is seen driving up to Wolfe's brownstone, which is located next to a giant forest full of trees, and parking his car in a little driveway, an image which is not possible considering the architecture of West 35th Street and the nature of brownstones in Manhattan.

The characters are also often depicted differently than their written counterparts, with Fritz (Wolfe's chef) and Theodore (Wolfe's orchid man) placed in more subservient roles. In the novels, Fritz and Theodore, while technically servants, are written as equals to Wolfe and Archie; just because Wolfe is their employer does not mean that his class status is markedly differentiated from theirs. In the Russian television series, however, both Fritz and Theodore are comically deferential to Wolfe, behaving in what one could imagine is a Soviet holdover of the stereotype of the exploited American servant. Archie and Wolfe have a more emotional relationship in the TV series, with Archie as a more sexualized character whom Wolfe has to rein in whenever he is interviewing a female suspect. This is exemplified by retitling *The Black Orchids* as *A Gift for Lily*. Archie's relationships with women are pushed to the forefront in order to add more romance to a plot that previously had little.

The police also play a more important role in the show than they do in the books; they have more control over murder scenes, and both murder suspects and Archie are more fearful of police authority. Archie, Wolfe, and Inspector Cramer are depicted as good friends working together as opposed to the back and forth, friend and foe relationship they have in Stout's novels. The heightened role of police authority reflects the tendency for the Russian *detektiv* heroes to be members of the police or military, not private investigators.

Then there are the minor inconsistencies, like the lack of a desk for Archie, the lack of red or yellow chairs in Wolfe's office, and the addition of to Wolfe of a mustache. In *A Gift for Lily*, the murderer does not die at the end, but becomes comically entangled in a gas mask contraption and then the whole cast of characters laughs into a fade out.[385] This kind of comical ending does not exist in the American Wolfe novels; while chapters sometimes end with Archie laughing at authority, murderers are rarely depicted as comedic.

The Russian TV version of *The Black Mountain* is vastly different than the novel in tone, plot, setting, and characters.[386] While solving the murder of Marko does still entail a trip to Yugoslavia for Wolfe and Archie, the motive for the murder is now connected to a past murder of Marko's brother and a secret hiding place of gold coins. The whole episode is virtually a comedy: Wolfe is jocularly referred to as Neron Wolfevich and spends most of the episode wearing a disguise of a tall black furry hat, fake goatee, and sheepskin coat, in which he is depicted stumbling around and looking confused in a foreign countryside. Archie and Wolfe's time in Montenegro lacks almost entirely the political intrigue of the Stout book; Black Mountain separatists

[385] Sergey Zhigunov, "Podarok dlia lili (A Gift for Lily)." in *Novye prikliucheniia Niro Vul'fa i Archi Gudvina*, directed by Viktor Sergeev and Igor' Muzhzhukhin, 2005.

[386] Sergey Zhigunov, "Posledniaia volia Marko (The Last Wish of Marko)," in *Novye prikliucheniia Niro Vul'fa i Archi Gudvina*, directed by Viktor Sergeev and Igor' Muzhzhukhin, 2005.

are mentioned in connection with Marko but are not central to the plot. Nor do Wolfe and Archie encounter any of the difficulties in illegally crossing borders or finding food—once off their boat from Italy, they casually walk up to a nice meal at an upscale restaurant. When they are taken to the political headquarters, it is so they can work with the political boss to find the murderer together instead of its being the close call with arrest and deportation in the original version.

The boss's secretary is a seemingly random choice for a love interest for Archie, and both are briefly shown on a horseback ride along a beach at sunset. This scene culminates in a dramatic reveal, for a friendly American they met earlier is seen behind a rock with a gun, waiting for Archie to get off his horse. When Archie moves to kiss his love interest, he inadvertently positions his horse between himself and his would-be assassin, causing the assassin to shrug his shoulders, lower his gun, and leave, apparently considering it impossible to wait the minute or so it would take until Archie gave him a clear shot again.

Wolfe is arrested midway through the episode, leaving Archie to be the real brains behind the operation in Yugoslavia (although they both receive medals from the political boss before they leave the country). The plot culminates in Archie's destroying a cement seal with a sledgehammer and gold coins falling from the sky, at which point the Yugoslav party boss says, "You really are an American": money literally falls from the sky at the American's feet. The episode ends with Archie and Inspector Cramer shooting the murderer dead just after he shoots Wolfe in the leg, which is what happens in the novel. However, the murderer in the television episode turns out to be a small-time thief from Cleveland rather than an ideologically-driven hit man from Yugoslavia, as Stout wrote him.

Such gaps between the Stout books and the Russian television series did not, however, diminish Nero Wolfe's popularity in Russia. It is just another case of the desire to make money in the new free market Russian economy leading some villain in the television industry to commit a crime (of bad taste).

Conclusion

One main question of my research is this: considering Stout's politics and politically charged plotlines, why was he ever published in the Soviet Union?

When I began my research, I had not thought it would include the Soviet period but would begin with the 1990s, and I turned out to be incorrect. It is surprising that Soviet censors did not seem to notice that Stout was such a strong political activist whose views were often directed against Communist ideology. The criticism of Stout by critics like Andzhaparidze was confined to problems with his plots, and more generally with the translation of Western detective novels as a whole; Stout's name on Freedom House documents passed unnoticed. It's possible that censors and critics did not bother to look into Stout's politics, or, more likely, did not care, because his books served a purpose in their Soviet publication – his plots critiquing racism in America and the FBI's abuse of power showed Soviet citizens that the US had real societal problems.

It is also possible that since Stout was one among many relatively minor (compared to the big names of Agatha Christie and Sir Arthur Conan Doyle) Western detective novelists published in Russian translation, he was merely overlooked in the crowd. Since not all of Stout's books had politics in their plots, it was not difficult to find Nero Wolfe novels that did not trouble the censors. And, when censorship was required, as in the 1994 publication of *The Cop Killer*, it was a relatively easy thing to do – just change a country's name. Cannon's thesis explores how Stout managed to write politically charged novels without losing literary integrity; his ability to weave political intrigue into murder mysteries in subtle ways also allowed for his publication in the USSR.

The next question I sought to answer was why, after the Soviet Union fell, Stout was so popular in Russia, arguably more so than in the United States, where his celebrity was waning. Not a single one of my friends in America had heard of Rex Stout before I started my research, but almost every person my age I met in Russia had. Why is Stout so much better known among the younger generation in Russia?

Russian speakers on the Nero Wolfe forum (whose existence is significant in itself) had varying answers to this question. Chervotkin writes:

> I read them [Stout's novels] for the atmosphere that the author creates. For me, it is analogous to what George Simenon did in his books about Commissioner Maigret. Stout (as well as some of his translators) manages to create the sense of presence. Everyone and everything

is almost palpable, as if you could touch them. There are jokes, epithets and short eloquent descriptions that sound very natural.[387]

User BleWotan also sees the books' literary value as the reason for Stout's popularity: "There is a kind of core in these books; the characters are outlined with vivid features that I enjoy as a reader. The detective part is secondary for me; the characters and their interactions come first."[388] Both of these answers support the idea that Stout's popularity simply rests in his literary talent. Zavgorodnii goes into more detail in relation to Stout and America:

> What I really like in Stout's books is not so much the plot but more the originality of the characters and the atmosphere created by the author. Now, as I am trying to read Stout in English, I begin to understand some of the nuances that were inaccessible to me when reading him in Russian. For example, I see that in everyday life Wolfe uses somewhat more sophisticated vocabulary than other characters, including some words that may be rarely used and unknown even to native speakers (his famous "flummery," for example). Some time ago, when we (users of this forum) were making a list of the books that Wolfe read in Stout's books...I was astonished by how diverse the character's (and his creator's, of course) interests were. Definitely, Stout's books (along with some other factors) evoked the interest for the United States of America in me.[389]

---

387 Sergey Chervotkin (user Avis), November 20, 2015.
388 User BleWotan, December 14, 2015.
389 Stanislav Zavgorodnii (user Chuchundrovich), November 23, 2015.

Another Russian blogger, Desh, writes that since Wolfe lives in "a utopia" where life is governed by sense and morality, one could contrast it with the world that Russian readers live in.[390] Clearly, the setting of the books attracts Russian readers' curiosity; New York especially is a draw for many Russians who will never go there (hence the way the Russian television series opens with the New York skyline and the Statue of Liberty).

The Stout cookbooks were also of interest to Russians, who enjoyed reading about the delicacies consumed by Americans; three editions in twelve years of *At the Table with Nero Wolfe* prove this point.

Stout's popularity can also be traced to the Russian trend of nostalgia for its past. Stout was wildly popular in the 1950s in America, the era of the Cold War, when anti-Communist sentiment was common and Senator McCarthy and HUAC were polarizing the American public. Stout's books reflected the political tensions at the time, but, while reading about the tense situation in America in real life, Americans could be entertained by mysteries with satisfying neat endings. His popularity expanded in 1965 when he went to new lengths to criticize the FBI. American nostalgia for the Cold War does not really exist, however, so it's not surprising that more young Americans don't read Stout today. Stout's popularity in the 1950s and 1960s cannot be denied, but his popularity did not continue after his death in a significant way in America.

In Russia, through 1970s censorship, the 1990s detective translation boom, and the 2000s retranslations and multiple cookbook editions, Stout has been part of every changing era in Russian memory back to Soviet times. He is woven into Russian nostalgia for past (and often worse) periods of history. Russians'

---

390 Dobavil Desh, "Klassicheskii detektiv protiv krutogo," in *Detektivnyi metod. Istoriia detektiva v kino i literature (The Detective Method. A History of Detektiv in Movie and Literature)*, 2014.

dissatisfaction with their society is longstanding. (Interestingly, they can be nostalgic for eras they mostly did not like.) Stout's honest critiques of American societal problems with race, the FBI, and McCarthyism are comforting for Russians to read because they too felt (and feel) dissatisfaction with their government, past and present. This is true of an older generation that is nostalgic for Soviet times, as well as children of the Brezhnev era who don't want to pay for their parents' mistakes. Marinina has things both ways – she appeals to her readers' nostalgia while appealing to the dissatisfaction of the younger generation with plots concerning economic corruption.

Stout's appeal in Russia varied from decade to decade. In the 1970s, Russians wanted to read the previously forbidden Western detective story and see what life was like in America. In the 1990s, Stout's attacks on Communism reached Russians willing to hear the message that their past system was bad. They also appreciated the way Wolfe and Archie locked up criminals and villains, for the turmoil of the 1990s created an atmosphere of fear and uncertainty that sent Russians running for this kind of comfort in literature. Most recently, in the 2000s, Stout's popularity can be seen as part of the Russian trend of appreciating and consuming more pop culture than ever before, both foreign and homegrown.

In tracing the trajectory of this one American author's impact on Russian literary culture, it is necessary to remember that Stout was a novelist first and a political activist second. Most Russians did not read his books for political insight but instead picked up a Wolfe novel because they wanted to be entertained. Stout's unique and unforgettable characters of Wolfe and Archie are the most important part of any analysis of Stout's popularity; when it comes down to it, the most basic explanation of Stout's popularity anywhere in the world is simply that he knew how to tell a really good story.

In 2015, at the annual Black Orchid banquet hosted by the Wolfe Pack around Stout's December 1st birthday, I was fortunate enough to meet Rebecca Stout Bradbury, Rex Stout's daughter. When I told her the topic of this book, she was very surprised. If you are a 76-year-old with a famous father, it is not often that someone is able to tell you something new about your parent that you don't already know, but I did that with Rebecca Stout Bradbury. Rex Stout's legacy in America is well known, but the extent of his fame and influence in both Soviet and present-day Russia was not known even to his own daughter. Research on Rex Stout and his legacy in Russia adds another layer to the already complex history of cross-cultural Cold War influences. With tensions between Russia and the United States on the rise once again, perhaps Nero Wolfe and Archie Goodwin will play yet another role.

And, with that, Wolfe would most likely say, "Pfui."

APPENDIX

Statistical Records of Printed Materials in Russia in 2014[391]

English-language books published:
1090 books, 2,389,400 copies in circulation, 27,297,400 printed pages

English-translations published:
6738 books, 39,492,900 copies in circulation, 638,452,700 printed pages

Top twenty authors published:
1. Darya Arkadyevna Dontsova: 95 books, 1,683,000 copies in circulation, 23,088,400 printed pages
2. Rex Stout: 72 books, 1,132,800 copies in circulation, 18,874,000 printed pages
3. Tatiana Viktorovna Polyakova: 58 books, 663,200 copies in circulation, 8,701,600 printed pages
4. Aleksandra Marinina: 50 books, 661,200 copies in circulation, 10,333,000 printed pages
5. Tatiana Vitalyevna Ustinova: 40 books, 593,500 copies in circulation, 7,891,900 printed pages
6. Oleg Yurievich Roi: 41 books, 542,000 copies in circulation, 8,243,900 printed pages

---

[391] Statisticheskie pokazateli po vypusku pechatnykh izdanii (Statistical Indicators for the Production of Publications)," collected by Rossiiskaia knizhnaia palata: filial ITAR-TASS (Russian Book Chamber: ITAR-TASS Branch), 2014.

7. Vladimir Grigorievich Kolychev: 41 books, 511,200 copies in circulation, 6,878,600 printed pages
8. Yulia Vitalyevna Shilova: 38 books, 506,000 copies in circulation, 6,127,000 printed pages
9. Steven King: 61 books, 453,500 copies in circulation, 12,224,800 printed pages
10. Yekaterina Nikolaevna Vilmont: 42 books, 424,000 copies in circulation, 5,549,600 printed pages
11. E.L James (Джеймс Эл): 3 books, 405,000 copies in circulation, 12,282,900 printed pages
12. Fyodor Mikhailovich Dostoyevksy: 68 books, 394,800 copies in circulation, 11,740,100 printed pages
13. Boris Akunin: 43 books, 377,500 copies in circulation, 6,349,500 printed pages
14. A. and S. Litvinovy: 41 books, 373,000 copies in circulation, 5,014,700 printed pages
15. Erich Maria Remarque: 48 books, 353,400 copies in circulation, 640,900 printed pages
16. D.I. Rubina: 53 books, 344,400 copies in circulation, 7,215,600 printed pages
17. Lev Nikolayevich Tolstoy: 49 books, 328,500 copies in circulation, 10,629,500 printed pages
18. N.N. Aleksandrova: 64 books, 324,000 copies in circulation, 4,072,700 printed pages
19. M.S. Serova: 38 books, 318,200 copies in circulation, 3,790,400 printed pages
20. Darya Aleksandrovna Kalinina: 43 books, 313000 copies in circulation, 3,928,700 printed pages

Stout Collections in the 2000s by Russian Publishing Houses[392]

Publishing House: Tsentrpoligraf

"Neizvestnyi Staut" (Unknown Stout) 2002
25 volume series, 26th is the cookbook
*rest of the titles cannot be found online

"Ves' Niro Vulf" (All Nero Wolfe)
2002
1. *Igra v bary (Prisoner's Base)*
2. Nepriiatnosti vtroine
3. *Zolotye pauki (The Golden Spiders)*
4. *Tri svidetelia (Trouble in Triplicate)*
5. *Esli by smert' spala (If Death Ever Slept)*
6. *Slishkom mnogo klientov (Too Many Clients)*
7. *Pravo umeret' (A Right to Die)*
8. *Pokovaia troitsa (Homicide Trinity)*
9. *Smert' chuzhaka (Death of a Dude)*
10. *Smert' schitaet do trekh (Death Times Three)*
11. *Gde Tsezar' krov'iu istekal (Some Buried Caesar)*
12. *Zanavees dlia troikh (Curtains for Three)*
13. *Krasnaia korobka (The Red Box)*
14. *Ne pozdnee polnochi (Before Midnight)*
15. *Troinoi risk (Triple Jeopardy)*
16. *Chernye orxidei (Black Orchids)*

"Reks Staut, Klassika detektiva" (Rex Stout, Classic Detective)

---

[392] Collection information was gathered from the following online catalogs: "The National Library of Russian Online Catalogue," (The National Library of Russia, 2014); "Russian State Library," (Federal Agency on the Press and Mass Communications of the Russian Federation, 2012).

2004
1. *Esli smert' navesegda usnet (If Death Ever Slept)*
2. *Krasnaia korobka (The Red Box)*
3. *Otzvuki ibiistva (The Sound of Murder)* *Alphabet Hicks novel
4. *Troinoi risk (Triple Jeopardy)*
5. *Zanaves dlia troikh (Death Times Three)*
6. *Pravo umeret' (A Right to Die)*
7. *Priz dlia printsev (A Prize for Princes)* *non-Wolfe novel, non-mystery
8. *Ubit' zlo (How Like a God)* *non-Wolfe, non-mystery

Publishing House: Eksmo

"Ves' Staut" (All Stout)- 2006, 2007, 2009
1. *Zolotye pauki (The Golden Rings)*
2. *Ubei seichas- zaplatish' pozzhe (Kill Now, Pay Later)*
3. *Okonchhatel'noe reshenie (The Final Deduction)*
4. *Ubiistvo- ne shutka (Murder is No Joke/Frame Up for Murder)*
5. *Chernye orkhidei (Black Orchids)*
6. *Krasnaia shkatulka (The Red Box)*
7. *Ne pozzhe polunochi (Before Midnight)*
8. *Vtoroe priznanie (The Second Confession)*
9. *Izcheznuvshii president (The President Vanishes)* *originally written anonymously, non-Wolfe novel
10. *Tol'ko cherez moi trup (Over My Dead Body)*
11. *Vmesto iliki (Instead of Evidence)*
12. *Rozhdestvenskaia vecherinka (Christmas Party)*
13. *Semeinoe delo (A Family Affair)*
14. *Dver' k smerti (Door to Death)*

15. *Vyshel mesiats iz tumana (Eeny, Meeny, Murder, Mo)*
16. *Bokal shampanskogo (Champagne for One)*
17. *V luchshikh semeistvakh (In the Best Families)*
18. *Prochitavshemu-smert' (Murder by the Book)* *two different translated titles are included in the collection
19. *Igra v bary (Prisoner's Base)*
20. *Zaveshchanie (Where There's a Will/Sisters in Trouble)*
21. *Povod dlia ubiistva (Omit Flowers)*
22. *Poslednii svidetel' (Murder by the Book)* *two different translated titles are included in the collection
23. *Vsekh, krome psa,- v politsiiu! (Die Like a Dog)*
24. *Slishkom mnogo zhenshchin (Too Many Women)*
25. *Chernaia gora (The Black Mountain)*
26. *Slishkom mnogo povarov (Too Many Cooks)*
27. *Eto vas ne ub'et (This Won't Kill You)*
28. *Pogonia za mater'iu (The Mother Hunt)*
29. *Smertel'naia lovushka (Booby Trap)*
30. *Esli by smert' spala (If Death Ever Slept)*
31. *Gambit (Gambit)*
32. *Smertel'nyi plagiat (Plot it Yourself)*
33. *Krov' skazhet (Blood Will Tell)*
34. *Umolknuvshii orator (The Silent Speaker)*
35. *Priglashenie k ubiistvu (Invitation to Murder)*
36. *Fer-de-lans (Fer-de-lance)*
37. *Snova ubivat'(The Rubber Band)*
38. *Znaiut otvet orkhidei (Might as Well Be Dead)*
39. *Pravo umeret' (A Right to Die)*
40. *Plokho dlia biznesa (Bad for Business)* *Tecumseh Fox novel
41. *Liga perepugannyx muzhchin (The League of Frightened Men)*
42. *Slishkom mnogo klientov (Too Many Clients)*

43. *Immunitet k ubiistvy (Immune to Murder)*
44. *Kulinarnaia kniga Niro Vul'fa (The Nero Wolfe Cookbook)* *cookbook

Publishing House: Amfora

"Velikie syshchiki" (Great Detectives) 2014
1. *Poznakom'tes' s Niro Vul'fom (Fer-de-Lance)* *new translation without abbreviations
2. *Krasnaya shkatulka (The Red Box)*
3. *Liga ispugannyx muzhin and S priskorbiem izveshchaem (The League of Frightened Men and Cordially Invited to Meet Death)* *new translation of *The League of Frightened Men*
4. *Umolknuvwii orator and Prezhde chem ia umru (The Silent Speaker and Before I Die)*
5. *Snova ubivat' (The Rubber Band/To Kill Again)* *new translation
6. *Gde Tsezar' krov'iu istekal (Some Buried Caesar)*
7. *Tol'ko cherez moi trup (Over My Dead Body)*
8. *Zaveshchanie (Where There's a Will/Sisters in Trouble)*
9. *Chernye orkhidei (Black Orchids)*
10. *Shlishkom mnogo zhenshchin (Too Many Women)*
11. *I byt podletsom (And Be A Villain)*
12. *Vtoroe priznanie (The Second Confession)*
13. *Dver' k smerti (Door to Death)*
14. *Ubiistvo iz-za knigi (Murder by the Book)*
15. *Igra v piatnashki (Prisoner's Base)*
16. *Zolotye pauki (The Golden Spiders)*
17. *Chernaya gora (The Black Mountain)*

18. *Ne pozdnee polnochi (Before Midnight)*
19. *Znaiut otvet orkhidei (Might As Well Be Dead)*
20. *Esli by smert' spala (If Death Ever Slept)*
21. *Prazdichnyi piknik (Fourth of July Picnic)*
22. *Bokal shampanskogo (Champagne for One)*
23. *Iad vkhodit v meniu (Poison a La Carte)*
24. *Slishkom mnogo klientov (Too Many Clients)*
25. *Okanchatel'noe reshenie (The Final Deduction)*
26. *Gambit (Gambit)*
27. *Pravo umeret' (A Right to Die)*
28. *Krov' skazhet (Blood Will Tell)*
29. *Smert' soderzhanki (Death of a Doxy)*
30. *Seminoe delo (A Family Affair)*
31. *Gor'kii konets (Bitter End)*
32. *Smertel'nyi dubl' (Double for Death)* *Tecumseh Fox novel
33. *Skverno dlia dela (Bad for Business)* *Tecumseh Fox novel
34. *Razbitaia vaza (The Broken Vase)* *Tecumseh Fox novel
35. *Otzvuki ubiistva (The Sound of Murder)* *Alphabet Hicks novel
36. *Ruka v perchatke (The Hand in the Glove)* *Dol Bonner novel
37. *Gornaia koshka (Mountain Cat)* *non-Wolfe novel
38. *Prezident ischez (The President Vanishes)* *originally written anonymously, non-Wolfe novel
39. *Pravosudie konchaetsia dom (Justice Ends at Home)* *pre-Wolfe novel with two archetypes of Wolfe and Archie
40. *Ee zapretnyi rytsar'(Her Forbidden Knight)* *pre-Wolfe novel orginally published in 1910, Stout's pulp fiction
41. *Ubit' zlo (How Like a God)* *non-Wolfe, non-mystery
42. *Za stolom s Niro Vul'fom (At the Table with Nero Wolfe)* *cookbook

Stout's Novels Mentioned in this Book[393]

English Titles	US Publishing Company and Year of First Publication in the US	Russian Titles	Russian Publishing House and Year of First Publication in Russia
Fer-de-Lance	Farrar & Rinehart 1934	*Ostrie kop'ia*	Unknown, 1993
Too Many Cooks	Farrar & Rinehart 1938	*Slishkom mnogo povarov*	Mysl', 1991
Some Buried Caesar	Farrar & Rinehart 1939	*Gde Tsezar' krov'iu istekal*	Petergrof, 1991
Over My Dead Body	Farrar & Rinehart 1940	*Cherez moi trup*	Pressa, 1994
"Watson was a Woman"	The Sunday Review of Literature 1941	*"Uotson byl zhenshchinoi"*	Unknown, 1998
Not Quite Dead Enough	Farrar & Rinehart 1944	*Smert' tam eshche ne pobyvala*	Unknown, 1994
Booby Trap	Farrar & Rinehart 1944	*Smertel'naia lovushka*	Tekst, 1992
The Silent Speaker	Viking Press 1946	*Umolknuvshii orator*	Intergraf Servis, 1990
And Be A Villain	Viking Press 1948	*I byt podletsom*	Ragua, 1991
The Second Confession	Viking Press 1949	*Vtoroe priznanie*	Tekst, 1992
In the Best Families	Viking Press 1950	*V luchshikh semeistvakh*	Intergraf Servis, 1992
Murder by the Book	Viking Press 1951	*Proghtiavshemusmert'*	Petergrof, 1991
Home to Roost	Viking Press 1952	*Ne roi drugomu iamu*	KUBK-a, 1994
The Cop Killer	Viking Press 1952	*Ubiistvo politseiskogo*	Kometa, 1990

[393] First year of translation in Russian and year of retranslation information is based on "The National Library of Russian Online Catalogue."

The Black Mountain	Viking Press 1954	*Chernaya gora*	Pressa, 1994
Method Three for Murder	Viking Press 1960	*Izbavlenie metodom nomer tri*	Amal'teia GMP, 1993
Poison à la Carte	Viking Press 1960	*Otpravlenie*	KUBK-a, 1994
A Right to Die	Viking Press 1964	*Pravo Umeret'*	Intergraf Servis, 1990
The Doorbell Rang	Viking Press 1965	*Zvonok v dver'*	Progress, 1973
The Father Hunt	Viking Press 1968	*Pogonia za ottsom*	Intergraf Servis, 1993
Death of a Dude	Viking Press 1969	*Smert' khlyshcha*	Olma-Press, 1993
Please Pass the Guilt	Viking Press 1973	*Pozhaluista, izbav'te ot grekha*	Venda, 1994
The Nero Wolfe Cookbook	Viking Press 1973	*Povarennaia knigi Niro Vul'fa*	Venda, 1995

Darya Dontsova's Ivan Podushkin Series[394]

Publishing House Eksmo:

2002:
    1. *Buket prekrasnykh dam (Bouquet of Beautiful Ladies)*
    2. *Brilliant mutnoi vody (Diamond of Turbid Water)*

2003:
    3. *Instinkt Baby-Iagi (The Instinct of Baba-Yaga)*
    4. *13 neschastii Gerakla (13 Sorrows of Hercules)*
    5. *Ali-Baba i sorok razboinits (Ali Baba and the Forty Female Thieves)*

2004:
    6. *Naduvnaia zhenshchina dlia Kazanovy (An Inflatable Woman for Casanova)*
    7. *Tushkanchik v bigudiakh (Jerboa in Curlers)*
    8. *Rybka po imeni Zaika (A Fish Named Stutterer)*

2005:
    9. *Dve nevesty na odno mesto (Two Brides in One Place)*
    10. *Safari na cherepashku (Safari for a Beetle)*

2006:
    11. *Iabloko Monte-Kristo (The Apple of Monte-Cristo)*
    12. *Piknik na ostrove sokrovishch (Picnic on Treasure Island)*

2007:
    13. *Macho chuzhoi mechty (A Macho Man of Someone Else's Dreams)*

---

[394] "V gostiakh u Dar'i Dontsovoi." Darya Donstova, http://www.dontsova.ru/hall/.

14. Verkhom na "Titanike"(Riding on the "Titanic")
15. Angel na metle (Angel on a Broomstick)

2008:
16. Prodiuser koz'ei mordy (Goat Face Producer)

2012:
17. Smekh i grekh Ivana-tsarevicha (The Laughter and Sin of Ivan Tsarevich)

2014:
18. Tainaia sviaz' ego velichestva (His Majesty's Secret Affair)
19. Sud'ba naidet na senovale (Fate Will Find in the Hayloft)

2015:
20. Avos'ka s Almaznym fondom (String Bag Full of Diamonds)

2016:
21. Koronnyi nomer mistera X (The Star Performance of Mister X)

Bibliography

"17 Writers Frame a World Law Plan." *The New York Times*, July 4, 1949, 2.

"Books and the Tiger." *The New York Times Book Review Spring Book Supplement*, March 21, 1943.

"Darya Dontsova." http://www.forbes.ru/profile/darya-dontsova.

"Nero Wolfe Vs. The F.B.I.". *Life*, December 10 1965, 127-34.

"Nero Wolfe." *Dublin Evening Herald*, August 22 1955.

"Niro Vul'f I Archi Gudvin." nerowolfe.info, http://nerowolfe.info/.

"Poka ya ne umer (2001)." IMDb.com, Inc., http://www.imdb.com/title/tt0368157/.

"Reks Staut (Rex Stout)." RTComm, http://lib.ru/DETEKTIWY/STAUT/.

"Russian State Library." Federal Agency on the Press and Mass Communications of the Russian Federation, 2012.

"Sherlock Holmes Is Favorite in Russia." *The Washington Post*, April 15 1967, A15.

"Some Quips That Flew in from the Air Front." *The Amarillo Globe*, April 26, 1945, 4.

"Statisticheskie pokazateli po vypusku pechatnykh izdanii (Statistical Indicators for the Production of Publications)." edited by Rossiiskaia knizhnaia palata: filial ITAR-TASS (Russian Book Chamber: ITAR-TASS Branch), 2014.

"Stout Nearly Causes a Riot at Fish Rally." *The New York Times*, November 3 1944.

"The Myth That Threatened the World." In *Rex Stout: Activist*: The Wolfe Pack: The Nero Wolfe Literary Society.

"The National Library of Russian Online Catalogue." The National Library of Russia, 2014.

"The New Shape of U.S.- Soviet Relations." In *The Report of a Conference of Foreign Affairs Scholars*: Public Affairs Institute of Freedom House. Undated. Rex Stout Papers. MS1986-096. John J. Burns Library, Boston College.

"The Wolfe Pack: The Official Nero Wolfe Society." The Wolfe Pack, http://www.nerowolfe.org/.

"U.S. Bids to China and Soviet, Though Hopeful, Inspire Concern for Freedom in Europe and Asia; American Gains Continued, Though Slower Paced." Freedom House. Undated. Rex Stout Papers. MS1986-096. John J. Burns Library, Boston College.

"V gostiakh u Dar'i Dontsovoi." Darya Donstova, http://www.dontsova.ru/hall/.

"Vypusk Knig V Rossii V 2014 Godu Sokratilsia Na 10% (Book Production in Russian in 2014 Decreased by 10%)." (2015). Pro-books.ru.

"The Black Mountain by Rex Stout." *Battle Creek Enquirer*. December 26, 1954. Michigan. Box 39, Folder 8. Rex Stout Papers. MS1986-096. John J. Burns Library, Boston College.

"Wild Places." *Daily Dispatch*. September 5. Manchester. International Press-Cutting Bureau. Box 39, Folder 8. Rex Stout Papers. MS1986-096. John J. Burns Library, Boston College.

100 American Crime Writers, Crime Files. Palgrave Macmillan, 2012.

Agence France-Presse. "Mihajlo Mihajlov, a Yugoslavian Dissident, Dies at 76." *The New York Times*, March 7, 2010.

Andzhaparidze, Georgi. "Bogachi-filantropy i belye 'Mersedesy': chto i kak my perevodim (Wealthy Philanthropists and White Mercedes: What and How We Translate)." *Literaturnaia gazeta.* January 20, 1971.

———. "Zhestkost' kanona i vechnaia novizna (The Rigidity of the Canon and Perpetual Novelty)." In *Detektivy veka*. Itogi veka, Vzgliad iz rossii. Polifakt. Itogi veka, 1999.

———. "Zigzagi belykh limuzinov (The Zigzags of White Limousines)." *Literaturnaia gazeta*. March 26, 1975.

Baraban, Elena V. "Russia in the Prism of Popular Culture: Russian and American Detective Fiction and Thrillers of the 1990s." The University of British Columbia, 2003.

———."A Little Nostalgia: The Detective Novels of Alexandra Marinina." *The International Fiction Review* 32, no. 1, 2 (2005). https://journals.lib.unb.ca/index.php/IFR/article/view/7802/8859.

Baring-Gould, William S. *Nero Wolfe of West Thirty-Fifth Street*. Penguin Books, 1982.

Bechtel, Marilyn. "The Soviet Peace Movement: From the Grass Roots": The National Council of American-Soviet Friendship, 1984.

Beiderwell, Bruce. "State Power and Self-Destruction: Rex Stout and the Romance of Justice." *Journal of Popular Culture* (January 1993): 13-22.

Beumers, Birgit. *Pop Culture Russia!: Media, Arts, and Lifestyle*. ABC-CLIO 2005.

BleWotan. December 14, 2015 (2:26pm). Comment on Molly Zuckerman, "Reks Staut iz Ameriki v Rossii." *O Niro Vul'fe, Archi Gudvine, i ikh avtore, Rekse Staute (About Nero Wolfe, Archie Goodwin, and their author, Rex Stout)* (blog). Translated by Gleb Vinokurov. October 18,

2015 (8:38pm). http://nerowolfe.info/forum/viewtopic.php?f=5&t=522&start=10.

Brooks, Jeffrey. *When Russians Learned to Read, Literacy and Popular Literature, 1861-1917*. Northwestern University Press, 2003.

Burns, Bobby Ray Miller and Ronald G. "It's Time Again for a New Nero Wolfe Detective Novel." Rex Stout Papers. MS1986-096. John J. Burns Library, Boston College.

Cannon, Ammie. "Controversial Politics, Conservative Genre: Rex Stout's ArchieWolfe Duo and Detective Fiction's Conventional Form." Brigham Young University, 2006.

Censored to J. Edgar Hoover. October 12, 1965. FBI Redacted File. Wolfe Pack online archives.

Chervotkin, Sergey (user Avis). November 20, 2015 (11:32am). Comment on Molly Zuckerman, "Reks Staut iz Ameriki v Rossii." *O Niro Vul'fe, Archi Gudvine, i ikh avtore, Rekse Staute* (*About Nero Wolfe, Archie Goodwin, and their author, Rex Stout*) (blog). Translated by Gleb Vinokurov. October 18, 2015 (8:38pm). http://nerowolfe.info/forum/viewtopic.php?f=5&t=522&sid=5578a875b87af5 7f1d929613a0f50979.

———.November 20, 2015 (6:54pm). Comment on Molly Zuckerman, "Reks Staut iz Ameriki v Rossii." *O Niro Vul'fe, Archi Gudvine, i ikh avtore, Rekse Staute* (*About Nero Wolfe, Archie Goodwin, and their author, Rex Stout*) (blog)/ Translated by Gleb Vinokurov. October 18, 2015

(8:38pm). http://nerowolfe.info/forum/viewtopic.php?f=5&t=522&sid=5578a875b87af5 7f1d929613a0f50979.

Cook, Fred J., *The FBI Nobody Knows*. New York: MacMillan Company, 1964.

D.W. "Crime Fiction." *Encounter*. August 1981, 26.

Desh, Dobavil. "Klassicheskii detektiv protiv krutogo." In *Detektivnyi metod. Istoriia detektiva v kino i literature (The Detective Method. A History of Detektiv in Movie and Literature.)*. 2014. http://detectivemethod.ru/laboratory/classicdetective-against-hardboiled/

Detektivy veka. Itogi veka, Vzgliad iz rossii. Polifakt. Itogi veka, 1999.

Dontsova, Darya. *Dobri doktor Aibandit*. Litres, 2015.

———. *Tushkanchik v bigudiakh*. Litres, 2015.

Dostoevsky, Fyodor. *Diary of a Writer*. Vol. 2, New York: Scribners, 1949.

Dover, J. Kenneth Van. *At Wolfe's Door: The Nero Wolfe Novels of Rex Stout*. James A. Rock & Co, 1991.

Dralyuk, Boris. *Western Crime Fiction Goes East: The Russian Pinkerton Craze, 1907-1934,* Brill Academic Pub, 2012.

Drummond, Roscoe. "Freedom Seeks Foothold Behind Iron Curtain." *The Philadelphia Inquirer*. June 17, 1966. Box

21. Rex Stout Papers. MS1986096. John J. Burns Library, Boston College.

Dubin, Boris. "Russian Intelligentsia between Classics and Mass Culture." Moscow: VCIOM (Russian Public Opinion Research Center), 1998.

Kaemmel, Ernst. "Literature under the Table: The Detective Novel and Its Social
Mission." Translated by Glenn W. Most. In *The Poetics of Murder: Detective Fiction and Literary Theory*, edited by Glenn W. Most and William W. Stowe: Harcourt Brace Jovanovich, June 1983.

Foley, Barbara. *Radical Representations: Politics and Form in U.S. Proletarian Fiction, 1929-1941*. Post-Contemporary Interventions. Edited by Stanley Fish and Fredric Jameson Durham: Duke University Press, 1993.

Frascina, Francis. *Art, Politics and Dissent: Aspects of the Art Left in Sixties America*. Manchester University Press, 1999.

Freedom House notes on Solzhenitsyn's exile. Undated. Rex Stout Papers. MS1986096. John J. Burns Library, Boston College.

Garrard, John Gordon Garrard and Carol. *Inside the Soviet Writers' Union*. New York: Free Press, 1990.

Gransden, Greg. "Yanks Write New Chapter in Soviet Publishing: Books: Onetime Propaganda Mills Still Carry the Works of Lenin. But American Favorites, Such as 'the Godfather,' Are the Top Sellers." *Los Angeles Times*, February 19, 1991.

Gryspeerdt, Sam Kinchin-Smith and Nancy. "Curious Incidents: The Adventures of Sherlock Holmes in Russia." *The Calvert Journal*, 2014.
http://calvertjournal.com/comment/show/2817/sherlock-holmes-in-russia.

Hartmann, Thom. ""The Doorbell Rang" – Thom Hartmann's Independent Thinker Review." In *BuzzFlash*, 2010. http://truth-out.org/buzzflash/commentary/thedoorbell-rang–thom-hartmanns-independent-thinker-review/8471-thedoorbell-rang–thom-hartmanns-independent-thinker-review.

Holquist, Michael. "Whodunit and Other Questions: Metaphysical Detective Stories in Postwar Fiction." In *The Poetics of Murder, Detective Fiction and Literary Theory*, edited by Glenn W. Most and William W. Stow: Harcourt Brace Jovanovich, June 1983.

Hoover, J.Edgar to Rex Stout. November 15, 1949. FBI Redacted File. Wolfe Pack online archives.

Ilyina, Natalia. "Detective Novels: A Game and Life." *Soviet Literature* 3 (1975).

———."Palitra krasok." *Vopros literaturyi* 2 (1975).

———. "The Last Days of Her Life." *Soviet Literature* 6 (January 1, 1989): 119-37.

Jones, M.A. to Mr. DeLoach. May 20, 1965. *"The Doorbell Rang" New Mystery Novel by Rex Stout*. FBI Redacted File. Wolfe Pack online archives.

Kiser, Marcia. "Nero Wolfe: a Social Commentary on the U.S." In *The Thrilling Detective,*, 2003. http://www.thrillingdetective.com/non_fiction/e002.html.

Knight, Stephen. *Crime Fiction since 1800 : Detection, Death, Diversity*. Palgrave Macmillan, 2010.

Kovaly, Héda Margolius. *Under a Cruel Star: A Life in Prague, 1941-1968*. Holmes & Meier Publishers, Inc, 1997.

Lezerson, Ilya, Tatiana Solomonik, and Sergey Sinelnikov. *Za stolom s Niro Vul'fom, ili sekrety kukhni velikogo syshchika: kulinarnyi detektiv (At the Table with Nero Wolfe or Secrets of the Kitchen of the Great Detective: A Culinary Mystery)*. Velikie syshchiki (Great Detectives). 3 ed. St. Petersburg. Amfora, 2015.

Lipovetsky, Mark and Lisa Ryoko Wakamiya*Late and Post-Soviet Russian Literature*. Perestroika and the Post-Soviet Period. Vol. 1: Academic Studies Press, 2014.

Lorika. December 22, 2009 (4:33pm). Comment on "Niro Vul'f i Archi Gudvin Reksa Stauta (Nero Wolfe and Archie Goodwin of Rex Stout)," *Mir liubvi i romantiki* (*World of Love and Romantics*) (blog). Translated by Gleb Vinokurov. http://world-of-love.ru/forum/archive/index.php/t-16988.html.

Lovell, Stephen. *The Russian Reading Revolution: Print Culture in the Soviet and Post-Soviet Eras* Macmillan, 2000.

Lynds, Gayle. "Nero Wolfe, the Spy." In *Bouchercon 2010 Rex Stout Banquet*, 2010.

Marakhovskii, Viktor. "Niro Vulf, pobeditel' gomofobov. Ob evolyutsii tsenostei." In *Kul'tpul't*: Mediya Tsel', 2015.

Marinina, Aleksandra. *Shesterki umiraiiut Pervymi*. Eksmo Press, 2000.

———. *A Confluence of Circumstances. The Soviet and Post-Soviet Review* 29, no. 1, 2 (2002): iv.-220.

———. *Stecheniie obstoiatel'stv.* Moscow: Eksmo Press, 1999.

McAleer, John J. *Rex Stout: A Majesty's Life*. Millenium ed.: James A Rock & Co. Publishers, 2002.

McBride, O.E. *Stout Fellow: A Guide through Nero Wolfe's World*. iUniverse, 2003.

McCann, Sean. "The Hard-Boiled Novel." In *Gumshoe America: Hard-Boiled Crime Fiction and the Rise and Fall of New Deal Liberalism*, edited by Donald E. Pease. New Americanists: Duke University Press, 2000.

Menhert, Klaus. *The Russians and Their Favorite Books*. Hoover Institution Press, 1983.

Mihajlov, Mihajlo to President Tito of Yugoslavia. Undated Correspondence. Box 21.

Rex Stout Papers. MS1986-096. John J. Burns Library, Boston College.

Mitgang, Herbet. *Dangerous Dossiers: Exposing the Secret War against America's*
Greatest Authors Open Road Distribution, 2015. Kindle Edition

Monroe, David. "The Doorbell Rang by Rex Stout – a Review." In *Seeking In The Zeitgeist*: Awesome, Inc., 2012. http://seekinginthezeitgeist.blogspot.com/2012/02/doorbell-rang-by-rex-stoutmy-rating-4.html.

Morgan, Lyndall. "Darya Dontsova's 'Sleuthettes': A Case of the Regendering of the Post-Soviet Russian Detektiv?". *Australian Slavonic and East European Studies* 19 (2005): 95-116.

Morris, Marcia A. "'Canst Thou Draw out Leviathan with a Hook?': Akunin Colludes and Collides with Collins and Christie." *CLUES: A Journal of Detection* 28, no. 1 (Spring 2010): 69-78.

Nepomnyashchy, Catharine Theimer. "Markets, Mirrors, and Mayhem: Aleksandra Marinina and the Rise of the New Russian Detektiv." In *Consuming Russia: Popular Culture, Sex, and Society since Gorbachev*, edited by Adele Marie Barker: Duke University Press, 1999.

Newton, Newton. *The FBI Encyclopedia*. McFarland, 2003.

Ol'ga T. January 27, 2013 (2:49pm). Comment on user MsBulavkapetek1855, "Blagodarnost.'" *O Niro Vul'fe, Archi Gudvine, i ikh avtore, Rekse Staute* (*About Nero Wolfe, Archie Goodwin, and their author, Rex Stout*) (blog). December 19, 2011 (2:48pm). http://nerowolfe.info/forum/viewtopic.php?f=8&t=301.

Olcott, Anthony. *Russian Pulp: The Detektiv and the Russian Way of Crime*. Lanham: Rowman & Littlefield Publishers, 2001.

Panichev, Sergey. Vkontakte message to author. March 15, 2016.

Polshikova, Lyudmila. "Bookworm-Sleuths." *The Moscow Times*, March 16 2001.

Quarles, Philip. *Rex Stout Writes Detective Stories, Makes Enemies of the FBI*. Text of podcast audio. WNYC.org. 1:00p, 2013.

RAMZES. "Biografiia Edgara Guvera." *O Niro Vul'fe, Archi Gudvine, i ikh avtore, Rekse Staute* (*About Nero Wolfe, Archie Goodwin, and their author, Rex Stout*) (blog). April 27, 2009 (10:33am). http://nerowolfe.info/forum/viewtopic.php?f=5&t=48.

Remnick, David. *Lenin's Tomb: The Last Days of the Soviet Empire*. New York: Random House, 1993.

———. "Letter from Moscow: The Hangover." *The New Yorker*, November 22 1993.

Roberts, Elizabeth. "Dr. Ekaterina Genieva." In *Russia: Lessons and Legacy- The Alexander Men Conference 2012*: Moffat Book Events, January 30, 2012.

Romerstein, Martin J. Manning and Herbert. *Historical Dictionary of American Propaganda*. Greenwood, 2004.

Rymko, Natalia (user Rymarnica). "A kak vy risuete loshad'?" *O Niro Vul'fe, Archi Gudvine, i ikh avtore, Rekse Staute* (*About Nero Wolfe, Archie Goodwin, and their author, Rex Stout*) (blog), March 28, 2013 (6:39pm). http://nerowolfe.info/forum/viewtopic.php?f=14&t=459.

———. April 1, 2016 (9:56am). Comment on Molly Zuckerman, "Reks Staut iz Ameriki v Rossii." *O Niro Vul'fe, Archi Gudvine, i ikh avtore, Rekse Staute* (*About Nero Wolfe, Archie Goodwin, and their author, Rex Stout*) (blog). Translated by Gleb Vinokurov. October 18, 2015 (8:38pm). http://nerowolfe.info/forum/viewtopic.php?f=5&t=522&sid=5578a875b87af5 7f1d929613a0f50979.

———. October 19, 2015 (8:33pm). Comment on Molly Zuckerman, "Reks Staut iz Ameriki v Rossii." *O Niro Vul'fe, Archi Gudvine, i ikh avtore, Rekse Staute* (*About Nero Wolfe, Archie Goodwin, and their author, Rex Stout*) (blog). Translated by Gleb Vinokurov. October 18, 2015 (8:38pm). http://nerowolfe.info/forum/viewtopic.php?f=5&t=522&sid=5578a875b87af5 7f1d929613a0f50979.

Shaginian, Marietta. *Mess-Mend: Yankees in Petrograd.* Translated by Samuel D. Cioran. Ann Arbor: Ardis, 1991.

Shearer, Benjamin F. *Home Front Heroes: A Biographical Dictionary of Americans During Wartime* Vol. 3: Greenwood, 2006.

Shenker, Israel. "Rex Stout, 85, Gives Clues on Good Writing." *The New York Times*, December 1, 1971.

Simkin, John. "New Masses." http://spartacus-educational.com/JmassesN.htm.

Stanley, Alessandra. "The World: In Its Dreams; Russia Solves Its Crime Problem." *The New York Times*, March 15, 1998.

Staut, Reks (Rex Stout). "Uotson byl zhenshzhinoi (Watson Was a Woman)." In *Detektivy veka*. Itogi veka, Vzgliad iz rossii. Polifakt. Itogi veka, 1999.

———. "Sovremennyi amerikanskii detektiv." Translated by Yuriya Smirnova. In *Zvonok v dver'* edited by Natalia Ilyina, 8-207. Moscow: Progress, 1973.

———. *Kulinarnaia kniga Niro Vul'fa (The Cookbook of Nero Wolfe)*. Translated by E. Zaitseva. Ves' Stout. Moscow: Eksmo, 2009.

———. *Ubiistvo politseiskogo (the Cop Killer)*. KUBKa, 1994.

———. "Ubiistvo politseiskogo (The Cop Killer)." In *Igra v piatnashki (Prisoner's Base)*: Amfora, 2014.

Stinnet, Caskie. "Rex Stout, Nero Wolfe and the Big Fish." *Herald Tribune*, October 10 1965, 10-11, 27.

Stout, Rex to His Excellency Josip Broz Tito. From the Ad Hoc Committee for Mihajlo Mihajlov. August 1, 1966. Box 21. Rex Stout Papers. MS1986-096. John J. Burns Library, Boston College.

Stout, Rex to Mihajlo Mihajlov. Undated Correspondence. Box 21. Rex Stout Papers. MS1986-096. John J. Burns Library. Boston College.

Stout, Rex to Mrs. Franklin D. Roosevelt. "Writers Board for World Government." January 15, 1951. Wolfe Pack online archives.

Stout, Rex. "The Case of the Spies Who Weren't." *Ramparts*, January 1966, 31-34.

———. "Watson Was a Woman." *The Saturday Review of Literature* (March 1, 1941): 3-4, 16.

———. "We Shall Hate, or We Shall Fail." *The New York Times*, January 17 1943.

———. *A Right to Die*. The Viking Press, Inc., 1964. Kindle Edition.

———. *And Be a Villain*. The Viking Press, Inc., 1948. Kindle Edition.

———. *Booby Trap*, in *Not Quite Dead Enough*. Farrar & Rinehart, 1944), Kindle Edition.

———. *Death of a Dude*. The Viking Press, Inc., 1969.

———. *Fer-De-Lance*. Farrar & Rinehart, Inc., 1934. Kindle Edition.

———. *Home to Roost*, in *Triple Jeopardy*. The Viking Press, Inc., 1952, Kindle Edition. Kindle Edition.

———. *In the Best Families*. The Viking Press, Inc., 1950. Kindle Edition.

———. *Murder by the Book*. The Viking Press, Inc., 1951.

———. *Not Quite Dead Enough*. In *Not Quite Dead Enough*: Farrar & Rinehart, 1944. Kindle Edition.

———. *Over My Dead Body*. Farrar & Rinehart, Inc., 1940.

———. *Poison Á La Carte*. In *Three at Wolfe's Door* Viking Penguin, 1960. Kindle Edition.

———. *Some Buried Caesar*. Farrar & Rinehart, 1939.

———. *The Black Mountain*. The Viking Press, Inc., 1954. Kindle Edition.

———. *The Cop-Killer*. In *Triple Jeopardy*: The Viking Press, Inc., 1952. Kindle Edition.

———. *The Doorbell Rang*. The Viking Press, Inc., 1965. Kindle Edition.

———. *The Father Hunt*. The Viking Press, Inc., 1968. Kindle Edition.

———. *The Second Confession*. The Viking Press, Inc., 1949. Kindle Edition.

———. *The Silent Speaker*. Viking Penguin, 1946. Kindle Edition.

———. *Too Many Cooks*. Farrar & Rinehart, Inc., 1938.

———. Undated Correspondence. Freedom House. Rex Stout Papers. MS1986-096. John J. Burns Library, Boston College.

———. Undated manuscript. *Home to Roost*. Box 15, Folder 5. Rex Stout Papers. MS1986-096. John J. Burns Library, Boston College.

Sussman, Leonard. Note to Executive Committee of Freedom House. October 18, 1967 Box 21. Rex Stout Papers. MS1986-096. John J. Burns Library, Boston College.

The Art of Detective Fiction. St. Martin's Press, Inc., 2000.

The Greatest Russian Stories of Crime and Suspense. Pegasus Crime. Pegasus Crime, 2012.

The Nero Wolfe Files. Wildside Press LLC, 2005.

Townsend, Guy M. *Rex Stout, an Annotated Primary and Secondary Bibliography*. New York: Garland Reference Library of the Humanities, 1982.

Unknown to J. Edgar Hoover. Undated Correspondence. FBI Redacted File. Wolfe Pack online archives.

Vishevsky, Anatoly. "Answers to Eternal Questions in Soft Covers: Post-Soviet Detective Stories." *Slavic and Eastern European Journal* 45, no. 5 (2001): 735.

Voronina, Olga, e-mail message to author, October 30, 2015.

Vronskaia, O., "Na podstupakh k 'zolotomu pistoletu.'" *Literaturnaia gazeta*. No.9 (1998).

Wachtel, Andrew. *Remaining Relevant after Communism: The Role of the Writer in Eastern Europe*. Chicago: University of Chicago Press, 2006.

Wikipedia Contributers. "Agatha Christie (Band)." Wikipedia, The Free Encyclopedia., https://en.wikipedia.org/w/index.php?title=Agatha_Christie_(band)&oldid=70 3557998.

———. "Clare Boothe Luce." Wikipedia, The Free Encyclopedia., https://en.wikipedia.org/w/index.php?title=Clare_Boothe_Luce&oldid=70726 5564.

———. "House Un-American Activities Committee." Wikipedia, The Free Encyclopedia., https://en.wikipedia.

org/w/index.php?title=House_UnAmerican_Activities_Committee&oldid=708565501.

———. "Karadorde." Wikipedia, The Free Encyclopedia., https://en.wikipedia.org/w/index.php?title=Kara%C4%91or%C4%91e&oldid=707060032.

———. "Progress (Publishing)." Wikipedia, the free encyclopedia, http://ru.wikipedia.org/?oldid=75511036.

———. "Sergey Markovich Sinelnikov." Wikipedia, The Free Encyclopedia . http://ru.wikipedia.org/?oldid=76834152.

———. "Strom Thurmond." Wikipedia, The Free Encyclopedia., https://en.wikipedia.org/w/index.php?title=Strom_Thurmond&oldid=7083556 84.

Wilkinson, Stephen. *Detective Fiction in Cuban Society and Culture*. Peter Lang, 2006.

Wilson, Edmund. "Why Do People Read Detective Stories?" *The New Yorker*, October 14 1994.

Winks, Robin W. *Detective Fiction: A Collection of Critical Essays*. New Jersey: Prentice Hall Inc., 1980.

Winterich, John T. and Frankel Haskel. "Private Eye on the FBI." *Saturday Review of Literature*. October 9, 1965.

Zavgorodnii, Stanislav (user Chuchundrovich). "Kubok luchshego detektiva- u Archi Gudvina." *O Niro Vul'fe, Archi Gudvine, i ikh avtore, Rekse Staute* (*About Nero Wolfe, Archie Goodwin, and their author, Rex Stout*) (blog). April 28, 2009 (9:55pm). http://nerowolfe.info/forum/viewtopic.php?f=5&t=49.

———. November 23, 2015 (4:40pm). Comment on Molly Zuckerman, "Reks Staut iz Ameriki v Rossii." *O Niro Vul'fe, Archi Gudvine, i ikh avtore, Rekse Staute* (*About Nero Wolfe, Archie Goodwin, and their author, Rex Stout*) (blog). Translated by Gleb Vinokurov. October 18, 2015 (8:38pm). http://nerowolfe.info/forum/viewtopic.php?f=5&t=522&sid=5578a875b87af5 7f1d929613a0f50979.

———. "O saite." *Niro Vul'f i Archi Gudvin*. http://nerowolfe.info/about.

———. "Rossiia, 2001-2002, 'Niro Vul'f i Archi Gudvin,' 2005, 'Novye prikliucheniia Niro Vul'fa i Archi Gudvina.'" *Niro Vul'f i Archi Gudvin*. http://nerowolfe.info/movies.

———. "Staut i staut." *Niro Vul'f i Archi Gudvin*. http://nerowolfe.info/beer.

Zuckerman, Ed. "Toast to Fritz." Paper presented at the The Black Orchid Banquet, December 5, 2015.

Zuckerman, Molly. "Reks Staut iz Ameriki v Rossii." *O Niro Vul'fe, Archi Gudvine, i ikh avtore, Rekse Staute* (*About Nero Wolfe, Archie Goodwin, and their author, Rex Stout*) (blog). October 18, 2015 (8:38pm) http://nerowolfe.

info/forum/viewtopic.php?f=5&t=522&sid=5578a875 b87af5 7f1d929613a0f50979.

Zueva, A., "Kto vy, pokupateli knig?" *Knizhnoe obozrenie.* 1996.

Made in the USA
San Bernardino, CA
31 January 2019